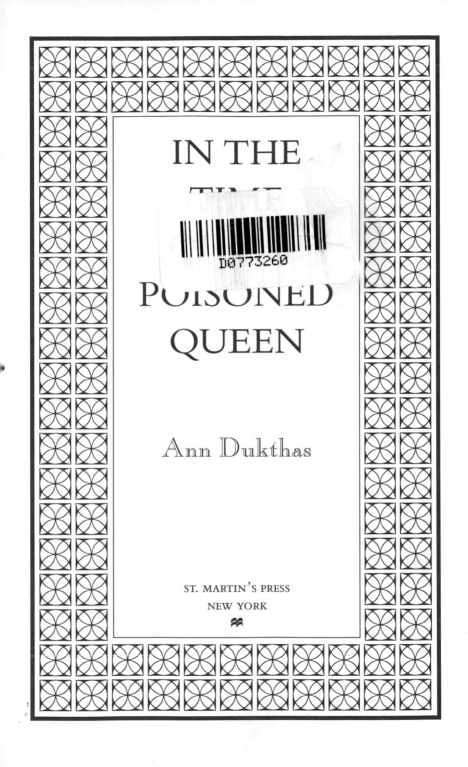

IN THE TIME OF THE POISONED QUEEN

Ann Dukthas

ST. MARTIN'S PRESS
NEW YORK

IN THE TIME OF THE POISONED QUEEN
Copyright © 1998 by Ann Dukthas
Printed in the United States of America. No part of this book
may be used or reproduced in any manner whatsoever without
written permission except in the case of brief quotations em-
bodied in critical articles or reviews. For information, address St.
Martin's Press, 175 Fifth Avenue, New York, N.Y. 10010.

Library of Congress Cataloging-in-Publication Data

Dukthas, Ann.
    In the time of the poisoned Queen / Ann Dukthas.
      p.   cm.
    ISBN 0–312–18030–6
    1. Great Britain—History—Mary I, 1553–1558—Fiction.
I. Title.
PR6054.O37I5   1998
823' .914—dc21   97–31614

First edition: May 1998

10 9 8 7 6 5 4 3 2 1

To my sister, Mary Ladyman,
and her husband, Peter

HISTORICAL NOTE

In 1547 Henry VIII died. He left three children: Mary, Elizabeth, and Edward. The latter succeeded Henry as King until 1553, when he died at a tender age. England slipped to the brink of civil war. Mary claimed the throne for herself, but the Duke of Northumberland, Edward VI's Protector, tried to advance the claim of his son, Guildford, who was married to the great-granddaughter of Henry VII, Lady Jane Grey. Mary won a crushing victory but instigated a repressive policy to bring England back into the Catholic faith. Her bishops, especially Bonner of London, began a systematic persecution of the Protestant faithful. Mary's reign proved to be a catalogue of disaster. The English lost Calais in France, whilst, at home, people rested their hopes on Mary's early death and the accession of Princess Elizabeth, Mary's half-sister.

On a number of occasions Elizabeth was brought under suspicion of plotting against Mary, but her motto was "Much suspected, nothing proven." By 1558 rumours that Mary would soon die an untimely death were circulating, not only in England but abroad. The finger of suspicion was pointed at Elizabeth, the French, even Mary's Spanish husband, Philip II. Into this maelstrom of political controversy, Nicholas Segalla was about to step. . . .

MAJOR HISTORICAL CHARACTERS
MENTIONED IN THE TEXT

Peter (Gian Pietro) Carafa: Pope Paul IV

Henry II: King of France

Catherine de' Medici: Henry's Italian wife

Diane de Poitiers: Henry II's principal mistress

Michael Nostradamus: astrologer and fortune-teller in the service of Catherine de' Medici

Henry VIII: King of England (1509–1547)

Catherine of Aragon: Henry VIII's first wife

Mary Tudor: Henry and Catherine's only surviving child

Anne Boleyn: Henry VIII's second wife, executed for alleged adultery with her brother George and Mark Smeaton

Catherine Howard: Henry VIII's fourth wife, executed for alleged adultery with Thomas Culpepper

Jane Seymour: Henry VIII's third wife

Edward VI: the only surviving son of Henry and Jane Seymour

Protector Somerset: Edward VI's first regent

John Dudley, Duke of Northumberland: He replaced Somerset as regent, but fell from power and was executed in 1553 when Mary succeeded to the throne.

Elizabeth Tudor: daughter of Anne Boleyn; later Elizabeth I of England

William Cecil: Elizabeth's principal secretary and most fervent supporter

Cardinal Reginald Pole (or de la Pole): leading Catholic churchman; Queen Mary's principal adviser

Philip II of Spain: son of Emperor Charles V; Mary Tudor's absentee husband

Mary Stuart: Scottish princess; Henry VIII's great-niece; married to Francis, Dauphin of France

IN THE
TIME
OF THE
POISONED
QUEEN

Prologue: Essex, June 1995

Ann Dukthas entered the lounge of the Roebuck Hotel. She ordered a dry white wine and sat on a comfortable chair in front of the roaring fire. The lounge was empty except for a family who had apparently travelled down for a midweek stay whilst visiting the sights in London and southern Essex. They were bemoaning the swift seasonal change, and Ann could see why. The weather had turned abruptly nasty. Winds lashed the latticed windows with rain. Ann was glad to be indoors. The journey from Central London by car had been hectic, the roads congested; there had been some hold-up virtually every five miles. The Roebuck came as a welcome relief: as usual, her stay was paid for by her enigmatic friend Nicholas Segalla. Ann did not know where he lived or what he did. Segalla was undoubtedly wealthy, able to pay for the best. Always dressed in the finest suits, shirts, and shoes, Segalla was discreet, not ostentatious. He stayed out of the limelight, always alone and aloof. For some strange reason he had chosen her to share his great secret. At first, Ann had found his claims difficult to accept, but Segalla had produced the evidence. He was a man who could never die. An individual who had moved amongst, and worked for, the great ones of history. Time and again Ann had seen the evidence: scattered references from the chanceries of Europe, eloquent testimony on how Segalla had worked for princes, dukes, kings, prime ministers, and popes. As Segalla had once explained to Ann:

"If you hold power you must exercise it to protect yourself. Governments do it today with their CIA, MI5, or KGB. Ann, times may change, fashions come and go, but human nature stays the same. Be they princes or popes, they always need their agents, their secret men on whom they can utterly rely. I am, I was, one of these."

On one occasion Ann had asked him why. Segalla, enigmatic as ever, had replied that he had been condemned by an ancient curse to wander the face of the earth. He could never grow old, he would never die. Apart from that, Segalla refused to elaborate. Nevertheless, he produced convincing evidence for his claim, whilst Ann, a professional historian, had done her own research without exciting the suspicions of colleagues. Slowly but surely she had come across references, be they in the Public Record Office in Chancery Lane, the Vatican archives in Rome, the Archives Nationales in Paris, or the manuscripts of the Escorial palace in Spain. All alluded to Nicholas Segalla, sometimes a monk, other times a priest, a Jesuit, a soldier. A man cloaked in secrecy. The manuscripts described him as "well beloved," "much trusted," "our most loyal clerk." Sometimes he was mentioned as carrying dispatches or being sent on a journey "pro negotiis secretis," on secret affairs. A successful man who won the trust of those he served, he was rewarded not with land but with gold, silver, and precious jewels.

Ann had learnt never to question Segalla. He was generous to a fault, charming yet sad. Ann wondered if she could ever be attracted to a man she knew so little about. It was like studying a fascinating oil painting in the National Gallery: there were impressions, colour, texture, but, in the end, these only intrigued her rather than resolved anything. Segalla came and went as he pleased; only once had he ever hinted why he had chosen her:

"Something is about to happen," he confessed. "History is going to change, and in a way you can never imagine." He smiled shyly. "But, there again, I've thought that before. Perhaps the reason I speak to you is prosaic. I've become lonely. I want to confess: purge myself of the secrets I hold. I wander into a bookshop and buy some historical study resolving a great mystery from history. I feel the urge to respond and explain what is wrong, or right, in its conclusions." He stared at her, as if convincing himself that she could be trusted. "And, of course, like everyone, I dream: the people I've met, those I've served. My relationships with them were intense: Mary of Scotland, Elizabeth of England, Catherine de' Medici of France, Marie Antoinette, Victoria. They were people, flesh and blood, with dreams and hopes. They trusted me. Sometimes they spoke to me as if I were their confessor. The years may pass, but memory doesn't dull. Death and the passing of the years do not draw a line in the dust. Relationships can survive the grave." He tapped the side of his head. "Sometimes I feel, yes, I feel like a haunted house."

"And I have to exorcise you?" Ann asked.

Segalla smiled, running slender fingers through his thick black hair. Ann had known him for three years. The passage of time always made its presence felt but not to Segalla. He could suffer cold or flu like anyone else, but he never changed.

"Why?" Ann had asked. "You are a man, vulnerable to poison, stiletto, the sword, the dagger in the dark. Surely many a crossbow bolt or bullet has been fired at you?"

Segalla had laughed. He'd taken off his jacket, loosened the gold cuff links and pulled back the sleeve of his silk shirt. His arm was brown with a mass of scars from shoulder to wrist.

"Death is not the only agony, Ann." He ran his finger along the pink marks and scars. "There are worse fates. Oh, I've been shot and stabbed. I've had garrotte strings round my neck. I've been lured into marsh and quagmire, thrown overboard from a pitching ship, cast into an icy river outside Moscow. I've known the agony of fire and sword, of rat-infested dungeons, and the terrifying darkness of oubliettes, yet I never die. I go to the limit. I have been in that twilight zone between death and life. I have hung 'twixt heaven and hell, between sky and earth, looking for the great darkness, yet I never travel into it."

"And do you want to?" Ann asked.

"Sometimes, yes: especially when you see those you love,

those you've grown accustomed to, leave. I was reading that doctors are producing drugs to make man live longer." Segalla laughed softly. "But does longer life mean happiness?"

"Are you happy?" Ann asked.

"I am happy to be working out my salvation," Segalla replied evasively. "But, like any man or woman, I have my fears. I do not have supernatural powers. I have nightmares, of being locked up in a dungeon, forgotten as the years pass."

"But surely some of those you have met in history suspected your secret?"

"Oh yes," Segalla replied. "There are those, the lords of the black arts, princes, men of power who would have loved to have seized me and force out my secret."

Ann picked up her glass of white wine and stared into the fire. She remembered that conversation with Segalla from when they had flown back from Vienna, one of the few occasions when he had spoken about his past and his great secret. Segalla had placed such trust in her that Ann, a Catholic, had sworn a great oath never to reveal or allude to it. She also suspected that Segalla kept a close eye on her and, in his own cryptic manner, ensured she kept the secrets he revealed.

Segalla always acted the same way. Ann would be invited to this city or that town and given a manuscript, written in the form of a novel, which always probed and revealed some great secret of history. In London it had been the murder of Lord Darnley, Mary Stuart's husband. In Paris the fate of the lost Dauphin, Louis XVII. In Vienna the truth about Prince Rudolph's supposed suicide at the hunting lodge of Mayerling. Ann sipped at her wine. So why Essex? What had happened here? What was so special? She was a historian, but, for the life of her, she could not recall any great mystery. True, there was the city or, further north, the great Tudor palace of Hatfield.

"Do you like that wine?"

Ann started and looked round. Segalla was seated at a table just to her right. He rose, came across, and shook her hand.

"How long have you been here?"

Ann saw the raindrops on his black woollen overcoat, and an umbrella in the stand near the door still dripped with water.

"Just a few minutes," he apologized.

"Don't you trust me, Nicholas?"

Segalla unbuttoned his coat, threw it across an empty chair, and sat down beside her.

"Old habits die hard, Ann. Every place I go into, I always stand or sit just within the door. Is it safe? I ask. If I want to leave, how can I? Is there an enemy here? It's like a game." He lifted his hand and called the waiter over.

"You've eaten lunch?"

Ann nodded.

"Then I'll just join you in a glass of wine."

Segalla opened his small leather briefcase, took out a manilla envelope, and pushed it across the table. He pulled back his cuffs and studied the face of his Rolex watch.

"It's two o'clock. We'll dine at eight. Yes?"

Ann agreed. Segalla tapped the package.

"There'll be time enough to read that."

"What is it about?" Ann picked the envelope up.

Segalla paused whilst the waiters served the white wine.

"It's about a murder."

"Of whom?"

"Mary Tudor."

Ann looked up in amazement. "But she was riddled with disease, anxiety, and phobias. Her brain and body just gave out!"

"Mary Tudor was a remarkable lady," Segalla replied. "A great queen married to the wrong king. A woman of outstanding courage and tenacity. She was barely forty when she was murdered. And"—he picked his wineglass up—"she was murdered in the most subtle and cunning way."

"But why have you brought me here?"

Segalla lifted the wineglass in a silent toast, then plucked a folded copy of the *Times* from his pocket and pushed it across the table. The article he'd ringed at the foot of the front page merely announced how archaeologists at Sinistrel Manor in Essex had discovered a secret room with a skeleton inside. The evidence indicated the person had been murdered some four hundred years earlier and its corpse hidden there.

"Tomorrow morning," Segalla said, "pathologists are going to study the remains. I want to be there."

"You knew the victim?" Ann asked.

"Aye, but, unlike *Hamlet*'s Yorick, I have no sweet memories. The remains belong to the assassin responsible for Mary Tudor's murder."

Chapter 1

The year 1558, according to all the chroniclers, letter-writers, and gossip collectors, was an ominous one. At night, flame-tailed comets and fiery stars seared the heavens; they were seen as the precursors of war, famine, and pestilence. The year had been ushered in by a freezing winter which lasted so long people muttered that God had forgotten spring. It was a time of change: the English had been driven out of Calais, and the Spanish fought to maintain their footholds in the Low Countries. Kings and princes came and went. Popular discontent seethed from the borders of Scotland to the wild rushing rivers of Germany. Religion was a cause of war, not peace. Every man believed that God spoke to him. Across western Europe, death by burning was now a common sight, the stench of charred flesh mingling with the odours of the cities. In England, Catholics burnt Protestants. In Germany, Protestants burnt those more radical than themselves. In Spain, Catholics burnt Catholics who could not agree with them. All of Europe was a maelstrom. Men waited to see what further horrors would emerge.

In her secret chamber at the palace of Fontainebleu, Catherine de' Medici lay face down on the floor, pulling back a secret shutter so she could watch her husband make love to the voluptuous Diane de Poitiers. Catherine, fair-haired and sallow-faced, watched intently as her royal husband and the father of her children squandered his seed on a woman Catherine dismissed as nothing better than a whore. She lay, breath held, and watched the twisting, writhing figures until the lovemaking was complete. Henry lay on his back staring up at the ceiling, not even suspecting that his wife, the Italian woman, was watching his every move. Henry turned on the bed and grasped Diane's long, silky hair. Catherine pulled the shutter closed. The Queen could not decide which was the more hurtful, the lovemaking or the subsequent pleasantries. After all, Henry was a beast of a man who had drunk deep of the pleasures of life. Catherine had come to accept this. The more Henry immersed himself in silken fripperies, the more power seeped into her own hands. Catherine sighed and clambered to her feet, brushing the dust from her dress. She smiled at the six ladies-in-waiting, her companions in conspiracy, chosen for both their beauty and their total loyalty to her.

"If I am going to spy on my husband," she announced drily, "I should at least expect a clean floor!"

She walked over, sat down in the heavily carved, high-backed chair, and glanced at the hour candle.

"He'll be here soon," she murmured. "See, the flame has nearly reached the fourteenth ring."

Catherine watched the flame dance. Her face had been

described as saintly, with large, lustrous eyes, smooth skin, and voluptous lips, but these didn't betray her emotions. A closed book was Catherine de' Medici, Queen of France: her woman's mind teemed with plot and counterplot. Yet she hid her anxiety well. Catherine was Italian: she could control today, but what about tomorrow? She had ideas, ambitions, and dreams for herself, her sons, her church, and France. Yet she required guarantees. She needed the curtain to the future pushed back to afford a glimpse of what tomorrow might bring. Catherine stiffened at a footfall outside followed by a gentle rap on the door. One of the ladies-in-waiting rose and went towards the door: she curtsied as a black-garbed, deep-hooded figure walked quickly into the room.

Michel de Notredame, or Michael Nostradamus as de' Medici called him, was neither a prince of Church nor a prince of State. Nevertheless, the ladies knew their mistress revered this man as a prophet.

"Madame." Nostradamus bowed.

"You may all go," Catherine declared. Her ladies-in-waiting rose, curtsied, and swept from the room. Once the door closed behind them, Catherine waved her prophet to one of the vacated seats. He sat down, pulling back his hood. Nostradamus had a pleasing face, one which intrigued Catherine. He had close-cropped hair, a large broad nose, high cheekbones, and a neatly clipped moustache and beard, but it was his eyes which always fascinated Catherine: large and dark, sometimes hard as flint, at other times full of life. He was fifty-four years of age but looked not yet forty. A doctor, the son of a Jewish convert, Nostradamus had come to Catherine's attention not only because of his ability to survive the plague in the towns where he had worked, but because of his uncanny ability to divine the future.

"You seek my advice, madame?"

"I rely on your advice, Michael." The Queen leaned forward. "You have used the mirror?"

Nostradamus nodded. "Last night, madame. I lit the candle and watched the flame grow."

"And what did you see?"

"Great changes, madame. In France and in England."

"For me?" Catherine asked greedily.

"For you, madame, a time of great power."

"Tell me again," Catherine urged.

"The young lion will overcome the older one in a field of combat and single fight. He will pierce his eyes in their golden cage. Two wounds in one, then he dies a cruel death."

"And that will usher in my time of power?"

"Yes, madame, but you must be careful."

Catherine's fingers flew to her lips. She kissed the magical stone in the ring on her finger. Nostradamus would tell her his prophecies but never explain them. He was diplomatic and cunning enough to leave that to her. Nevertheless, when she had heard that prophecy, Catherine had thrilled with excitement. She was certain, deep in her heart, that the old lion was her husband; for wasn't Henry's personal sign a golden lion rampant? And the young lion who killed him? Would that be one of his sons? If she had been alone, Catherine would have closed her eyes and moaned in pleasure. Her sons she controlled. She was their king, their father, their mother, their tutor and confessor.

"And it will happen soon?" she insisted.

"Within months," Nostradamus replied. "But, madame, how many I cannot tell you."

"And what else have you seen?" Catherine asked.

"As I have said, madame, a time of great change. Within two years all the rulers of Europe will fall."

Catherine's hands clasped tighter.

"Every one?" she whispered.

"Every one, madame, except you!"

Catherine closed her eyes and breathed out a long, lingering sigh. If Nostradamus was correct, and there was no reason to disbelieve him, what would it mean? That old fanatic in Rome, Pope Paul IV? If he died, who would succeed him? A Frenchman? Someone she could control? And the emperor Charles V? That king-monk who lurked in his shadowy chambers in some monastery listening to his clocks instead of controlling his far-flung empire. And in France? Henry II: If he died he would be succeeded by her eldest son, Francis, married to Mary the the Scottish princess, the only woman in Europe with a claim to thrones of three countries: France, England, and Scotland.

"And England's ruler?" Catherine opened her eyes. "Mary Tudor?"

Nostradamus allowed himself a slight smile.

"Madame, I am a physician as well as a prophet. I do not have to divine the future to tell you that Mary is unwell."

Catherine nodded. Mary Tudor, married to an absent husband, Philip of Spain, had never been a healthy woman. How had Noailles, the French ambassador in London, described her? A small creature, yes, that was how it was: thin and slightly built with reddish hair, harsh-faced though kindly eyed. A woman marked by misfortune. Catherine felt a pang of sympathy for Mary. Daughter of Henry VIII and Catherine of Aragon, rejected by her father, that uxorious, corpulent king, Mary had, at last, succeeded her sickly brother Edward VI to the throne of England. She was consumed with one ambition: to turn back time, to make England Catholic again. She had married Philip of Spain. To her it had been a love match but to Philip a marriage of convenience. He was always absent, either in Spain or plotting to take over Charles V's empire in the Low Countries, burning heretics and threatening France's northern border. Catherine had studied the dispatches from England: how Mary was beset on every side by enemies. How the Londoners hated and resented her Catholic ways, mocked her Spanish consort, and ridiculed Mary's pathetic attempts to beget an heir. The English queen's constant proclamations that she was enceinte were already a stale joke in the courts of Europe. Mary would never conceive. She was barren and dry as an old fig. Now fresh gossip was reaching the court in Paris: Mary was sickening, this time grievously. Some said her mind and body were breaking. Others whispered that she was being slowly poisoned.

Catherine moved in her chair. She twisted the ring on her finger so that it caught the light. And if Mary died? If she was helped into the Purgatory in which she so fervently believed, who would succeed her? Elizabeth? Henry VIII's daughter by Anne Boleyn: green-eyed, cat-faced, red-haired Elizabeth with her stubborn character and secretive ways? But she had been declared a bastard. Henry VIII himself had repudiated her when he sent her mother, Anne Boleyn, to the scaffold for adultery. And what was the great secret that was now on sale? Catherine leaned down, unlocked the small coffer on the table beside her, and pulled the parchment out. It was creamy and thick in texture, the handwriting clear and precise: a courtly, clerkly letter. She studied the writing once again. Three lines:

Ave Maria sepulta. Hail to Mary (buried).
What price the Crown of England?
Mark 15.34.

Catherine narrowed her eyes. She took the small eyeglass from her dark, burgundy-coloured dress and studied the cryptic letter. Noailles, her ambassador, had received this at his house in London. That city was seething with proclamations, ballads, and scurrilous news-sheets, but Noailles had apparently been interested in this particular one. The parchment was very expensive, the handwriting scholarly, but, more importantly, the letter referred to two important matters. First, that Mary would soon be dead and buried, and, secondly, that the Crown of England could be bought. But what did Mark 15.34, a verse from the Gospel, refer to?

"Madame?"

Catherine raised her head.

"Madame, have you finished with me? Should I go?"

"No, no, I have not, Michael." Catherine smiled. "I like you with me. Your very presence helps me think."

Nostradamus looked down at his hands in acceptance of this most gracious compliment.

Catherine went back and reread the letter again. Noailles would not have sent this, but, in his covering note, he claimed that he had learnt from his spies that similar letters had been dispatched to the Spanish Embassy as well as to Princess Elizabeth at Hatfield and the Queen at Greenwich. According to Noailles, the Spanish were deeply interested, whilst the letter had caused consternation at Hatfield and Greenwich. Catherine looked at the signature on the bottom of the letter: the Four Evangelists. "Matthew, Mark, Luke, and John," she murmured.

"Madame?"

Catherine shook her head. "I am thinking aloud, Michael, about this letter from our envoy in London." She passed it over. "I have shown it to you before."

"Yes, madame, you did."

"And what do you think of it?"

"If I follow your thoughts, madame, a very clever game of blackmail."

"We think the same, Michael," Catherine declared triumphantly. "Somebody in England or, if the letter is to be believed, four people in England are cleverly telling our English cousins that they know a secret. But what, eh? More important, is the time. Mary Tudor is sickly. What happens if she dies, Michael? What if she is being poisoned? By whom, eh? Philip of Spain, her errant husband? Is he tired of her? Does he have thoughts of marrying Princess Elizabeth? Or—" Catherine paused. Was Elizabeth poisoning her half-sister? she wondered. Was Elizabeth tired of waiting? Was she frightened that, before Mary died, the Queen would remove her, marry her off to some foreign prince? Or did some other group, still in the shadows, also play a deadly game? "If games are to be played," she murmured, "then France must play its part. What if, Michael, Mary Tudor dies? The English would never accept Philip of Spain."

"Princess Elizabeth, madame?"

"Elizabeth is illegitimate, a mere girl!"

"You were younger, when you became Queen."

"Aye," she replied. "But I am me, and Elizabeth . . ." Catherine shrugged as if she had said enough. "What happens, Michael, if Elizabeth does not become Queen? What happens if Mary Stuart, our little golden princess, emerges on the scene as true queen of England, Scotland, and France?"

Nostradamus blinked. He knew where Catherine was leading.

"Such a monarch, madame, would need careful advice and close management."

Catherine de' Medici nodded, hiding her thrill of excitement. I was born for this, she thought, to control, to conspire, to plot, move, and countermove. And why not? Other monarchs had their dreams. Mary, her daughter-in-law, Queen of England, Scotland, and France, with Catherine de' Medici controlling her! Was that too preposterous?

Catherine's mind raced ahead. A de' Medici on the thrones of England, Ireland, Scotland, and France. The Queen rose to her feet and extended her hand for Nostradamus. He knelt and kissed it. She stroked his hair.

"Keep close, Michael. Keep very close to me! That prophecy, about the lions, it's a matter only between the two of us?"

"You have my solemn word, madame."

Catherine waited until he left the chamber. She then went across, pulled back the picture on the wall, and opened the secret cupboard beyond; her chamber of potions, small phials and glasses of poisons which could take a person's life in seconds or in months. Catherine stared for a while, closed the door, and put the picture back. She went and knelt on the prie-dieu, praying for guidance in her plans, before going back to lie on the floor to spy on her amorous husband.

Elizabeth, daughter of Henry VIII and Anne Boleyn, sat in a cushioned window seat at the royal manor at Hatfield and gazed out over the park. A buzzard with a wounded wing had seized a rabbit but, mobbed by crows, had been forced to drop it. The crows closed in, cawing in triumph. Elizabeth waited.

"It will happen," she murmured.

Sure enough a grey, feathery shape appeared above the crows, floating on the shifting wind currents. The male buzzard had come to the assistance of his mate. He dropped like a stone, scattering the crows, seized the rabbit's corpse, and soared off in a display of triumph.

"A fascinating scene, eh, my lady?"

Elizabeth closed the Greek New Testament she had been studying and gestured at her personal secretary, Master William Cecil, to sit beside her. Cecil gazed around the beautifully polished, small hall. Servants at the far end were cleaning the tables of trenchers and goblets after the midday meal.

"I wonder which one is a spy?" he murmured.

"Oh, don't worry." Elizabeth laughed, her eyes still following the buzzard as it faded out of sight. "They are all spies."

"How do you know?" Cecil asked curiously.

Elizabeth studied her secretary's small, smooth face, rosy cheeks, and neatly trimmed moustache and beard: with his carefully coiffed hair and the sober dress of a clerk, Cecil reminded her of a little bird. Elizabeth, however, had learnt not to judge by appearances.

"You are a man of great subtlety, William. They must be spies!"

"Why?"

"Because they can all be bought. Everyone has a price: that's what you taught me, William."

"Even me, my lady?"

"You have a price, William."

Now Cecil studied his mistress: her small, narrow, pale face, the beautiful red hair hidden under a bejewelled cap. The veil which hung down on either side of her face gave his mistress the look of a madonna he had seen in a painting on his travels. Her dress of dark blue, with its white starched cuffs and neck, only heightened the impression of sanctity, except for her sea-green eyes, full of mischief and dancing with life as they glanced coquettishly at him.

"Perhaps I taught you too well, my lady."

"Much suspected, nothing proved," she retorted. "That's your doing, William. Mary can sit in London and suspect me of this or that, but she can't prove anything unless she buys you."

Cecil's face became so serious, Elizabeth threw her head back and pealed with laughter.

"My lady," Cecil gasped, "that's no jest!"

"Master Cecil, that's the truth. But you haven't asked me what your price is; it's me!"

Cecil smiled and relaxed.

"I'm the only thing that can suborn you." Elizabeth tapped him playfully on the knee with her copy of the New Testament.

Cecil hid his confusion in apologetic smiles and flurries of his hands. So sharp, he thought, so quick, so changeable. He quietly conceded that, at twenty-four, Elizabeth was now the master. He never knew from one hour to the next what mood she would take.

"I was watching those crows," she continued. "William, it's a short parable on politics. You must be strong to hold what you have and rely on the strength to seize back what has been snatched from you." Elizabeth smiled, though her eyes remained glass hard. She leaned closer. "Smile, William, when I talk to you, so that servant, who is taking overlong to clear the trenchers, thinks we are amusing each other! So, let us talk about that housewife, you know, the one who is sick in London?"

"On second thought"—Cecil rose to his feet, eager to assert himself—"if he does overhear us, he'll wonder what is so interesting about a housewife. Let us walk in the park."

They left the hall and went down a winding staircase. Cecil, trailing his fingers along the balustrade, stared at the crucifixes and statues which filled the stairwell as well as the entrance way at the bottom. If Mary dies, he thought, if Elizabeth becomes Queen, I'll change all this. I'll rebuild Hatfield as a monument to my mistress's tenacity.

They walked out across the lawn; only a wood dove cooing, the raucous cawing of the crows, and the occasional shriek of a peacock from the water gardens nearby shattered the afternoon silence.

"Now"—Cecil breathed in deeply—"this is the situation. The Crown of England, Madam Elizabeth, belongs to you. You are Henry's heir." He tapped the rosary slung round his neck. "A supporter of the Protestant church, yet, like me, you have to play the part. We both must play it well until Mary dies."

"When will she die?" Elizabeth retorted. "William, she must die soon! I am twenty-four years of age. A supporter of the reformed faith as my mother was." Elizabeth paused, staring into the middle distance. "Mary may be sickly," Elizabeth continued, "but she's only forty-two years of age. She could reign for another twenty years, and all the time she'll watch me, like those crows watched the buzzard. Any weakness, any mistake and she'll pounce, as she did after Wyatt's rebellion."

Elizabeth hid her shiver and wished she had brought a cloak out with her. She would never forget the aftermath of Wyatt's rebellion when she'd been implicated in it: Mary's soldiers and commissioners arriving, that dreadful journey in a black-draped barge down to Traitor's Gate and the Tower, then the interminable questions. For a few hours Elizabeth's very life had hung in the balance.

"I never want to make that journey again," she murmured. "Mary must die." Elizabeth grasped Cecil's wrist. "Will she die, William?"

Her secretary pulled a face. Even though they were in the middle of the lawn he was still nervous. If anyone overheard this conversation it would be the Tower for both of them: even imagining the Queen's death could be construed as treason. Cecil squeezed Elizabeth's slender fingers: he felt a thrill of excitement as he recalled those same fingers grasping the orb and sceptre. Cecil had never really made up his mind on his true relationship with Elizabeth. Secretary to a princess? Close counsellor? Father? Brother? Kinsman? Even lover? Cecil smiled to himself: that was Elizabeth's genius, she could be all these and yet nothing. A woman attracted, and deeply attractive, to men, but never once allowing any of them close. Only himself, yet even Cecil, who had learnt so much, could never be sure.

"Mary will die," he whispered.

"You said that two years ago. Do you remember,

William? We travelled down to the Queen at Richmond? She even lent us her own barge, festooned with garlands of artificial flowers and covered with a green silk canopy." Elizabeth half closed her eyes. "All her attendants were dressed in golden damask and blue and royal satin. My sister received us in a rich pavilion set up in a garden maze built in the form of a castle!" Elizabeth paused. "Yes, it was decorated in a checker pattern with silver lilies and golden pomegranates. William, I still dream of that occasion. All that wealth, all that glory. My sister, Mary, sitting there so sickly. I curtsied but thought, God forgive me, why don't you die! All this should be mine. Then there are other times, like this morning; I heard a milkmaid sing and I wished I was as free as her." Elizabeth gestured back at the house. "A lovely mansion, William, with its Irish oak beams, panelled walls, wainscoted chambers, and leaded windows." Her voice rose alarmingly. "But it's still a prison."

Cecil tugged at his cuffs. He walked over under the outstretched branches of a great oak tree. He gazed up, even now ensuring that no one was hidden there, listening.

"Sit down, sit down," he murmured. "Open your Greek Testament."

"Why?" she asked.

"Because I am sure Sir Thomas Pope, whom the Queen has placed here at Hatfield, is watching us from a window." Cecil strained his eyes and watched the doorway. "I wager one gold piece . . ."

"I never bet on certainties," Elizabeth joked back.

A figure appeared in the doorway. Elizabeth giggled behind her hand. Sir Thomas Pope, resplendent in a red-brocaded jerkin and light yellow hose, waddled across the lawn, his satin slippers providing a poor foothold on the wet grass. White-haired, cheery-faced, with his chest pushed out, he resembled a plump, jovial pigeon, kindly and fussy. Elizabeth had secretly vowed that, when she took the throne, she would reward him for his gentleness.

"I wonder if he'll slip?" she whispered.

Sir Thomas, however, had given up dignity for safety. He waddled across slowly before doffing his bonneted cap.

"I heard your voice raised. Is all well?" Pope's watery eyes scrutinized the Princess anxiously.

"Sir Thomas, Sir Thomas," Elizabeth replied soothingly, "I was deep in argument with Master Cecil here on the true meaning of the Greek *kalos*. He claims it can only be translated as *beautiful*. I believe, as did Dean Colet, that it can have the meaning of *agathos,* or *merciful.* "

Sir Thomas stared, open-mouthed. Elizabeth touched Cecil with her shoe, a warning not to smile or laugh: Sir Thomas Pope knew as much about Greek as a dog did about flying.

"It's a very important matter, Sir Thomas," she insisted. "And one dear to Her Majesty's heart."

Sir Thomas, an authority only on horseflesh and good claret, nodded reassuringly.

"It is about Her Majesty," he spluttered, "that I am here."

Elizabeth's heart skipped a beat.

"Tomorrow she celebrates Maundy Thursday. She wishes

you to join her at the Maundy ceremony and the great pontifical Mass to be celebrated later."

"Tell Her Majesty"—Elizabeth shook her head—"that her kindness is too much. However, I do not feel well, Sir Thomas." Elizabeth's fingers scrabbled at her brocaded stomacher. "A few pains. I'm totally unfit to travel. Please convey to Her Majesty my deepest regrets."

"Of course, of course," Sir Thomas reassured her. "But, my lady, if you are sickening, a physician . . . ?"

"No, no." Elizabeth wafted her hands. "I was a healthy person, Sir Thomas, until I met physicians!"

Pope realized this might be a witticism, so he smiled.

"In which case, my lady." He stepped back, nearly slipped, but managed to bow. "Ah, Master Cecil." He straightened up.

Sir Thomas always found it easier to talk to men than women: they were like horses, he could always read their minds, but women, especially this red-haired princess whom no one knew what to do with. . . . Pope regarded her as mysterious as the Greek she studied.

"Yes, Sir Thomas?" Cecil asked kindly.

"A man's waiting in the kitchen. Stephen Orslett. He says he knows you."

"Ah yes, Orslett! Sir Thomas, ask him to wait for a few minutes and then send him out."

Pope, happy to have learnt something he understood, smiled and waddled off.

"I don't want to go to Mass!" Elizabeth hissed. "I don't

want to sit for hours and be watched by Mary and her Catholic bishops, with those dark-garbed Spaniards waiting for me to make a mistake or say something I shouldn't. William." She gripped her secretary's hand. "Mary could live for years. Her belly grows big but there's nothing inside. One day there might be, and how will I end my days? An ageing, single woman being carted like a hogshead from one manor to another? Or married off to some imbecilic Italian prince to burn away under the hot sun?"

"The Four Evangelists," Cecil replied coolly, "are a more pressing danger."

Elizabeth wrapped her arms across her chest. If the future was a nightmare, she thought, it held no greater terrors than that letter Master Cecil had received only a week ago.

"Who are they?" she asked. "Master Cecil, who are they?"

"I don't know," Cecil replied. "But you must act as if it means nothing to you. I am, my lady, spending every last coin on finding out. If this goes on, I'll take all my wealth to the pawnbrokers. Talking of which, here comes Orslett."

The man who walked across the lawn was as different from Sir Thomas Pope as chalk from cheese. His black, oily hair swept back over his ears, and he had a swarthy face, dark slit eyes, and a slightly broken nose over full red lips. Orslett was dressed in a brown leather jerkin, leggings, and war boots on which the spurs clinked merrily. The war belt slung round his waist was weighed down slightly on one side by a sword with a basket hilt and a short stabbing dirk. He carried studded gauntlets and tapped these gently against his thigh as he strolled leisurely across. He nodded to Cecil but gave the Princess the most flattering bow.

"Well, Master Orslett?" Elizabeth studied this most secretive of Cecil's agents. A former priest, so they said, a soldier, an assassin: mice-eyed, quiet as a cat, venomous as a snake. Cecil often called on him for what he termed his "delicate tasks," yet they also knew he worked for the Queen.

"I have been to London, Sir William." Orslett's voice was cultured, like that of a courtier. "I have wandered many a dank alleyway and drunk in the shabbiest and filthiest of taverns. No one knows who the Four Evangelists are, not a peep, not a whisper. The same at court. The parchment is undoubtedly good," Orslett continued, "the writing most elegant: it contains a threat, does it not?"

"That is our business!" Elizabeth snapped.

"Of course, my lady." Orslett bowed. "But, if I knew more . . ."

"You won't," Cecil intervened. "Master Orslett—" Cecil wondered whether he should feed more secrets to this most duplicitous of men. "Master Orslett, you will go to the Tower."

"On what charge, sir?"

"I'm not jesting," Cecil retorted. "I wish you to bring back a list, it's easy enough to find, of all those who served in or visited the Tower between 1529 and 1535."

"And then?" Orslett asked.

"I shall find our Four Evangelists," Cecil replied. "In the meantime, Master Orslett, I shall give you, and you alone, one name, Philip Savage."

"Who's he?"

"You'll find out if you ever manage to dig him out of his lair." Cecil got to his feet. "He might lead you to the Evangelists!"

Chapter 2

Mary Tudor sat on her throne in the main hall of Greenwich Palace. The Queen was dressed in a gown of burgundy velvet with a white jewelled veil covering her russet hair: she tried to look as relaxed as possible.

I must remember, she thought, to keep my fingers away from my stomach. If people see me clutching they'll think the gripes and pain have returned. Or worse, that one of her false pregnancies had begun. Mary blinked quickly to hide her tears. So desirous was she of bearing Philip an heir, her belly had swollen up, but, in fact, there was no child, no heir. Now no husband: Philip had absented himself from England, claiming that pressing business in the Low Countries delayed his return.

Mary stared around the great hall. Benches were set, and in front of each bench, were stools for forty-two old and poor women to put their feet on; forty-two being the number of the Queen's years. In accordance with the Catholic rite, to celebrate the Lord's last supper, the feet of these poor people were to be cleansed by the almoner and subalmoner of her household and then washed by her. On either side of the Queen, the rest of the court watched the ceremony being carried out. Antoine Noailles was present, the foxy-faced, russet-haired French envoy. His presence was barely tolerated, but Mary had conceded that Calais was lost and her policy of helping Spain against England's old enemy had brought nothing but ruin. The envoy now stood one leg slightly forward, thumb between his lips, eyes half-closed. Now and again he would glance sideways, smile, and go back to licking the end of his thumb.

"He's crowing with triumph!"

Mary turned to the dark-haired, ivory-faced young woman sitting on her right: her principal lady-in-waiting and closest friend, Jane Dormer. Mary stared wistfully at Jane's beautiful face; so delicate, so exquisitely formed, full generous lips, lustrous, sea grey eyes, hair as black as a raven's wing. Jane, because of Lent, was garbed in dark colours, but these only emphasized her elegant beauty.

If I were as beautiful as you, Mary thought as she glanced quickly down at Jane's bosom, if my body were as rich and as tender as yours, would Philip have stayed?

"Madame, are you all right?" Jane leaned so close Mary could smell her perfume. "Monsieur Noailles," Jane continued, "stands like a barnyard cock."

"Let him crow for a while," Mary whispered, conscious that others were now looking towards her, wondering what was happening. Jane's gloved hand caught at the Queen's fingers.

"You are well, my lady?"

"A case of the rheums. My teeth ache and I feel as if a fire has been lit in my belly."

Mary breathed in and sat back on the throne. Of all the courtiers in the hall, her household officers, members of the council, Mary trusted none of them: only Jane. Mass had been celebrated in the palace chapel, and, throughout, Mary had been racked by doubt and guilt. She had sent Protestant bishops to the flames: Cranmer, Latimer, Ridley, Hooper. Others of the common sort had also died in terrible agonies in the fires of Smithfield. Mary had brought the old faith back: the monks, the friars, the priests, the Mass, yet it was all to no avail. The people did not want it. Mary believed that most of those present were only there as a pretence, a show. They were just waiting: waiting for her to die; waiting for Elizabeth, that little vixen, to ascend the throne and wear the crown of Edward the Confessor. Mary's stomach clenched in pain; her hand went beneath her cloak. Mary glanced to her right. Dr. Theophilus, that learned physician who had studied in the schools of Italy, was watching her with concern. She half smiled. Theophilus himself did not look well: his hair and beard looked straggly, unkempt and unwashed. He had an unhealthy pallor and his constant blinking seemed to have grown worse. Medice sane teipsum, Mary thought: Doctor heal thyself. She closed her eyes and muttered a prayer for forgiveness. Theophilus was a good physician and the potions and powders he provided often eased her pain.

"Madame?"

Her chamberlain had now approached the throne. A

buzz of conversation grew round the hall. Mary looked down and realized that the almoner and subalmoner had finished their task. Mary rose quickly and walked down the broad steps of the dais. Servants hurried up. Mary took off her robe, a purple cloak lined with marten fur. A long, linen apron was placed round her middle, a towel laid across her neck so it hung down either side like a priest's stole. Mary went towards the first old woman. She knelt and, with Jane Dormer and her other ladies-in-waiting around her, the Queen began washing the feet prepared by the almoner. Jane held a silver ewer, and another lady-in-waiting held a gold pot full of sweet-smelling, medicinal herbs. Mary washed the feet carefully, dried and crossed them, and fervently kissed the old, wrinkled skin. Mary, shuffling on her knees, moved to the next woman: all the time she prayed that Christ would recognize her humility, her act of self-denial, and, in his great wisdom, grant her some peace. Mary was also determined to show the throng of peacock courtiers, sniggering behind their hands at the top of the hall, that she was not as sick and infirm as they considered her. Mary the Queen had steely determination, yet Jane Dormer hovered over her like an anxious mother hen. The Queen moved round the hall, washing one pair of feet after another. Despite the preparations of the almoner and the heavy perfume of her ladies, the stench from these old women made Mary gag. She glanced up at Jane.

"After the ceremony," she murmured, "these women must be given a bath, fresh raiment, good food, and wine!"

Jane nodded. Mary went back to the washing of feet. She

tried to keep her mind on the ceremony. She was imitating Christ's actions at the Last Supper. She, who was showing mercy, fervently prayed that she would be shown mercy. Her tired mind wandered away. If only Philip would come back. If only they could live like man and wife. If only she could bear a healthy son. If only she had not given the order to burn so many. If only the Londoners would show her some love. If only the balladeers and pamphleteers would stop their hail of invective. If only Calais had not been lost. If, if, if . . . Mary found she couldn't stop the tears. The watching courtiers thought these were the result of spiritual fervour, but Mary felt her mind was balancing on the edge. She felt an irresistible urge to stop what she was doing, lie down on the floor, and rest. She paused, breathing in deeply. She was the daughter of Catherine of Aragon, granddaughter of the great Isabella of Spain. If she showed any weakness, her enemies would strengthen. The Queen looked up and sighed. The end of the washing was in sight.

Mary moved and began to wash another pair of feet, pouring the water gently, drying them with a towel. Mary stiffened. Something was wrong. These feet were soft and supple, the skin smooth and warm. Only old women were supposed to be here. Mary glanced up in alarm. The grey hair was a wig; the face it shrouded was young and hard. The woman's hand was coming up. Jane Dormer screamed as the knife appeared. Mary lifted the bowl, the cold water splashing down her dress, and blocked the parry. The woman tried to strike again, but Mary caught her wrist and glared into the hate-filled eyes.

"Jezebel!" the woman screamed. "Great whore of Babylon! You murdering bitch!"

Mary gripped the arm. She heard, as if from afar, the sound of running footsteps. The woman kept pressing down. Mary prayed her grip wouldn't slip, and then the royal yeomen were all about her. One punched the woman in the face, another gripped her by the neck. All was confusion. The would-be assassin was dragged away, kicking and screaming. Mary had never seen such hate. Jane Dormer was beside her. The noise in the hall was like waves breaking about her, and then she swooned.

She came to in her own private chamber. Above her was the red-and-gold tester of the great four-poster bed. The room was warm; chafing dishes full of burning coals glowed on pewter dishes, and the fire in the hearth had been built up. Jane Dormer was smiling down at her.

"My lady. Madame?"

The Queen blinked and pulled herself up against the bolsters.

"God forgive me," she declared. "I fainted!"

"God forgive you indeed."

Jane Dormer shooed the other ladies-in-waiting out into the chamber. Coming back, she sat on the bed and took Mary's hand in hers; it felt like a block of ice.

"Dr. Theophilus has been here. He said that it was only shock and exertion." Jane pointed to the smelling salts on the side of the bed. "He was more agitated than me so I told him to go."

Mary smiled feebly. "They will see it as a weakness."

"They will see it as God's design," Jane replied tartly.

She hid her despair. The Queen looked dreadful. Over the last few months Mary's face had taken on an ashy pallor, there were dark rings round her eyes, the tip of her nose was red, and a rash of spots on her chin showed beneath the paste. Jane looked at the Queen's neck; her ruff had been unloosened, and the skin was thin and sinewy. Mary sensed Jane's desperation. If only Philip were here! Mary smiled as she realized she was on the verge of what Jane called her "litany of if's."

"I'm being selfish," she said. "You, too, miss him, don't you?"

"Not Philip." Jane threw her head back and laughed. "But his envoy, yes!"

The Queen felt a pang of jealousy as Jane's beautiful face lit with pleasure. A most unexpected match, she thought: Jane, so vivacious, full of laughter, ever ready to giggle at the stuffy protocol of court etiquette, had fallen deeply in love with Count de Feria, the sober, astute, dark-eyed, olive-skinned envoy of Philip of Spain. De Feria was cool and precise in all his movements. A born diplomat, court etiquette even seemed to govern the way de Feria dressed, walked, spoke, ate, and drank. At first, Mary thought it was a match of ice and fire. However, as the months passed, Mary realized that this was all a mask. De Feria was a loyal, warmhearted, and dedicated man with a mordant sense of humour and a sharp wit. He adored Jane. Mary used to sit fascinated on court occasions as de Feria was locked in a battle to adopt the poise of a diplomat while, all the time, his eyes would shift to Jane Dormer; she, of course, always played the minx.

"He'll be here soon," Mary said. "Don't worry, Jane. I want to dance at your wedding!"

Jane leaned over and kissed the Queen on her brow: it was cold and clammy.

"You should rest, my lady." Jane made to get up, but Mary pulled her back.

"The assassin?"

"Margaret Fotherel," Jane replied. "The guards have her in the dungeons below."

"Has she been interrogated?"

"She has been questioned."

"Roughly?" Mary asked.

Jane glanced away. "She's been questioned. Madame, she tried to kill you. You are the Lord's anointed. God knows how she got in."

"No one is to be blamed," Mary interrupted. "She fooled the guards, she fooled the almoner, and she nearly fooled me. I want to know." Mary tried to fasten up her ruff. "I want to know why this woman tried to kill me!"

Jane made to refuse, but Mary's face had a stubborn set to it. Jane knew she was not to be put off. She helped the Queen make ready, put some fresh paint on her face, and made sure her apparel was correct. In the antechamber beyond, other ladies-in-waiting and members of the household came fluttering, all concerned. The Queen stilled their clamour.

"I am well and unhurt," she declared. "I thank you for your concern. It was just the heat!"

The courtiers clapped.

"Captain of the guard!"

The embarrassed, red-faced Sir Henry Grantchester, helmet under his arm, pushed his way through and went down on one knee in front of the Queen. Mary allowed him to kiss her fingers, a sign that she bore him no ill will.

"Madame." Sir Henry bowed his head. "I was at fault."

"You are not at fault."

Mary stroked the young man's head. Try as she might, she couldn't stop the tears welling. If only this soldier were her son, tall, upright, honest! Why? Mary thought. Why won't God give me a son?

The soldier stood up.

"The assassin, Madame . . .!"

"Would-be assassin, Sir Henry," Mary warned. "She never killed me."

"She's in the dungeons, Madame. Tomorrow morning she will appear before the justices at Westminster."

"And then what?"

"She is guilty of treason, Your Grace. She will be hanged and drawn!"

"London stinks of death!" The Queen made a cutting movement with her hand. "I wish to see her."

The captain of the guard was about to object, but Jane Dormer caught his eye and shook her head. The soldier led the Queen out of the royal chambers. As they did so, other guards joined them. Soldiers stood along the galleries, at the top of the stairs and below. Courtiers hurried up to offer their congratulations, but Mary just shook her head and the crestfallen time-servers withdrew. Mary was tense, her back stiff as a ramrod. She wanted to meet this Margaret Fotherel. She wanted to know why the woman despised her so much. Why so many Londoners hated her. When she stepped into the dank, mildewed dungeon which lay in the caverns beneath the palace, Mary ignored the smells, the hideous stench, the murky gloom. Fotherel had been manacled to the wall, her face was a mass of bruises, her shabby gown had been torn. The captain of the guard took a torch and held it close. Mary, ignoring his protests, stood as near as possible. Fotherel had not lost consciousness. She simply watched Mary out of the corner of her eye.

"You've come to gloat?"

"I've come to talk."

"Kill me."

"Why?" Mary asked. "Why should I kill you?"

Fotherel now looked at her directly, her wild-eyed look replaced by puzzlement.

"What, more papist trickery! You and your bishops, your limbs of Satan!"

"Just tell me," Mary asked, ignoring the protests of the guard and Jane behind her, "just tell me why you tried to kill me, the Lord's anointed?"

"You are not the Lord's anointed. You are a usurper, a Jezebel." Fotherel's voice broke. "You killed my father. He was a merry man, a tailor in Cripplegate but, because he refused the host and wine, your singing bread, your sacraments, my father was taken before bloody Bonner!" Fotherel's lips curled at the mention of Mary's old but ruthless bishop of London. "Tried and found guilty he was! Put in a coat of tar and burnt at Smithfield, not even a bag of gunpowder round his neck. I watched his eyes bubble and his skin crack like peeling paint under a summer sun!"

Mary's stomach clenched with pain. She gasped. Fotherel leaned forward in a clash of chains.

"God's judgement on you!" she hissed. "God's judgement on all of yours!"

Mary put a fist to her mouth. She felt like crying out, sinking down on the rotting, wet straw, letting the rats which scrabbled in the corner come and crawl their slimy bodies all over her. Five years she had been Queen! Five years holding the sceptre and orb, and it had all come to this. She was hated and despised because she had tried to bring back the old religion, the Catholic faith which had flourished in this island before the legions ever left.

"She'll hang!" Sir Henry declared. "Or burn!"

Mary felt tired. "Let her go," she murmured.

Fotherel's head came back.

"Give her ten strokes of the cane. No, don't even give her that!" Mary flicked her hand. "Let her go! Let her go! Let her go! Captain of the guard, carry out my order!"

Mary swept from the cell. She walked rigidly, back straight, head erect, allowing the servants to go before her. Only when she returned to her chamber, and Jane Dormer closed the door behind the rest, did Mary crumple to the floor, her skirts billowing out around her. She sat and sobbed into her hands.

"They hate me." She lifted a tear-stained face; a fiery stab in her innards made her wince and brought Jane Dormer hurrying beside her.

"Madame, get up! Please, get up!"

Jane helped the still wincing queen to a couch, silver-edged with blue and gold cushions with small mother-of-pearl fleurs-de-lie embroidered there. The room was now darkening. Mary shivered. Her father had been here once. Yes, she remembered coming in here, and Henry, his legs apart, thumbs stuck in his silver brocaded belt, had seemed to fill the room with his great frame. He'd walked towards her in slippered feet and stared down at her. He'd then given her the rough edge of his tongue about her refusal to accept the Act of Supremacy which made him head of the English Church. Eventually Mary had given in to her father's wishes. She had betrayed her mother's memory and her faith. Mary had vowed never to do that again. She closed her eyes.

"I hate you!" she hissed. "I hate you! I hate you!" Her fist went to her mouth. "Mother's heart is as black as a rotten pear!"

Jane Dormer, bringing across one of Dr. Theophilus's potions, abruptly stopped. Mary was now lost in her own nightmares. Jane trembled: Mary's mind was wandering too close to the darkness. The Queen had never forgotten how the physicians, when they had embalmed her mother's heart for burial, had found it black and rotting. Some had mentioned poison: others, more knowledgeable, had named ar-

senic. And there were other stories: how, when Mary became Queen, she and her close councillor Reginald Pole,
now also very ill, had, as an act of vengeance, secretly in the
dead of night, dug up Henry's corpse from his tomb in
Windsor and cast his bones into the Thames.

"My lady, you should rest!"

Mary opened her eyes quickly, like shutters being thrown
back. At first she seemed not to recognize Jane.

"Madame, the Queen," Mary declared dreamily, "will go
and see her councillor."

"Madame, madame!" Jane knelt beside her, the small cup
of potion in her hand. "Cardinal Pole is ill, he's sick, his mind
is wandering."

"Then I am alone." Mary gasped.

"You have me!"

Mary forced a smile.

"Madame, look at your present situation," Jane continued. "You are ill. Your belly troubles you again."

"It is nothing." Mary waved a hand. "Nothing but the
passing of the year."

"Madame, have you ever thought of poison?" Jane
steeled herself, playing deliberately on Mary's nightmares
about her own mother. "Madame, you are a Tudor of good
stock: the granddaughter of Isabella of Castile. These stomach pains, they come and go. Dr. Theophilus is mystified."

"Poisoned?" Mary asked. "Poisoned?" she repeated.

The room suddenly filled with ghosts: her mother,
Catherine, dressed in black, her belly swollen, her face podgy
and pale with pain. Had Father poisoned her? And Henry?

Balding, his great carcass rotting, lying in bed with his council gathered like crows around him. Was it true that some of them had helped him on his way? Put a cushion over his mouth to stop his breath? And, beside him, "God's little imp," her half-brother Edward VI, pale and sickly, large dark eyes in a thin, pinched face. There were rumours that old Northumberland had a finger in his death.

"But who would poison me?" she asked.

"There are those at court." Jane Dormer let the words hang in the air like a scaffold noose.

"I know. I know." Mary finished the sentence for her. "There are those who flock to Hatfield around little, red-haired Elizabeth. She and Master Cecil sit like little spiders in a corner of a room, spinning a web which might kill us all. But, I ask you, Jane, how could they poison me?"

"She sends you gifts," Jane replied. "Wine and sweetmeats. You eat and drink them! Her men, her spies are here. How do we know which cooks, scullions, chamberlains, and chambermaids are not with her? You hired Dr. Theophilus because he has an allegiance to no one. How do we know that?" Jane took a deep breath and continued. "Then there's the French; Monsieur Noailles is constantly sending you this and that. And, madame, what does it mean, Mark 15.34?"

Mary half smiled to herself and shrugged. Jane stared at her mistress. There are others who want you dead, she thought. But I dare not mention their names. First the English, and their number is legion. The woman in the dungeons, Fotherel, was simply one amongst a multitude. Jane dared not tell the Queen her worst suspicions about Philip of Spain. Philip, who had married Mary to keep England in the Spanish camp. Did Philip want Mary out of the way? Were the rumours true? Even Juan, her betrothed, had hinted that Philip's eyes were now wandering to Elizabeth. Jane closed her eyes and said a short prayer. She could not taste and drink everything the Queen did. Yet Jane was alarmed. She really believed her mistress was being poisoned, slowly murdered, but by whom? And the words of that anonymous letter from the Four Evangelists: "What price the Crown of England? Ave Maria sepulta. Mark 15.34." Jane gripped Mary's fingers.

"I saw the message," she said. "Madame, someone sees you dead and hails your memory."

"Mark 15.34," Mary muttered, then smiled. "The phrase is apposite, is it not? The words Christ screamed out on the cross when he felt forsaken. 'Eloi, Eloi, lamma sabacthani? My God, my God, why have you forsaken me?' " Mary gave a short, barking laugh. "I could say that of myself."

Another wince of pain; the Queen took the medicine from Jane's hand and drank it in one gulp.

"Some wine?" she muttered.

Jane went across, filled a silver filigree cup, and brought it back. The Queen sipped at it. She glanced up, a mischievous twinkle in her eyes.

"So, what do you propose, Jane? Shall I bring Elizabeth back to the Tower and put her on trial for high treason? But on what charge? I am not my father. I do not wish to kill my relatives!"

"You could pack her off to Ludlow in Shropshire!" Jane

snapped. "And send Master Cecil to inspect our fortifications on the northern march or, even better, on an embassy to France: your cousin Mary is now wife of the Dauphin." Jane glanced away. Aye, she thought, and there's another who has a claim to the throne of England. "And then, Mary." Jane very rarely lapsed into first-name terms with her mistress. "Come away with me! Come to Sinistrel Manor in Essex!"

"A gloomy place with a gloomy name!" Mary retorted.

"It's always been called that." Jane laughed. "Because it stands on the left side of the road to Epping. It's moated and surrounded by a high wall, so it's secure and peaceful. Let your mind and body rest. After Easter, madame; the almanac says it will be a good spring, the air will be cool and crisp. You can hunt the deer or stroll in the park. Forget London and its politics, Dr. Theophilus and his medicines. You need to sleep, to rest."

Mary sat back on the couch, and Jane took a deep breath. She could tell by her mistress's face that the prospect was pleasing. She cursed when there was a loud rap on the door. The captain of the guard came in.

"Madame, there is a man here who wishes to see you, Stephen Orslett."

Jane hoped the Queen would refuse, but Mary leaned forward.

"Oh yes, let him come in. And, Sir Henry, make sure no one listens at the keyhole."

Sir Henry bowed and withdrew. A few minutes later Orslett entered, soft as a cat slipping through the half-open door. He nodded to Jane, who now took a chair beside the

Queen's couch, then he went down on one knee before Mary and kissed her hand.

"Madame, you show me great kindness."

Mary laughed. "Master Orslett, you are a skilful and subtle man: the more I know of you the less I like."

"I am Your Grace's most humble servant."

"You are also Cousin Elizabeth's most humble servant!" Mary retorted.

Orslett lifted his head and smiled.

"Oh, for heaven's sake, man, sit in a chair!"

Orslett obeyed, his leather jacket and leggings creaking. He removed his war belt as every man who entered the Queen's presence had to. He pushed his black leather gauntlets down the side of the chair. Jane noticed how his fingers were long and slender like those of a harpist or seamstress.

"Madame, can I congratulate you on your escape? The news has already swept through to London."

"Thank you, Stephen. Jane, put a few more coals on the fire!" Mary rubbed her arms. "I feel cold."

Jane got up reluctantly. Orslett had a foot in every camp and a finger in each man's pie. A professional spy, a Judas man. The type who met under the eaves of houses, locked in hushed conversation with shabby strangers. Jane did not know whom he really served, Mary, Elizabeth, both, or just himself.

"And how is Cousin Elizabeth?" Mary asked.

Orslett's eyes slid towards Jane putting coals on the fire; his mouth watered. She was a beautiful woman with her piled-up black hair and slim waist; her every move was elegant. Orslett's eyes returned to the Queen.

"She is well, Your Grace. Much frightened by Mark 15.34, though I don't know why."

"Neither do I," Mary replied.

"Cecil suspects something. He has instructed me to go to the Tower to make careful listing of who visited there between 1529 and 1535."

"That should be easy for you," Mary replied. "You are a trained clerk, Stephen. There are even whispers that you once were ordained as a priest and celebrated Christ's mysteries on the altar."

"I am to hunt down the Evangelists," Orslett continued evasively. "But who they are, madame, and where they could be?" He shrugged one shoulder.

"And when you find them?"

"I suppose Master Cecil will tell me to kill them, Your Grace."

Mary leaned forward, steepling her fingers in front of her mouth. So, she thought, the hunt is on. Orslett was her best Limner, a greyhound of a man, swift and ruthless.

"Your Grace, what are your orders?"

Mary stared at this man who had played such a vital role when her brother, Edward, had died and Lady Jane Grey had raised the standard of rebellion. It was Orslett who'd hurried to Framlingham in Suffolk: he had been one of Northumberland's henchmen but confessed he could not stomach the Duke's treason. He informed Mary and her council of the rebels' plans and the strength of her enemies, and Mary had taken careful note before making her brave march on London. In the end, Northumberland and all his coven, his son, Guildford, and Lady Jane Grey had all gone to the block. Mary took her hands away from her mouth. More ghosts! Northumberland had to die, but Lady Jane should have been spared; a stripling, a mere girl!

"Too much blood!" she murmured.

"Your Grace?"

"Nothing, Orslett." Mary did not know whether to trust this man. "Go to the Tower. Do what Master Cecil says. Hunt down the Evangelists but do not kill them: their lives are in my hands." Mary lowered her face. Perhaps she would help Orslett, whet his appetite.

"Your Grace?"

"Yes, Orslett. You could help me in this matter. I cannot," the Queen lied, "do anything myself."

Orslett undid the top of his leather jerkin; the shirt beneath was white and crisp. Mary wondered if Orslett had a woman.

"Are you married, Stephen?"

"Yes, Your Grace. I have a house in Poultry. My wife, Alice, and three children."

Mary's mouth gaped. She did not expect that from such a man. He was lustful; his hot eyes secretive and sly.

"And you love them?" Mary tried to keep the envy out of her voice.

"Yes, Your Grace, I do." Orslett smiled mice-eyed at Jane. "But I am much tempted."

Jane turned away.

"Go to the Tower," Mary declared. "Of course, I can give you no documentation." She bit her lip and hid her grimace at the sore she had created there. "Search out, be busy on my half-sister's behalf. But, of course, Stephen, you are doing that, aren't you? You have a way of searching things out."

"Your Grace, of course, is right. I am also looking for someone else, Philip Savage."

"Ah!" Mary put her hand down. "I wondered when that name would surface. Philip Savage?" she mused. "I met him once, you know. When Father, in one of his rages, had committed me to the Tower. Philip Savage, the controller, a greasy, little ball of a man with his flickering tongue and that journal in which he kept notes of all his visitors." She looked narrow-eyed. "I thought he had retired, even died?"

"Rumour has it, Your Grace, that he is still alive. He may have the key to the secret of Mark 15.34."

Mary hid her fear. "If you find him, Stephen, you are to come back here." She extended her hand as a sign that her audience was over. Orslett kissed it and left.

"Why do you trust him?" Jane asked, coming to sit beside her mistress.

"I trust him for three reasons," Mary retorted. "First, I have to. Secondly, I have no proof that he's a traitor and, thirdly, he keeps an eye on my little half-sister and her wizard Master Cecil. Hatfield's a hotbed of sedition."

"You have other spies there?"

"Yes, but Elizabeth knows they are spies."

Jane went to kneel before her mistress and grasped her cold hand.

"Mary," she whispered, "what is so important about these Four Evangelists? What does Mark 15.34 mean? Why should the Saviour's dying words on the cross mean so much to Elizabeth and her familiar, Cecil?"

Mary steeled herself against the lie.

"It means everything to her, I think, and, therefore, Jane, everything to me!"

Chapter 3

On the feast of Saints Peter and Paul, 29 June 1558, Peter Carafa, known to Europe as Pope Paul IV, Servant of the Servants of God, 221st successor to St. Peter, Bishop of Rome, and recognized as Pope by the Catholic powers, knelt in his small private chapel in the castle of San Angelo overlooking the Tiber. Carafa stared up at the simple, stark crucifix: his severe, lined, bearded face twisted in annoyance. He had just passed his eighty-first spring, yet he cursed the passing of the years; how his ageing body could not keep up with his mind, as subtle as any which governed the chanceries of Europe. The Pope often came here, away from the glories of the Vatican, of St. Peter's, or the basilica of St. John Lateran; the castle of San Angelo was safe, heavily fortified against those Roman noble families who loved to plot and block his every move. Paul's snakelike eyes closed momentarily. They were nothing but dirty froth on a pond! Christ's Vicar on earth had other more important matters to resolve: Spain! Carafa's thin lips tightened even further. How he hated the power of Spain! That little, thin-faced viper Philip who proclaimed he was a Catholic, the Church's most loyal son! In reality, Philip was no different from the great arch-heretics who ruled their countries and seized the property and wealth of the Church. Carafa regarded Spain as a spider, spinning its web here in Italy, the Low Countries, the Empire, France, and now England. It was England which concerned Carafa. What was Philip plotting to do? What would happen when Mary Tudor, Henry VIII's sick daughter, died? And Carafa knew Mary was dying. . . .

The Pope heard the door open. Two men entered the chapel. Carafa did not turn: he knew he was safe. His bodyguard of handpicked cut-throats would never allow anyone in unless they had been scrupulously searched and Carafa specifically wanted to see them. He listened to the soft footfalls: the one standing behind him on his right must be Dr. Cesar, one of his personal physicians. A small, Italinate man, he wore his silver hair neatly coifed back and had a pointed face with a closely trimmed military moustache and beard. A merry-eyed soul, Cesar put his faith in strange potions but cheerfully confessed that he had no cure for death. The Pope closed his eyes. Carafa trusted Dr. Cesar as he hoped he could his other visitor, who must be standing just to his left: Nicholas Segalla, black-haired, sallow-faced, dressed in the robes of the newly founded Jesuit order. He was Carafa's confidant and special counsellor, emissary and envoy. A man with no family and very little past.

The Pope joined his hands in prayer, bowing his head so

he looked like a saint kneeling there on the heavy cushions before the altar. Yet he was not meditating or praying. Carafa regarded God as an equal to whom he could talk whenever and wherever he wished. Carafa's mind teemed like a box of worms. Segalla was for England, but could he be trusted? Carafa had only been Pope for three years. He had chosen Segalla from the household of his predecessor. He had set traps, but, at every turn and twist, Segalla proved his confidence and trustworthiness. Carafa was intrigued: he had searched amongst the archives and sometimes he listened to the stories about Segalla. Was the Jesuit a magician? A man with special powers? Other Segallas had worked for popes, decades, even centuries, ago. Segalla claimed his family had always been servants to the papacy, so Carafa couldn't argue any different, but sometimes he wondered. . . . He heard a cough.

"Your Holiness!"

The Pope crossed himself and, groaning and moaning, got to his feet. He grasped the silver-topped cane the young Jesuit put into his hand.

"Thank you, Nicholas," he whispered.

Carafa nodded at Dr. Cesar, who looked resplendent in his blue and silver lace, velvet doublet and jacket. A man for the ladies was Dr. Cesar, with his easygoing smile, courtly ways, and the lavish spending of his accumulated wealth. The doctor gave his most exquisite bow.

"Your Holiness looks in the best of health."

"Your Holiness," Carafa retorted, "is not in the best of

health!" He tweaked Dr. Cesar's cheek, squeezing it tightly between finger and thumb until he saw the light blue eyes wince with pain. At the same time Carafa's other hand tapped the cane on the paved stone floor. "I've got pains in my back, my arse, my thighs! My nose is blocked, my eyes are streaming! It pains me to pass water and my stools! Well, you've seen my stools so we won't talk about them now!"

Carafa took his hand away and walked over to the pontifical chair set against the wall. He sat down and gestured that his two visitors occupy the bench opposite. Cesar obeyed with alacrity, rubbing his cheek where the Pope had tweaked it. Segalla, dressed as usual like a crow, black from head to toe, was as cool and distant as ever: no trace of expression in those soulful eyes, no watchfulness or nervousness. Carafa smiled to himself. He had been a prince of the Church for decades. He always looked for nervous, little gestures, the hallmarks of a traitor. Try as they might, anyone who played the Judas could never really keep their treachery hidden. Segalla could be trusted. The Pope glanced at the heavy-lidded eyes of Dr. Cesar; and as for the good doctor? Well, Carafa held enough on that exquisite fop, that subtle little assassin, to send him to the dungeons far below or even to the execution ground which swept down to the Tiber.

"Your Holiness is in the best of health," Dr. Cesar repeated. "Your Holiness is past his eightieth year, yet you have the vigour of a young man. Philip of Spain," Cesar continued, knowing how Carafa loved to hear about his fellow rulers' misfortunes, "has a ruined digestion; he's liverish and sickly. His father, Charles V, is ill with gout and the rheums: his haemorrhoids are so enlarged he can't sit on a cushion without wincing with pain."

"And Mary of England?" Carafa broke in. "Mary of England is dying, is she not?"

"I have listened to what Your Holiness has told us," Cesar replied. "Mary's body is ill, her mind teeters on madness."

"Could she become pregnant?" Carafa broke in.

"She needs a man," Cesar jibed back. "Yet Philip of Spain is not at home and Mary is not the sort of woman to allow another to plough—"

"Thank you, thank you," Carafa interrupted. "Mary Tudor is a devout Catholic queen, not one of your court whores, Dr. Cesar. Isn't that right, Nicholas?"

"A goodly woman," the Jesuit replied, his eyes never leaving those of Carafa. "Virtuous and kindly, but, Your Holiness, how does this concern us? I know we are to go to England."

Carafa gazed round the chapel. "I like this place," he whispered. "Look at it, Nicholas. Apart from the crucifix on the wall, no pictures, no paintings." He banged his cane on the floor. "No drains, no holes, no gaps! No place where someone can scurry and listen in. Yes, Nicholas, you are off to England, Dr. Cesar with you. He is to treat the Queen," Carafa continued in a hurry. He paused and examined the silver top of the cane. "Mary is being poisoned, by someone very close to her!"

Segalla shifted on the bench and stared at this most ruthless and cunning of pontiffs. Segalla had been drawn into his service. He accepted that Carafa was a man of vision committed to reforming the Church, but he was also of devious wit and subtle mind. Segalla hid his smile: a man, indeed, who would make a good Jesuit, the end always justifying the means. Segalla also knew that Carafa nursed an intense hatred of Spain and feared that, under Philip II, Spain would be prepared to elect an anti-pope under its own direction. Carafa had mentioned, only two days ago as they had sat sipping dark red Falernian, how important it was for Segalla to go to England. Now Carafa was going to open his mind, here in this chapel, where no one could eavesdrop.

"Mary is almost forty years younger than me," Carafa continued. "Her father had a rotting carcass, but Mary was a young and healthy woman: the poisoner must be someone close."

"Her half-sister Elizabeth?" Segalla offered.

"It's possible." Carafa narrowed his eyes. "Elizabeth could be becoming impatient. She's been caught flirting with traitors before. A second such flirtation might prove fatal. More important"—Carafa dipped his finger into a stoup of holy water at the side of him and wetted his lips—"is Philip of Spain. Maybe he tires of Mary. Perhaps he'd like to bed young, red-haired Elizabeth and keep England with him in the Spanish camp."

"Your Eminence," Segalla interrupted. "Are you implying that Philip of Spain would poison his own wife?"

"Philip of Spain," Carafa spat the words out, "would poison his own mother if it suited him! Can you imagine, Nicholas"—Caraffa held up a clawlike hand—"a world where Spain controls the Netherlands and the Empire, parts of Italy and England. What would come next, eh?"

"But Spain would keep England Catholic."

"Would it really?" Carafa snorted with laughter. "Mary has been burning heretics by the cartload. She has tried to bring back our faith. Every day, it grows weaker and she with it!"

"What about the French?" Segalla replied. "They, too, might wish Mary Tudor dead. Elizabeth is regarded as illegitimate, excluded from the succession."

"Aye!" Carafa declared, leaning back in the chair. "My good friend Catherine de' Medici in Paris has ambitions for her daughter-in-law Mary of Scotland." Carafa applied more holy water to his lips. "Leave that for the moment," he murmured as if speaking to himself. "Nicholas, Dr. Cesar, you are to leave Rome tomorrow morning. A Venetian galley at Ostia will take you to one of the Channel ports. No, not in England but in France; probably to Calais or what's left of it!" He smirked. "Now the English have been driven out. Outside there's a small hunting lodge, Blanchetaque, on the river Somme. The French queen will meet you there. You are to give her my official good wishes and most solemn blessing: more importantly, you are to find out what her intentions are regarding England. Now, when you get to England"—Carafa eased himself out of the chair—"you are not to communicate with me but act as you think fit." Carafa waggled a finger. "Always remember, Nicholas, your actions must be governed by one thought only: the safety and security of the Roman Church in both this city and the world, not just for today, but for tomorrow." Carafa hobbled across to a window. "Ride out into the countryside. Italy is a beautiful place, a defenceless maid which the great kingdoms can rape whenever they wish. What is plotted in London, Madrid, or Paris might come to fruition here." Carafa turned and came back. "I want to know what is happening in England. I want to know about Mary Tudor. Above all, I want to know what Spain intends!"

"The poisoner must be someone close," Dr. Cesar spoke up. "There are many potions, but, if Your Holiness is correct, and I am sure you are," he added hastily, "the poison used must be one of a long term: a small bit here, another there."

"Her doctors?" Segalla smiled drily at Dr. Cesar.

"She has many," Carafa replied. "One of them, Dr. Theophilus, or that's what he calls himself, studied here in Italy and held posts in Ferrara and Florence. But why should he poison his Queen? On someone else's orders? And, if it is Elizabeth, that means she has someone very close to the Queen. If it's Philip?" Caraffa clicked his tongue. "You'll meet Lady Jane Dormer, Mary's principal lady-in-waiting, a beautiful woman, much taken by the Count de Feria, Philip's envoy to England."

"But I thought," Segalla declared, "you said that Jane was Mary's close friend?"

Carafa threw his head back in a loud neighing laugh.

"In politics there are no friends. Everyone at the English court is suspect!"

Carafa beat his fist on the arm of the chair as if relishing the joke, then the laughter died. He ran his tongue round his mouth searching for a morsel of food which was irritating his gum. As he did, Carafa watched Segalla out of the corner of his eye. The sly old prelate recalled his own advice: Trust no one! Not even Segalla must know the full picture.

"Ah well! Ah well!" The pontiff stared down the church. How long do I have? he thought. How long before I die and join the other pontiffs in that great mausoleum beneath St. Peter's? And who will come after me, eh? He smiled to himself. He had nearly been beaten to the tiara by Reginald Pole, Mary's confidant, but Carafa had taken care of the Englishman, revoking his legatine powers in England. Moreover, Pole was dying: Carafa closed his eyes at the thought which came next. No, that was sinful, he must not think of that!

"Your Holiness?"

Segalla was leaning forward on the bench.

"Your Holiness, there is more . . . ?"

"Yes, Segalla, there is." Carafa pulled a scroll from his voluminous sleeves and tossed it at the Jesuit.

Segalla unrolled it and read the courtly hand:

Ave Maria sepulta? What price the Crown of England?

Mark 15.34.

The Four Evangelists.

"Before you ask," Carafa added, "the numbers are a reference to St. Mark's Gospel, the dying words of Christ on the cross: 'Eloi, Eloi, lamma sabacthani? My God, my God, why have you forsaken me?' Such a letter has been posted all over

London and has caused consternation both at court and amongst Elizabeth's entourage at Hatfield. God knows who the Four Evangelists are."

"Why does such a message cause such excitement?" Segalla asked.

"I don't know," Carafa replied. "But they are now searching London for a former controller of the Tower, Philip Savage. A sly-eyed knave called Stephen Orslett leads the hunt. God knows whom he works for, but he has decided to concentrate on people at the Tower of London when Savage was controller."

"Why?" Segalla asked.

"I don't know!"

Carafa now got up and walked to the door. He turned and lifted his hand in benediction. Immediately Segalla and Dr. Cesar went down on their knees.

"I've told you what I know. Go in peace, my sons. My chancery will deliver all the documents and money you need. You are to be on board the galley at Ostia by this evening. God be with you!"

The Pope sketched his blessing and quietly left the chapel.

On the feast of the Assumption, 15 August 1558, Nicholas Segalla and Dr. Cesar left Calais and took the road to the royal hunting lodge of Blanchetaque. They had arrived at Calais two weeks earlier, seasick, suffering from rheums and aching in every joint after a slow, boisterous sea voyage. Segalla didn't know who had suffered more, himself or Dr. Cesar. Indeed, the physician had become so grey-faced that Segalla feared he might suffer some seizure and bit his tongue as he recalled the old aphorism, Doctor heal thyself. Nevertheless, once they were ashore in a comfortable tavern, in that part of Calais not burnt during the recent war, Cesar had soon recovered his usual good humour. Segalla, taciturn by nature, was much taken by the little physician, witty, charming, a source for all the scandal in the courts of Europe: who had seduced whom; who took bribes; which party was plotting against another; who was in favour; who was out of favour. A droll companion, Dr. Cesar, once he'd recovered, used all his medical knowledge to nurse Segalla back to health.

"It's all a matter of sleep, food, plenty of rest, fresh air, and keep well away from dirt." Dr. Cesar wagged a finger at Segalla. "Never eat tainted food. Stay well away from the black rat. Water, too, is forbidden unless it comes from a clear spring. Wine may give you a headache but, in this godforsaken place, water can bring you death! Oh, and be on guard against the pox!"

Segalla nodded wisely, keeping his face straight. He tried not to recall the previous evening when, from the good doctor's chamber, had come the most rapturous squealing as the honourable physician entertained two ladies from the town. Of course their arrival in Calais had been noticed, the port bailiffs carefully studying their warrants and letters. Twelve days after their landing, a royal messenger wearing the silver fleurs-de-lis had arrived and informed them at what hour to present themselves at the royal hunting lodge.

They had left in good time, hiring horses from the tavern stables. They reached Blanchetaque early, but they were let through onto the narrow gravel path which swept past trees and small copses up to the main door of the hunting lodge. This was a fairy-tale residence with its pointed towers, coloured glass windows, and polished oaken door, and the ivy creeping up the walls. Servants took their horses. A beautiful young woman, one of Queen Catherine's ladies-in-waiting, came out and curtsied: she flirted with Segalla but, when he gazed stonily back, turned all of her attention to Dr. Cesar. They were taken into an antechamber where two more beautiful damsels served them strips of vension covered in mushroom sauce, soft white loaves, and some of the best claret Segalla had drunk for many a year. When they had finished, Dr. Cesar just gazed beatifically round the oak-panelled room. Segalla went to talk, but Cesar shook his head, raising his eyes heavenwards.

"I just want to make some calculations," the good doctor declared.

He got up and crossed to an escritoire. Cesar sat down as if drawing some figures then handed a piece of parchment to Segalla.

"I think, monsieur, that's how much you owe me," Cesar declared. "You did lose the wager."

Segalla gazed back in puzzlement but then read the note.

> Say nothing that can be dangerous. There are more eye-
> lets and peepholes in this room than there are in a brothel.

Segalla screwed the piece of parchment up and put it into his jerkin.

"Dr. Cesar, I thank you for reminding me. I'll pay you on our return."

They discussed their voyage: the violence of the seas in the Bay of Biscay. Segalla was growing bored when the door was abruptly flung open. A chamberlain announced Cather-ine de' Medici, Queen of France. Cesar and Segalla went down on their knees. Segalla smelt a fragrant perfume and glimpsed a grey taffeta dress. A hand stretched out, cool and soft; the purple amethyst in the ring winking like some fairy light. Segalla brushed this with his fingers and glanced up: Catherine de' Medici's sallow face was covered in a little paint, and her lips were parted in a smile, but the eyes were hard and watchful. She exuded power in every small ges-ture: the lifting and dropping of her shoulders, the clutching at her skirt, and, all the time, those eyes never moved, as if she were searching Segalla's soul. A dangerous woman, Segalla thought. The Queen moved over to greet Dr. Cesar. She then went and sat in a high-backed chair against the wall, in-dicating with her fingers for them to sit. She was unaccom-panied except for one lady-in-waiting who stood near the door. Segalla noticed with amusement how the young woman's body blocked both the keyhole and what he thought was a small eyelet in the woodwork.

"We are safe here." Catherine laughed, low and throaty. Her eyes slid to Dr. Cesar. "Don't worry, the eyelets and peepholes have now been covered up. And you are right, Dr. Cesar, there are more in this room than there are in a brothel." She raised her hand and giggled. "It's such fun," she lapsed into Latin, "to watch people act when they think they are unobserved."

Cesar bowed low in the chair. "Madame, you are most perceptive!"

"Dr. Cesar, don't flatter me. My husband used to flatter me with the fragrance of his whores still on his body. Once that happens to you no compliment is worth a sou." She ran her hand along the arm of her chair and gazed at the speck of dust on her fingers. "Moonbeams," she muttered. "Nothing substantial. Nothing is substantial except power. Isn't that right, Segalla?"

"It depends," he replied.

"Yes, of course it does," Catherine retorted. "It depends very much on who is wielding it, when and why. So, let's not waste time, the Pope sent you here. He wants to know what will happen if Mary Tudor dies? It's quite simple. The only legitimate successor to the English throne is my daughter-in-law Mary of Scotland."

"The English will not accept her," Segalla replied.

"They accepted Philip of Spain," Catherine retorted. "I have written as much to His Holiness: he encourages me in this design."

"Is Mary Tudor dying?" Segalla asked.

"She was sick at Easter and the malady grows worse."

Catherine looked quickly at Dr. Cesar. Segalla could have sworn that she blinked slowly at the doctor, but then she turned her head and did the same to him, as if they shared some secret.

"Do you have a hand in the Tudor's illness?" Segalla asked abruptly.

Catherine laughed and put her finger in her mouth to clean her teeth.

"If I did, monsieur, I certainly would not tell you."

"And Mark 15.34?"

"Oh, the dance has moved on since then," Catherine replied.

She opened the small, black samite bag which hung from a velvet cord round her waist and handed over the small scroll.

"Our envoy in England, Monsieur Noailles, sent us that, copies also being sent to any who'd like to read."

Segalla undid the red cord. The manuscript was thumb-marked, but the parchment was of very good quality and the letters formed in a good, courtly hand. "What price the Crown of England?" it began.

Ave Maria sepulta! Why do you look in the Tower? The tower is empty. Why not look for the truth? It lies in Mark 15.34. Thirty pieces Judas asked when he be-trayed that which he should not. A thousand pieces of gold and we shall give that which we have.

The Four Evangelists.

"Our clerks have studied this," Catherine interrupted.

Segalla lifted his head. Catherine was sitting forward in her chair, eyes bright with excitement.

"Copies of this have been given to Elizabeth at Hatfield, Mary at Greenwich, the Spanish ambassador, as well as ours. What does it mean, eh, Segalla?" Catherine got to her feet and walked over to a small, diamond-shaped window. "You are to be out of France within a day," she declared. "I agreed that with His Holiness. An English ship, allowed in under the truce, will leave tomorrow morning." She turned. "But, until then, you are my guests. Dr. Cesar, your medical knowledge interests me." Catherine turned and glanced slyly at Segalla. She walked across and ran her finger down his smooth, olive cheek. She kept her back to Cesar. Segalla was chilled by the look of this most cunning of queens. She leaned down and whispered in Latin. "One day, Segalla, one day, when both you and I have the time, we must sit down and talk."

"About what, madame?" Segalla replied softly.

"About life, about death, about legends of a man who can avoid it?" Catherine straightened up and gave him a dazzling smile. "But, for now, you have my reply to the Holy Father. If Mary Tudor dies, France will advance the claims of Mary Stuart."

Philip Savage, formerly controller in the Tower, moved his spindly legs wearily along Eel Pie Lane, which ran under the towering mass of St. Paul's Cathedral. Savage was a ruined man with no trace of his former glory or pomposity. He should have been given a generous pension, but dabbling in politics had cost him that. He'd had to give up his house which overlooked the Thames and move to a shabby, mean tenement in Dog Leg Lane, a squalid little chamber at the top of rickety stairs. His only visitor was the burly oaf who came to collect the rent on the last day of every month, and woe betide Savage if he was not there to pay. Savage came to the end of the alleyway. He stopped and watched enviously as a group of maidens danced on a small, grassy plot around their makeshift dance pole. Savage, with his shabby jerkin, hose, and patched boots, was a sorry sight, his thin face dirty and unshaven. Nevertheless, Savage still had his appetites: a cup of claret, a tender piece of beef, and one of those young wenches. Savage's fingers went to his lips. He moaned in quiet pleasure. In his days of glory, when the sun had shone and he had scurried round the Tower with a look of importance on his face! Those had been the days! The great prisoners of state—Stafford, Duke of Buckingham; Thomas Cromwell, Earl of Essex; Anne Boleyn; Lord Rochford—they'd all tried to catch his eye. The silver had streamed in like water, and Savage had lived the life of a splendid hog: fine wines, tasty foods, and young strumpets from the city, fresh and sweet, who would sit on his lap and share a cup of wine as he played with the strings of their bodices.

One of the young girls caught Savage looking at her, and she started to laugh, pointing to him in disdain. Savage shuffled on. All those days were past. No one bothered him, except. . . . Savage stopped, wrinkling his nose. He'd heard rumours: Savage had gone back to his grand house near the river and an old man who'd once served as porter had told him that someone was looking for him; a mysterious man cowled and hooded. Savage didn't like that: he knew it wasn't the others. They, too, were in hiding, and Savage had, for safety's sake, usually ignored their invitations. He reached Dog Leg Lane and scuttled down the dirty, vermin-ridden runnel until he reached the door to his narrow tenement.

"Master Savage?" The young woman waiting in the stinking hallway was brown as a berry; her hair, shining and lustrous, fell down to her shoulders; her swelling, generous breasts were barely covered by a tight-fitting smock. Savage looked at the painted face and licked his lips.

"I have nothing for you," he croaked. "Take your custom elsewhere."

"But I have something for you, Master Savage." She held up the small flask of wine. "Both this and its bearer are gifts for you."

"For me?" Savage went forward, even as the juices started in his mouth. "Who would want to send gifts to a man like me?"

"An old friend, Master Savage." The wench drew towards him, hips swaying. "Someone who knew you in your former glory and wishes to thank you for kindnesses received."

Savage, for the life of him, couldn't remember giving

anyone kindnesses. He beckoned the girl forward and watched her go langorously up the stairs, the tilt of that beautiful head, her slim waist and broad hips. He glimpsed clocked stockings and a trim ankle above decorated shoes. At the top of the stairs Savage trembled as he turned the key in the lock, almost pushing the girl into the dingy chamber within. As he fumbled in the dark, Savage heard the girl chuckle merrily: he quietly promised she would make a different sound before long. He lit two thick tallow candles; the flame burnt a blueish yellow. Savage sat on his cot bed and snatched the flask from the girl's hand. He poured the wine into a battered pewter cup: it tasted like honey to his dried, parched throat.

"Well, go on," he slurred. "Let's see what the bearer has brought!"

The girl slowly undid the laces on her bodice, pushing down her skirts; Savage could barely restrain himself. It was so long, and he could have enjoyed all this if he hadn't been so stupid. If he and the rest hadn't tried to sell that secret to the mysterious Mr. Clarence. Savage drank a second cup more slowly than the first. The girl was almost naked; Savage became aware of another sensation: a burning in his stomach, terrible pains leaping up. He felt he was going to be sick. Savage dropped the cup and started forward, hands gripping his belly. He tried to retch, but his throat seemed to be closing up, depriving him of air. The room had grown so hot and stuffy. Savage, unable to bear the pain any longer, closed his eyes, slumping back on the bed, legs and arms jerking as the deadly poison raced through his body. So quick, he thought. The girl was bending over him, her face no longer smiling. She was the last thing Savage saw before he died.

Chapter 4

Segalla sat at the high table in the main hall of Greenwich Palace. He and Dr. Cesar had arrived from Calais eight days beforehand. They had made their way along the dusty, winding tracks from Dover to Canterbury and then up the old pilgrims' way into London. Segalla and Cesar had been Catherine de' Medici's guests at a splendid supper in the hunting lodge. Despite her whispers, the French queen had raised no contentious matters but seemed more intent on extolling the virtues and merits of the grey-faced, dark-garbed man who sat beside her, Nostradamus. Segalla had studied this most enigmatic of prophets. Nostradamus's reputation was already known in Rome, and Segalla wondered if Nostradamus was a member of the cabala, that very secret coven of great magicians, men and women who knew how to use their hidden powers to determine the future and control the present. Segalla had retired early, alarmed that Catherine de' Medici might draw him into conversation down paths which he did not wish to go.

They had left early the following morning, Dr. Cesar

not much the worse for drinking deeply and being entertained by one of Catherine's ladies-in-waiting. They had reached Calais. French officials already had their baggage packed, but sudden squalls swept the Channel and another week passed before a high-powered cog took them across into the port of Dover. Harbour masters and port reeves had checked their warrants and baggage. Again there was little trouble, and Segalla was pleased that their journey to London had proved uneventful.

They had arrived at Greenwich and been given suitable quarters. Later that same day they were granted a brief audience with the Queen. Mary had been gracious but aloof. She had introduced Jane Dormer, to whom Segalla had taken an immediate liking. The lady-in-waiting had also been pleased to see him. A devout Catholic, she had fussed Segalla and expressed hopes that Dr. Cesar would, with his skill and expertise, be able to help her mistress. Segalla suspected that Dormer was responsible for their luxurious chambers in the second gallery overlooking the Lion Court. The lady-in-waiting herself had come to ensure they were comfortable as well as to present the Queen's invitation to this small, splendid supper to which the Count de Feria, the Spanish ambassador, and Antoine Noailles, the French envoy, had also been invited. A small, select group: Segalla recognized de Feria as one of those professional court officials who so efficiently and effectively served Philip of Spain and his far-flung empire. De Feria was clothed in a suit of dark satin with white lace ruffs at the collar and cuffs. He was a sober-sided man, with dark deep-set eyes, a narrow, pointed face, and a moustache and beard clipped in the military fashion. De Feria spoke elegantly and quietly, but Segalla caught the fire in his eyes whenever he looked at Jane Dormer whilst she, with her flushed cheeks and glittering eyes, made no pretence at hiding her passionate love for this most elegant Spaniard. Noailles was different: overdressed in gaudy colours like a peacock, he was a fussy, little man with red hair and beard, constant high-pitched chatter, and eyes which never stayed still. Segalla realized this was a pretence. In Rome Noailles was known as a skilful and ruthless diplomat, totally dedicated to the interest of his master Henry II and Catherine de' Medici.

Others were also present: Sir Henry Grantchester, the captain of Mary's guard; and Dr. Theophilus, a small, worried-faced man, who from the start regarded Segalla and Dr. Cesar with some animosity. The supper had begun at eight. Segalla himself had given the blessing, and, at first, the conversation had been about Pope Paul's view of the European scene. Segalla answered quickly and quietly, making sure he never mentioned Calais; the loss of that town, held by the English for over 250 years, had been a grievous blow to Mary. Segalla always tried to move the conversation away from himself, paying more attention to the Queen. She was dressed in blue and gold with a jewelled cap to match. Segalla judged her to be very tense. Her face was pallid beneath the paint; now and again the Queen would cough or clutch her stomach as if in pain. Dormer sat on her right, Dr. Theophilus on her left. Occasionally the doctor would pick up a small phial and pour drops into the Queen's cup of watered wine. Segalla suspected it must be some opiate to deaden pain and perhaps soothe the Queen's nerves.

"It's a pity Dr. Cesar couldn't have been here." Theophilus glanced spitefully at Segalla.

"Monsieur," Segalla replied courteously, "the Queen's health is safe in your hands. The only thing Dr. Cesar can do is advise."

"How is the good doctor?" The Queen glanced across the table at Segalla.

Segalla noticed how Jane Dormer, as soon as the Queen's attention was diverted from her, turned to whisper something to de Feria. The Spaniard laughed and dabbed at his lips with a napkin. Across the table Noailles, who had been watching his Spanish counterpart most closely, now glanced at Segalla, intrigued by Theophilus's questions.

"Dr. Cesar is not well," Segalla replied. "Slightly discomfited after his voyage."

Segalla, indeed, had been disturbed by Cesar's appearance: pale and clammy-skinned, the physician had excused himself from the festivities, saying he was suffering a chill.

"I have had a chance to talk to him," Theophilus continued. "A well-qualified man, but His Holiness could have at least informed me that Dr. Cesar was about to arrive."

Segalla shrugged.

"You can never have too many good physicians," the Queen intervened tactfully. "Master Segalla." She looked under her eyebrows at him. "Why have you come?"

Immediately all conversation around her died.

"The Holy Father," Segalla replied, "is concerned, Your

Grace, at the cause of your illness. He sends you his most apostolic blessing and has asked me to represent him here in London."

"He could do more!" the Queen replied archly. She bit her lower lip. "My good friend and councillor Cardinal Reginald Pole is sick, his body is weak, his mind is failing. There is no need," she continued in a rush, "for His Holiness to show such displeasure. . . ."

Segalla sipped from his wine cup. The intense dislike and rivalry between Pole and Pope Paul was well known: not only Paul's rival for the papacy, Pole was seen as a liberal, a man who believed in open dialogue with the Lutherans and the other so-called heretical states in Europe. Paul IV, however, like Philip of Spain, believed that opposition should be crushed by dungeon, fire, and sword.

"His Holiness is also old," Segalla replied. "But, soon, Your Grace, I hope to present his compliments to His Eminence Cardinal Pole. I am sure these difficulties are temporary."

Mary nodded and was caught up in another fit of coughing. She dabbed her mouth with a napkin and smiled at Segalla as if apologizing for her outburst. Segalla bowed perceptibly and returned to cutting up the exquisitely cooked, sliced pheasant in the silver platter before him. Jane Dormer, eager to break the tension, now began to openly wonder who was the most courtly? A Spaniard? A Frenchman? Or an Englishman? She gazed flirtatiously at Noailles whilst impishly nudging her Spanish fiancé. Everyone joined in. Sir Henry Grantchester openly declared that, on the field of love, an Englishman would always carry away the honours. Segalla let this conversation go by him. He gazed round the ostentatious hall with its glazed windows, coloured tiles, and timber roof craftily carved and decorated with red and gold roses. Above the wainscoted walls gilded medallions were carved into the brickwork; these bore the painted eschutcheons, mottos, and emblems of former kings and queens of England.

Now and again Segalla glanced at his companions. Noailles was hotly holding forth, but Segalla sensed everyone was acting. They all wore masks and, now and again, lifted them to peep at each other. The more he looked at the Queen the more certain he became that she was very ill. Lady Dormer was feverishly excited, but her worry and anxiety for her mistress were apparent. De Feria also was subdued: whenever he could, the Spaniard leaned forward and looked down the table as if to study the Queen more closely. Noailles also kept Mary under close scrutiny, as a cat would a mouse hole. Only Sir Henry Grantchester, the bluff young soldier, seemed unaware of the tensions swirling beneath the festivities.

Servants came out of the shadows to refill goblets. More dishes were brought in: slices of venison, salmon and leeks in almond sauce, roast tongue of beef, and chicken livers. Mary hardly touched her food. Segalla, who had eaten enough, simply took small portions to satisfy the chefs and cooks who came out to receive the guests' thanks and cries of appreciation. Segalla hoped the meal would not last too long. The Queen had promised a private audience with him whilst, before the meal, Noailles and de Feria had intimated that they would like to "discuss the current situation" with him.

Segalla pretended to sip from his wine cup; the task the pontiff had set him was a difficult one. How could he determine if the Queen was being poisoned? How could he sniff out the traitor at court where, secretly, everyone was waiting for the Queen to die? And the envoys to the great powers, what did they intend? De Feria seemed to be an honourable man, but was Philip of Spain determined to rid himself of one Tudor to marry another? And were the French so eager to advance the claims of Mary Stuart that they would stoop to regicide? So they could all cry out "ave Maria sepulta!" and bow to greet the new monarch. But who would this be? Mary Stuart? Or Elizabeth at Hatfield? Segalla was determined to meet Elizabeth as soon as possible. Moreover, if any of these parties were engaged in murder, who would they hire to help them? An envoy like Noailles would not dare to resort to such nefarious practices as poison, but he might hire those who would. And that strange message, Mark 15.34? And the enigmatic Philip Savage the Holy Father had mentioned? How on earth could Segalla, newly arrived in England, act with any hope of success?

Segalla fingered the rosary beads in the breast pocket of his robe. He'd been most careful in the few days he had been here, acting like a stranger, a foreigner, an alien. He dared not slip and reveal how, in previous years, he had often galloped along the old pilgrims' route from Canterbury to London. Or how, fifty years before, he had sat here and been entertained by Henry VII and his wife, Elizabeth of York. Segalla gazed round. So much had happened. What was a crisis then was now the dust of history. He heard a sound and looked up. Dr. Theophilus had pushed back his chair; the physician's head was down, his hands clutching his stomach. The doctor had eaten well and drunk deeply. At first Segalla thought it was a touch of colic, but then Theophilus half rose, body straining, head going back, his mouth opening and closing.

"Dr. Theophilus!" Segalla leaned across the table, his shout deadening all conversation around him.

Sir Henry Grantchester sprang to his feet, his chair falling back. Theophilus was now lurching towards the door, lost in his own terrible pain. He suddenly fell to his knees with a loud cry; his body jerked, then he fell sideways, his head crashing against the red tiled floor. Confusion broke out. Servants, scullions, and soldiers on duty left their posts. Sir Henry Grantchester ordered the doors to be sealed, driving the servants away, shouting at one of the cooks to fetch the captain of the watch. Segalla went and turned Dr. Theophilus's body over. His face had turned a liverish grey, the lips discoloured, the eyes half-open; a trickle of saliva mixed with food snaked out of the corner of his mouth. Segalla felt for the pulse in his neck, but this was very faint. Theophilus's eyes opened. He made a rasping, cluttering sound at the back of his throat. Segalla tried to help him up, but the physician's body jerked again in one final spasm of pain and his head fell back. Segalla laid him down. Again he felt for a pulse in the wrist, but this was now gone. He studied the physician's face, but the half-open eyes showed no sign of life; his skin was cold and clammy to the touch. Segalla looked over his shoulder at the other guests.

"Dr. Theophilus is dead," he declared. "Sir Henry, please send for Dr. Cesar."

Segalla took a cloak from a peg, put it over the corpse, and walked back to the table. The other guests had resumed their seats. Segalla looked for any suspicious reaction, but there was none. The Queen and Jane Dormer were horrified, the two envoys aghast. Sir Henry Grantchester was busy, a typical soldier, more concerned with clearing the hall. Jane Dormer absentmindedly picked up a silver fork, a piece of beef on the end.

"My lady," Segalla broke in, "I think it's best if we eat and drink no more. Sir Henry, order the scullions and servants to stay in the kitchen. No one is to leave the palace." Segalla caught the look of annoyance in Noailles's eyes. "Your Grace," he addressed the Queen, "I am sorry, I have no authority to give orders here."

"No, no, Nicholas," the Queen murmured, half-smiling. She pushed her own silver tray away. "What you say is right."

"It may have been a seizure," De Feria spoke up.

"I doubt it," Segalla replied. "Theophilus was poisoned." Segalla gazed round in desperation and decided to seize his opportunity. "Your Grace." He leaned across the table, not caring if the other envoys overheard him. "Your Grace, may I have a word in private?"

"Of course, Nicholas. No, Monsieur Noailles"—the

Queen raised a beringed hand—"don't object; I would ex-
tend the same courtesy to you."

Mary rose and went to the end of the table away from
where the corpse lay. She sat on a window seat and patted the
cushion beside her. The Queen was glad to have an opportunity to study this enigmatic Jesuit. Mary, blessed with a
marvellous memory, had recalled tidbits of gossip from her
youth. Hadn't her own mother praised a father called Segalla?
A priest? Or was it a courtier in the service of her grand-
mother Isabella of Castile? Mary quietly admitted she was
much taken by the Jesuit as well as curious. Mary had sur-
vived by her wits in the cut-throat intrigue in her father's and
brother's courts. She had withstood the wiles and cunning of
men like Cromwell, Somerset, and Northumberland. She
had, as she quietly confided to Jane, a nose for treachery, and
this priest seemed loyal. He had a scholar's face; smooth olive
skin, except for the furrows between the eyebrows and sharp
marks etched on either side of his mouth; and sad, rather
mocking, but not cynical, eyes. Mary blinked and squeezed
the priest's hand.

"I'm sorry, Segalla, I was just thinking. Well, you asked to
speak to me?"

"Your Grace, I am here on behalf of His Holiness the
Pope. I am not too sure what my task is. His Holiness is
subtle."

"He's as crafty as a fox," Mary interrupted. "But, there
again, perhaps he has to be. So, why did he send you,
Nicholas?"

"To protect your interests," Segalla replied. "Your Grace, I think Dr. Theophilus was poisoned. We do not know whether that poison was meant for you."

What colour remained in Mary's cheeks drained away.

"Your Grace, I do not mean to frighten you, but platters were changed; one goblet put down, another picked up. It stands to reason; why should anyone wish to poison Theophilus . . . ?"

"Continue!"

"I am floundering about, Your Grace. I am a stranger in London. His Holiness mentioned, as did the Queen of France, these anonymous letters from the Four Evangelists: their insistence about Mark 15.34. His Holiness also mentioned a man, an official from the Tower. . . ."

"Philip Savage?" Mary finished the sentence for him. "Controller at the Tower. I believe my Lord of Northumberland and others searched for him but could not find him. Some say he is dead, others that he has changed his name and appearance and is still in hiding."

"I could go out on the streets of London." Segalla successfully hid his smile. "I could wander the alleyways for a hundred years but discover nothing. Madame, you are under attack. The letters of the Evangelists hail you as dead and buried. They hint at some dangerous secret?"

"And the last one mentioned blackmail." Mary looked through the latticed window at the darkness outside. "I think I can trust you, Nicholas. I have my own man, Stephen Orslett." She sighed. "But he works in the shadows, a man of great stealth." She lowered her voice. "I know he also works for my sister. Where his loyalties lie I do not know. I cannot bring him into the light." She touched the wooden cross hanging round Segalla's neck. "But you are different."

Segalla watched the Queen's tense, slightly harsh face: she no longer met his gaze and she kept blinking as if fighting back tears. She knows more than she's telling me, Segalla thought, and he glanced to where the others were watching him curiously.

"My court is full of spies." Mary flailed her hands in her lap. "And I do not know whom to trust. Except for you and Jane. My sweet cousin Reginald Pole is sick in mind and body. Philip will not come back. . . ."

Mary would have continued but the door opened. Dr. Cesar, swathed in a heavy, military cloak, came in. He looked brighter than when Segalla had last seen him; he rubbed his eyes, stifling back a yawn. Segalla excused himself and went across to pull back the cloak covering the corpse.

"Poor Theophilus," Cesar murmured. "Such is life, in the midst of which, we are all in death."

He sighed and crouched down on the other side of the corpse. He undid the dead physician's tunic, studying the face now turned a liverish hue, the half-open eyes, the slightly purple lips. Cesar pulled up the shirt beneath the doublet and pressed the slightly swollen stomach. Segalla noticed the blotchy stains.

"Birthmarks?" he asked.

"Death marks," Cesar retorted. "Dr. Theophilus was poisoned. How, or by whom, I don't know." He ran his finger down the dead man's cheekbone. "The body humours have been severely changed; the clammy skin, the discolouration of the face and the lips." Cesar opened the dead man's mouth.

Segalla hid his distaste: Theophilus's tongue had turned a slightly blackish colour.

"What poison?" he whispered.

"God knows, Nicholas. There are so many new potions on the market: the juice of deadly toadstool, belladonna, foxglove, potions mixed with potions. There are at least six types of arsenic being sold on the streets of Rome. Some kill immediately, some within hours, days, or even years."

"So how can we tell?"

"We can't," Cesar replied, getting to his feet.

He covered the dead man's face and went and sat at the table. He pointed to all the dishes.

"Your Grace." He addressed the Queen, who had taken her seat. "As I have said to my companion here, Dr. Theophilus was poisoned. But how and by whom I do not know." He drummed his fingers on the table. "Madame, what did you share with Dr. Theophilus?"

The Queen shrugged. "We all ate from the same dishes."

"And the wine jugs?"

Dr. Cesar leaned over and took a large, silver embossed one, its handle shaped in the form of a snarling griffin. It had the royal escutcheon emblazoned on the side.

"There are four of these." He pointed down the table.

"That's right," Jane Dormer spoke up. "The Queen and Dr. Theophilus would have used that one." She pointed at the jug Cesar held.

"It's true." Noailles spoke up, plucking at the loose skin

of his lower lip. "The servants served up our plates, but, as for the wine jug, Dr. Theophilus would fill his own and did not wait for a servant."

Cesar raised the wine jug and sniffed, wrinkling his nose. He asked Segalla to bring him one containing the white Rhenish and sniffed that but dismissed it. All the other jugs were collected for his scrutiny.

"Your Grace, you drank wine tonight?"

Mary, pale, touched her stomach and shook her head.

"I dared not," she whispered. "I only pretended." Her eyelids fluttered. "It's the same with the food."

Segalla could see the Queen was clearly embarrassed. He now realized why she kept dabbing her hand with her napkin; the little she had chewed had probably been spat back into it.

"Dr. Cesar." De Feria leaned over. "Do not keep us in suspense. Is there something wrong with that wine?"

"Sir Henry." Cesar called over the Queen's captain, who was standing at the door.

The young man looked visibly shaken, and Segalla could understand why. He had heard rumors about the attack on the Queen on Maundy Thursday, and, if Dr. Cesar was to be believed, this was a second attempt. Sir Henry was directly responsible for the Queen's safety.

"Your Grace," Dr. Cesar continued in a flat voice, "I apologize I was not here tonight. By tomorrow morning I shall be recovered and I'll give you my best attention: those gripes in your stomach must be attended to. What did Dr. Theophilus prescribe?"

"A slight opiate," the Queen retorted. "Something to take away the pain."

"That will end," Cesar said confidently. "Now, Sir Henry"—he pushed the wine jug into the soldier's hand—"you have a rat-catcher in the palace?"

Sir Henry nodded.

"Tell him to trap two. It won't take long. Go to the kitchen and soak some beef in this wine. Wear some gloves, which you should destroy later, and, when the rats are caught, push the meat into their cage." Dr. Cesar stood up, cradling the wine jug in his hands. He bowed towards the Queen. "Your Grace, the only advice I can give you now," he added drily, "is that I would not eat or drink anything here until this matter is settled."

They all sat in silence as Cesar followed Grantchester out of the hall.

"Who could it be?" Noailles spoke up. "One of us? A servant? Even Theophilus himself?"

"What do you mean?" Segalla asked.

"The man drank deeply," Noailles retorted. "Did he become confused?"

The Queen put her face in her hands and cried. Jane Dormer stood and put a protective arm round her shoulder. For a while the Queen sobbed uncontrollably and, when she took her hands away from her face, the tears had blotched the paint on her cheeks. Segalla's heart skipped a beat. The Queen did look very ill. By her own confession she had eaten and drunk nothing. He quietly admired her courage at being able to sit and pretend to enjoy herself.

"I apologize," the Queen gasped. She dabbed at her face with the cloth Jane Dormer gave her. "I feel so ill. I am so tired. Why does the good Lord allow people to hate me so much?"

"Arrest the servants!" de Feria declared. "They should all be questioned."

"I would advise against that," Segalla retorted before he could stop himself. "Your Grace, we have no proof of who poisoned that wine, if it is poisoned. Servants come and go; wine is poured; jugs are moved around the table." He leaned across and picked up the dead physician's goblet. Segalla sniffed carefully at it, beneath the burgundy, he caught a sweet-sour smell, slightly musty, like that from an unwashed cup. He put the goblet down.

"Why?" Jane Dormer spoke up. Her pale face looking even more beautiful, a fierce protective look in her eyes. "Why can't the servants be questioned?"

"Segalla is correct." The Queen fluttered her hands on the tablecloth. "We can question, we can rack, we can interrogate and, in doing so, make more enemies, spread the circle of hate and resentment. In the end, all we do is punish innocent people."

"Then what can we do?" Jane Dormer snapped. "My lady, you must eat, you must drink!"

"I will taste everything in future," Segalla replied. He breathed in deeply. "I shall taste whatever you eat or drink at such banquets."

"Master Segalla, that is not necessary."

"So shall I," Jane Dormer declared, dazzling Segalla with

a smile. She clapped her hands. "And you are right, sir, the more we publish this abroad, the worse it becomes. If we let it be known that Her Grace has someone to taste her food and drink, it might make others think before they act."

Mary now sat straight in her high-backed chair.

"The hall is clear," she declared. "I know Sir Henry has guards outside. I tell you this and, yes, my enemy may be sitting next to me. Yet I do wonder how long this can go on. My troops have been driven out of Calais." She glanced sharply at Noailles. "But, thank God, we have a truce with France. My husband is in the Low Countries and will not return. My womb is barren and bears no fruit. My attempts to bring back the Catholic faith"—she shrugged—"have died in the fires of Smithfield. The people hate me for that, for marrying a Spaniard, for losing Calais." Her voice dropped to a whisper. "My good friend and close councillor Cardinal Pole is sickly. I do not think he will see another spring." Mary tightened her lips. "Now my enemies hunt me and I don't think I will live much longer." She stilled any clamour with a sharp movement of her hand. "But, whilst God gives me strength, I shall continue to do what I think is right. If I catch the man who is trying to kill me, be he high- or low-born, he'll suffer the full rigours of the law at Tyburn." She rose abruptly to her feet, and the others hurried to do likewise. "There shall be no more feasts," she murmured, "no more such banquets."

The Queen allowed de Feria to pull back her chair and went to stand beside Theophilus's corpse.

"Have him removed," she declared.

Segalla watched her go and stared at a wine jug winking in the candlelight. He suddenly remembered he had drunk wine, but from which jug? Whom had the assassin really been hunting?

Chapter 5

Segalla made his excuses and left the hall. He went along a moonlit gallery which overlooked one of the rose gardens. In one of the window seats he found a sleepy-eyed page, on duty until the palace chamberlains rang the bell for all retainers to retire. The boy was surly; but when Segalla pressed a coin into his hand, he soon remembered his manners and led the Jesuit up a flight of stairs to the late physician's chamber. These were opulent quarters: a small anteroom and chancery with a bedroom beyond. The page lit the candles with a taper and then left, closing the door behind him. Segalla immediately made an extensive search. He found chests of philtres and potions, clothing, and other belongings, but, the more he searched, the more convinced he was that someone had been here before him. Virtually all the physician's papers had been removed. There was no journal, no personal letters or memoranda. Dr. Theophilus appeared to be a tidy man who kept everything in place, but the chancery desk he had used was completely empty. Segalla reasoned that someone must have just come in and collected every piece of parchment, yet Theophilus had undoubtedly been a man of letters: the chancery desk was covered with inkpots, disused quills, pumice stone, red wax, seals, and ribbons of different colours. In a small chest beside the writing desk, Segalla found fresh leaves of parchment and vellum ready for use. Segalla went to the door, pulled it open, and listened. Whoever had come here might return, or had he left already?

Segalla closed the door and went back to the bedroom. He took a candle and examined the bedding: the state of the quilt and bolster indicated that these, too, had been carefully searched for any hidden manuscripts. Segalla sat in the chair and watched the flame of the candle dance in the draughts seeping through the shutters. He fingered the cross round his neck and tried to place what else was missing. Theophilus had certainly been poisoned. Downstairs the other envoys believed that the intended victim had been the Queen, but it now looked as if Theophilus himself was the real victim. Somebody had poisoned that wine and knew that Theophilus would never leave that supper alive. That's why his chamber had been searched, but for what? Had Theophilus been a friend and ally of the Queen? Did he know something about those who plotted against her life, and so the conspirators had decided to remove him? Or had they tried to suborn him and been rejected, hence the need to silence him forever? Or was Theophilus a traitor? Someone whom the conspirators had used but who had now outlived his usefulness, so his chambers were searched for any manuscripts which might incriminate them?

Segalla eased himself into a chair. Or was Theophilus a blackmailer? Was he one of the Evangelists, those mysterious writers who wrote about Mark 15.34 and hailed Mary as if she were already dead? Segalla heard a sound and was about to rise when he heard the click. He froze, his hand going to the small dagger he kept beneath his jerkin.

"Welcome to England, Father."

The voice was low, indistinct, so soft Segalla couldn't decide whether it was male or female, man or boy.

"Sit where you are," the voice continued, soft and lisping. "Do not turn round, Father, or spring to your feet or search for the dagger which undoubtedly you have somewhere about your person. I mean you no harm. And you are intelligent enough to realize that if you stand, the candlelight will only illuminate you, a good target."

"What do you want?" Segalla asked.

"Why, the same as you, Father!"

The mysterious visitor was deliberately disguising his or her voice. Sometimes it was high, sometimes deep; the person must also have a muffler across his or her mouth.

"If you mean me no harm," Segalla replied, easing the dagger from his pouch, "why not let me face you?"

"Oh come, come, Father. Are you going to tell me why you are really in England? Of course not! So why should I tell you my business?"

"Someone is plotting against the Queen."

"That is true."

"And the Four Evangelists and their letters about Mark 15.34?"

"I agree," the voice replied. "Such seemingly innocent but cryptic remarks seem to cause great consternation."

"So, why are you here?"

"The same as you, Father. I am looking for what Theophilus may have written, but it looks as if it has already gone."

"Did you have a hand in his death?"

"Of course not!"

"Do you know where Philip Savage is?"

"If I did, I'd be a wiser man."

"But there's nothing here!"

"I can see that, Father. You are just like me, wondering what is going to happen."

Segalla heard a sound: he strained, wondering if the person was still there or had left. He heard the far door close and rose slowly to his feet. The room behind him was empty, as was the small chancery and anteroom, and, when Segalla went out into the gallery, there was nothing except the squeak of a rat and the dust motes which danced like little imps in the moonbeams sloping through the unshuttered windows.

Segalla walked back to the top of the stairs and down into the main gallery. Sir Henry Grantchester had apparently been busy; guards were now posted at different places. Segalla was stopped on several occasions. He was explaining to one officer when the page boy he had met earlier came running up and breathlessly announced that Sir Henry and Dr. Cesar were waiting for him in the hall. Segalla followed the lad down. He expected to see that the envoys had left, but, apart from the Queen, all were still seated round the now cleared table. Jane Dormer, who explained that she had been to see the Queen, had also rejoined them, bringing a jug of wine which, she announced, she had tasted herself. Dr. Cesar sat at one end of the table. He smiled as Segalla took his seat, then, stooping down, he picked up a cage and placed it on the table. Inside one rat lay dead; the other was still weakly moving.

"We fed them the meat soaked in the wine," Sir Henry declared, "as the good physician told us to. At first, the rats seemed vigorous and inquisitive, but, as you can see. . . ."

"How long did it take?" Segalla asked.

"Well, the rats were caught and they instantly ate the meat. I would say, within half an hour, whatever they ate worked its effect."

Jane Dormer wrinkled her nose and made a sign with her hand. Cesar apologized and put the cage back on the floor.

"There is no doubt," the physician announced, "that the wine was poisoned. I would hazard a guess that this took place at the beginning of the meal, and, whatever the potion was, it took probably an hour and a half to have its effect."

"But whoever poisoned the wine," de Feria said, "must have known which jug the Queen would use?"

"That is impossible!" Noailles snapped. "Jugs are passed backward and forward."

"It might have been possible," Jane Dormer declared. "You see, all of the jugs are placed along the table. These are refilled by the servants. One of these could have put the poison in as he or she replenished it. Or"—she shrugged her beautiful shoulders—"the poison could have been put in the jug by one of us at the beginning of the meal. Do you remember, before we took our seats, when we all milled about . . . ?" Her voice trailed off. "However, Her Grace needs me." She rose to her feet. "Gentlemen, I bid you good night."

De Feria followed her out, and Noailles, eager not to miss anything, bustled out of the chamber, throwing his farewells over his shoulder, determined not to let de Feria out of his sight. Sir Henry Grantchester sat for a while, face cupped in his hands. Segalla studied the young officer. Grantchester had an open, honest face, and his hair, moustache, and beard were neatly cut. He had thick lips and a slightly broken nose, but his expression was one of complete bemusement and bewilderment. A man out of his depths, Segalla concluded: an honest soldier more interested in the parade ground than the silken subtleties of court intrigue. The captain looked at Segalla and let his hands fall away with a sigh.

"I have offered the Queen my resignation," he declared. "I was her appointment. My father and brothers were with her at Framlingham when she was hailed as Queen. I decided to march on London against Northumberland." He got to his feet and put on the war belt he had looped over the arm of a chair. "Her Grace, of course, has refused!"

"Sir Henry," Segalla asked, "if the Queen dies, God forbid, what would happen to you?"

The soldier pulled a face. He swung his cloak round his shoulders, fumbling with the silver clasp.

"The rewards of this post, Segalla, are many. I have the Queen's ear. I have my wages, lodgings, and preferment, but, as you say, if the Queen died, God forbid, I would be replaced."

"Why?" Segalla asked. "You are a good soldier, loyal. Let us say Mary's half-sister, Elizabeth, succeeded?"

Grantchester threw his head back and laughed.

"If Elizabeth becomes Queen and is closeted with Master Cecil and others of his ilk, believe me, my good fellow, I wouldn't suffer, but they'd remove me."

"Because you served Mary?"

"No, Segalla, because, like you, I serve the Pope. My family are Catholic and always have been. Two of my cousins were executed by King Henry and my father was imprisoned by Northumberland for six months in the Fleet because of his faith. I was born a Catholic, Segalla, I have lived like a Catholic, and I will die a Catholic. Elizabeth will have nothing to do with me." He leaned across the table, his face tense, eyes watchful.

Segalla realized Grantchester was not as open or as naive as he had first thought.

"You sit there, Master Segalla, watching us all, and I

watch you. You wonder if I would have the malice or the treachery to work against my Queen. If you said it openly, I would challenge you to a duel, but, remember this, Segalla"—Grantchester tapped the tip of Segalla's nose with his finger—"Theophilus died when you arrived. You may watch me, but, as God lives, sir, I shall watch you."

Grantchester left the hall. Dr. Cesar yawned and twirled the end of his moustache.

"A basket of worms, eh, Nicholas, a basket of worms!"

"Did you know Theophilus?" Segalla asked.

"By reputation," Cesar replied. "Like all of us"—he smiled wryly—"like all physicians, he worked in France and Italy travelling from court to court."

"What nationality was he? Was Theophilus his real name?"

Cesar pulled a face. "By birth an Englishman, but the English with their dull-sounding names; I suppose Dr. Theophilus sounded grander. Why do you ask?"

"I have been up to his chambers," Segalla replied. "There is no documentation, nothing whatsoever!"

"But that's preposterous!" Cesar exclaimed. "Theophilus was well past his fiftieth year. A man such as he would accumulate memoranda, files of letters."

"Do you know how he was poisoned?" Segalla asked. "I mean, can't you guess?"

Cesar shook his head. "It's about as useful as wondering how many angels can sit on the tip of a pin. Nicholas, there are so many poisons about. All you need is a few grains sprinkled into a pot. But why these questions?"

"I honestly believe," Segalla retorted, "that the Queen was not the intended victim. It was Theophilus."

Cesar smoothed his moustache and sipped at his wine.

"Why should someone want to kill him?"

"I don't know," Segalla replied. "But the hour is late and you, my good physician, should practise what you preach and get a good night's sleep. I intend to see if the Queen will grant me an audience."

In the end Segalla found the Queen had not retired. She had changed into a robe of ivory silk lined with fur and was seated before the fire, her feet on a footstool, Jane Dormer on cushions at her feet. Grantchester, on guard in the antechamber, at first protested, but the Queen, on hearing Segalla's voice, told the soldier to let Segalla in. He was invited to pull up a cushioned stool; in the flames of the dying fire, the Queen looked even more aged and sickly than Segalla had seen her at the banquet.

"She'll not sleep," Jane whispered, tapping her hand on the Queen's chair. "She tells me to look after her, but how can I?"

"Your Grace, you should sleep," Segalla declared. "And, in my view, you should not worry: the assassin did not strike at you but at Theophilus. Who was he?"

"Oh, he came with letters of accreditation from Italian bishops, from the French court. Good physicians, Nicholas, are very rare. There are many quacks and leeches."

"But you must have known about his background?"

The Queen cupped her face in her hands. "Dr. Theophilus was not his true name," she declared. "Like many of his profession, he changed it to enhance his reputation and public status. I understand it's quite common in Germany. I know he was a graduate at the Halls of Cambridge and that he studied physic at Salerno and Padua as well as Montpellier and Paris. You should see Cardinal Pole." Mary swiftly changed the conversation. "You can do so tomorrow. My squire Orslett," the Queen continued, "will take you along the river to Lambeth in the morning. He will also bring you Theophilus's real name."

"There's something else," Jane Dormer added. "Theophilus was a lecherous old man. Father, I am no flirt. I keep my eyes and my thoughts to myself."

"But Theophilus thought you were?"

"Yes. He was hot-eyed and, when his face became wine-coloured and those lips slobbered, he liked to boast. He said he had a pretty Doll Tearsheet."

Segalla looked askance.

"A courtesan," Jane explained, "whom he'd set up in a chamber above a baker's shop in Bowyers Row. A young girl, Nicolette, of French extraction. Sometimes he'd refer to her as if to show he was a young man of the world, much liked by the ladies."

"Orslett will take you there tomorrow." The Queen got slowly to her feet and extended her hand for Segalla to kiss. "He will take you there, then by barge down to Lambeth to see Cardinal Pole. Orslett will also bring you a warrant, a licence to travel where you will. I know," she added drily, "the

Holy Father is interested in my good sister's welfare. I am equally sure that my good sister, Elizabeth, may be interested in what the Holy Father has to say."

"Madame, I will be honest with you," Segalla retorted. "His Holiness has no great love for your half-sister."

"Neither do I," Mary replied. "But I was raised in a hotbed of intrigue. My father's court crackled with conspiracy and gossip like freshly lit charcoal." She sighed. "I can see the signs already: 'Ave Maria sepulta.' As the psalmist says, 'In some men's eyes, I am already dead.' " Mary ran her hand down her face. "And the road to Hatfield is now busy with visitors and well-wishers."

Segalla kissed her hand and withdrew. He was in the gallery outside when he heard the door open behind him and his name called. Jane Dormer stood in the shadows. Segalla went back.

"My mistress is not well," she murmured.

"Dr. Cesar may be able to help," Segalla replied.

"Perhaps. But there's something else you should know." Lady Jane took him by the arm away from the door. "I am betrothed to Count de Feria. He loves me deeply, as I love him. He's brought the Queen messages from King Philip of Spain, but he has also secret instructions." Jane bit her lip and fought back the tears. "The Queen is right, many see her as dead already, and that includes her husband."

"What?"

"The Count de Feria," she continued, "has been secretly instructed by King Philip"—she paused to choose her words carefully—"to sound out the Princess Elizabeth on her marriage: not to some foreign prince but to himself!"

Segalla gasped.

"Philip is a cold man," Jane continued. "He has his mistresses and his whores. Wives are simply pawns to him. He believes Mary is dying; she may not even last the winter. Philip coldly plans to marry her half-sister."

"Elizabeth would be a fool to accept."

"Elizabeth may have no choice. French troops now occupy Calais, their ships patrol the narrow seas. What happens, Segalla, if the Queen dies and French troops cross to Dover, bringing the Scottish Mary with them? The French would also receive support from Scotland, where Mary's mother is regent."

"But if Philip strikes first?" Segalla interrupted.

"The English army and navy are in a poor state," Jane declared. "Philip could have troops on the Canterbury road within days. If Spanish troops were needed to hail Elizabeth as Queen and keep out the hated French, such a marriage match may not be unpopular."

Segalla stared out of the window. The palace was now silent. He could hear a door close, the tramp of a guard or the call of a sentry down near the gate; pinpricks of light could be seen at some windows. Queen reflected on what Jane Dormer was saying. At the same time he realized why the Pope had sent him to England: Mary Tudor was losing control. Greenwich was her mausoleum. In the city beyond, the merchants and bankers, the printers and preachers, the lawyers who sat in Parliament, and the great lords with their retinues, obeyed Mary but kept one eye firmly on the Hatfield road. They were waiting for something to happen. Now it looked as if the great powers had reached the same conclusion. And, like scavengers, were gathering to see what pickings they could make. And it was oh so easy to reach the next conclusion. Why maintain the tension? Why make the waiting any longer than it had to be? If Mary died, who would mourn her? Jane Dormer, a few of her friends, some Catholic lords, the likes of Sir Henry Grantchester? Who would look for anything suspicious? And, even if they found it, demand vengeance? Philip, as far away as possible, already forgetting Mary and plotting to climb into Elizabeth's bed? Or the French? Eager to spread their rule from the forests of Lorraine to the great, cold seas north of Scotland? Philip would hate that. If the French, or their allies, controlled England's southern coast, they could close the Channel to Spanish shipping and cut off Spain from the Netherlands, depriving Spanish troops there of money, supplies, and ammunitions. It would all be a matter of time: whoever moved fast and boldly could win the entire game. No wonder old Caraffa in Rome, with his spiteful hatred of Spain, was prepared to ally papal interests to French ambitions. So what could Segalla do? Hunt down the assassin? Perhaps check, obstruct, but what then?

"Father?"

Segalla broke from his reverie. Jane Dormer was staring up at him.

"The Count de Feria has told me this," she continued, "because he is an honourable man."

"There is only one fly in the ointment," Segalla replied. "Or should I say two? First, it all depends on the Lady Elizabeth, what she intends."

"And secondly?"

"Ave Maria sepulta," Segalla replied. "Men may dismiss the Queen as sickly, at death's door, but they could be wrong. Her mother was of good constitution and, despite King Henry's cruelty, lived a long and full life. Mary could recover and live a decade or two."

"She is sick in mind and body," Jane replied. "Yet, if some relief could be given to these symptoms, the pains in the head and the stomach, the feeling of listlessness, then perhaps. . . ."

She was about to turn away, but Segalla grasped her hand and lifted the unresisting fingers to his lips. Jane blushed.

"Quite a courtier for a Jesuit!"

"No, my lady, I salute you. I am in the dark and around me vipers curl and wait, but you I trust."

"Do you, Father? Some people even murmur that I am Philip's spy."

Segalla laughed. "Because you are in love with his ambassador?"

Jane shrugged. "If the Queen dies then I will be English no longer. I will not stay to watch the victors crow over a corpse before being dismissed to some damp castle on the Welsh or Scottish march."

"And this Mark 15.34?" Segalla asked.

Jane Dormer sighed. "Now, that is strange: the Queen puzzles me. I am sure she has some inkling about what it means."

"Could she be the author?"

Jane shook her head. "For some reason the reference alarms her, but she won't say why. I cannot fathom that. Some mystery from the past."

"Tell me." Segalla looked over his shoulder down the gallery. "You talk of possibilities of the future. Yet, from what I know of English law, Mary will have some say in her successor. Has she indicated whom?"

"There is only one choice," Jane replied. "Her half-sister Elizabeth. Mary may hate to utter her name in the same sentence as the Crown Imperial of England, but don't mistake my mistress, she is Henry's daughter. She is proud of the name Tudor. She would not leave the Crown to any other claimant. Mary is a conscientious woman: a Tudor with all that family's hatred of civil war and nobles squabbling over the throne. In the end, she will see it as her duty to ensure that Elizabeth, whatever her faith, whatever her plots and treachery, is crowned as her successor at Westminster. And, yes, before you say it, Mary has no love for her: 'Boleyn's wench,' that's what she calls her half-sister."

"Do they ever meet?" Segalla asked.

"Rarely. The Queen will invite her half-sister to this function or that. However, Elizabeth is a sharp-witted minx and plays the part accordingly. She is not well or the roads are too difficult, or she intends to come when this or that thing happens."

"Would Elizabeth poison her sister?"

Jane breathed in deeply and took a step nearer the window: the poor light gave her face an ivory sheen.

"I don't know," she replied. " 'Much suspected, nothing proved': that's Elizabeth's motto about herself. There are those around her who certainly would." Jane walked back down the gallery, then turned. "You should sleep, Father. Tomorrow is another day."

Segalla climbed the stairs to his own chamber. A sleepy-eyed soldier informed him that Dr. Cesar had retired for the night. Segalla smiled his thanks and went into his own room where he undressed, bathed his hands and face, and sat on the edge of the bed. He stared at the portrait of King Henry set against the far wall. Segalla felt sleepy, but what Jane Dormer had told him made his mind teem with possibilities: he would have little sleep until he put his suspicions into some order.

"What do we have here?" he murmured, as if the fat-faced monarch in the portrait could answer him back. "Mary Tudor has no heir and is sickening. The French and Spanish have ideas about the succession. They see themselves as controlling the game, perhaps even its masters."

Segalla picked at a loose thread on the bed coverlet. We have threatening letters, he reflected, making veiled references to Mary's death and some secret contained in those lines of Mark's Gospel, Chapter 15, Verse 34. An old man, Philip Savage, may be able to help, but no one can find him. An assassin is loose in the English court. Mary may be poisoned, but the real victim tonight was her physician

Theophilus. Why? And who had gone to the dead man's chamber and removed all his documents and papers? Segalla sighed and climbed into bed. For a while he composed himself, muttering a prayer before extinguishing the candle, and, lying down, stared into the darkness.

In her chamber above the baker's shop in Bowyers Row, the French courtesan, Nicolette, sat on the edge of her bed and stared at the saddle panniers she had packed so carefully earlier in the evening. Dr. Theophilus had visited her the previous morning. Usually he couldn't wait to fondle her breasts or throw her back on the bed. Nicolette didn't mind. Theophilus might not be virile, but he was clean and smelt fragrantly; his purse was always full of silver and he was a generous patron. He was old, and Nicolette often had to work hard to satisfy him. Even more, the doctor had told her he loved her. Nicolette, who had known Theophilus for months, had become intrigued. Men always said that, but he seemed to mean it. Nicolette stood up and took off her shift and stood admiring her rounded body in the shiny piece of metal which served as a mirror. Theophilus had said he would come back later this evening, and tomorrow they would leave England.

"Why?" Nicolette had asked.

Theophilus had refused to meet her eye but murmured something about warmer climes and how he was finished with the English fog and mists. Nicolette knew he held a high position at court. He would often preen himself and give her juicy tidbits of gossip. Nicolette swallowed hard and looked at the small box Theophilus kept full of potions, herbs, and different concoctions. Theophilus had told her never to open the box or have anything to do with it. She tapped it with her foot. One day, when they were married, perhaps Theophilus would tell her the truth about things, such as his silly name which Nicolette could not get her tongue round. Why not use his proper name, John Gresham; wasn't he proud of that? Indeed, there was a lot Nicolette needed to know about her patron. Perhaps she'd make him beg: refuse her favours. One day when, as Theophilus had described, they lived in a mansion or opulent house in Italy. Yes, that's where Theophilus said they would return to: take ship to Ostia and live in some city. For the time being, however, Nicolette had to wait. Theophilus had left strict instructions that he would come back, and, tomorrow morning, they would leave. Everything must be packed ready to go.

Nicolette began to dress slowly and sat combing her long, lustrous red hair. She heard a noise outside and went to look out of the arrow-slit window, but the street below was cloaked in darkness. The shop was quiet: the passageway leading down to the front door would always tell her if someone was approaching. The stairs creaked and groaned like the worn mattress on their bed when she and Theophilus cavorted there. Nicolette began to apply paint to her face. She reckoned it must be well after midnight. Where was Theophilus? Nicolette froze. The stairs outside creaked. Perhaps it was Theophilus? Should she sit here tapping her foot? Or lie langorously on the bed and pretend to be asleep? More creaks and groans from the stairs outside. Nicolette's heart skipped a beat. She always recognized Theophilus's footfall, but whoever was there was walking slowly. Perhaps the good physician was drunk? She went to the door and opened it.

"Theophilus!" she called.

The stairwell was dark and musty. A cold breeze wafted her face, and Nicolette realized the door below must have been left open.

"Theophilus!" she called. "Don't play games!"

Whoever was on the stair had now stopped climbing and must be hiding in the shadows. Nicolette became frightened. She closed the door, slamming across the bolts.

"You can stay there!" she shouted, "if you are going to tease me!"

Nicolette was frightened. The shop below was deserted. The baker and his family lived across the street. No one used the garret above. Nicolette ran across and picked up a dagger she kept in an embroidered pouch on top of one of the chests. She pulled this out. London was infested with night walkers, cat-eyed men looking for easy prey. Nicolette heard the stairs creak and groan again; she sighed with relief. Whoever it was, he was now going back down. She heard the door slam shut and sat on the bed, wondering whether it was safe to go outside and see what had happened. She was about to return to her mirror when she saw the first tendrils of smoke curl under the door. Nicolette's throat became dry. Fingers to her mouth, she walked to the door. The handle felt hot, and, when she opened it, the draught from her room only strengthened the flames racing up the stairs.

Chapter 6

Aservant woke Segalla early, saying that Master Stephen Orslett was waiting for him in the vestibule below. Segalla washed and dressed quickly in sober attire, dark velvet green hose, white shirt, a quilted, padded jacket, and a broad-brimmed hat. The streets of London would be muddy, so he put on leather walking boots and wrapped a thick leather sword belt round his waist. Orslett smiled when he saw him.

"You look anything but a priest, Father."

Segalla shook the outstretched hand.

"What do I look like, Master Orslett?"

"Stephen is my first name. You look like me, Father: a jack of all trades and master of none."

Segalla smiled. "The same could be said of any good Jesuit. And call me Nicholas. You are the Queen's man?"

"Her equerry, her squire. I carry out errands."

Segalla studied Orslett's dark face and close-set eyes. The man was clean-shaven, dressed in black from head to toe, charming, though his eyes were watchful. A fighting man, Segalla concluded. He had seen the likes in many households in Rome and France. Dangerous men, mercenaries who, like him, worked in the shadows. However, at least Orslett was honest; a jack of all trades. Segalla wondered if blackmail and murder were part of these. Orslett seemed an educated man, his voice and speech devoid of any accent, soft and measured. Was he the person he had met in the dead physician's chamber the previous evening?

"Have we met before, Stephen?"

"I don't think so." Orslett smiled, as if savouring a secret joke. "Although I'll be honest, Father, as soon as you arrived in London, I was following you."

"On whose orders?"

"Why, the Queen's."

"And who else do you work for?"

Orslett smiled widely. "I am the Queen's messenger between the court and Hatfield. Princess Elizabeth also honours me with her favours."

"But does she trust you?"

"I said, in my excess," Orslett replied, quoting from the psalms, "All men are liars."

"Aye," Segalla replied. "And there's nothing new under the sun. Or so the preacher has it."

"My orders," Orslett replied, "are to take you to Lambeth to meet his eminence, Cardinal Pole, but, before that, we have two other tasks. One, I have been busy this morning in the cellars and sewers beneath Greyfriars." He shook his head at the puzzlement on Segalla's face. "The other concerns a young lady I wish to meet. Nicolette, the dead physician's whore?"

"You've seen his corpse?" Segalla asked.

"Of course. I have no skill in physic, yet it appears that Master Theophilus was poisoned: how, why, and by whom. . . ." He shrugged. "Of course," he added, "Theophilus may have killed himself."

"What do you mean?"

"Why, Nicholas, these physicians sometimes eat and drink what they prescribe. It may have been a mistake."

"Do you believe that?"

"No, I don't." Orslett rubbed his face. "But the Queen is still agitated. I had to give her what little comfort I could. Do you wish to break fast?"

Segalla agreed and they stopped at the palace buttery for some bread, ale, and strips of boiled ham. Segalla noticed how Orslett blessed what he ate and drank.

"I was once a priest myself," Orslett explained. "Trained in a seminary in France. I came back during Edward's reign to minister to the faithful."

"And you were caught?"

"Yes and no. Not by the authorities, but by a young woman. I fell in love with her, left my priesthood, and married." Orslett wiped his lips on the back of his hand. "When I was abroad I did some service as a soldier. I know Latin, Greek, Italian, and French, but what can a priest do when he gives up his priesthood? A scrivener? A clerk? Not for me." He clapped Segalla on the shoulder. "But, come, I wish to show you something."

Horses were saddled and ready in the courtyard. The day was a fine one and the trackway underfoot firm and easy. Segalla suddenly realized he had left Greenwich without saying farewell to Dr. Cesar. He reined in, wondering whether he should go back.

"My colleague will wonder where I am."

Orslett, still chewing on a piece of ham he had taken from the buttery, shrugged.

"Dr. Cesar will be busy enough," he declared. "I understand the Queen wants him to take a fresh look at Theophilus's corpse. A merry rogue, Cesar. He already has a reputation with the palace chambermaids!" Orslett glanced up at the light blue sky. "But come on, Nicholas, we have a miracle waiting for us in London!"

After that he refused to elaborate but turned the conversation to the Jesuit order and its speed in spreading throughout Europe. Segalla found his companion personable but also an actor playing a part. A former priest, a sword and dagger man, yet he referred to his wife and young children, proud as any merchant or burgess in the city.

A man of treachery? Segalla wondered. Orslett could ingratiate himself with anyone. Indeed, the more the fellow spoke, the more convinced Segalla became that it was Orslett who had been in the doctor's chamber the previous night.

The country lanes were quiet, running through heath and marsh, sometimes fields bordered by high hedges or pales of newly enclosed lands. They passed sleepy villages buried deep in woodland or waste, the only sign of life being lazy spirals of smoke. As they approached the city, the atmosphere changed. Mummers, their shabby carts decorated with flags and streamers, thronged the highway. Cattle and oxen were being driven down to the slaughterhouses. Peasant farmers walked with handcarts full of produce for the markets. Wandering scholars, a cavalcade of soldiers, beggars, sometimes entire families, the mad, the landless, the infirm, all streamed into London to see what profit could be made.

Segalla and Orslett entered the city by Fleet Street. Orslett, now riding ahead, forced his way through, the Queen's badge high on his jerkin. People drew aside reluctantly. There were muttered curses and the occasional shouted obscenity, but Orslett, with sword and dagger hanging down from his war belt and garbed like a crow, rode his horse through. They passed the Fleet prison, crossed the old city ditch, and entered the area under the dark mass of St. Paul's Cathedral. The crowds were dense, flowing like shoals of fish by the stalls and booths set up on every street. The air dinned with the shouts of the apprentices, carters, hucksters, the cries of children, and the barking of dogs. Men and women shouted from the open windows of the high-storied houses. Segalla had to keep his wits about him. The streets were clogged with dirt and rubbish and reeked pungently of the saltpetre laid down to cover some of the stink. Some streets had broad sewers clogged with waste; the trackways on either side were equally hazardous because of the low and heavy signs of the taverns, ale shops, houses, and shops which stood along every street.

They dismounted near the old lich-gate of the cathedral. Orslett led him down Carter Lane and across into the ruins of Greyfriars, the great Franciscan monastery ransacked by Henry VIII, now taken up by stalls and booths. A group of shabby scholars stood clustered like songbirds on a broken-down wall and sang goliards' songs for alms. A seller of broadsheets walked up and down, his shoddy news-sheets clutched in his hands as he proclaimed marvellous news and doings. At the far end of the monastery ruins a great scaffold had been set up on which a thronelike chair, draped in a white, shabby sheet, had been placed. A young girl dressed in a Lincoln green smock, her blonde hair covered by a gold-edged, blue veil, sat there; arms across her chest, head down as if in deep meditation and prayer.

"What's happening here?" Segalla asked.

"Wait and see," Orslett whispered.

The crowd were becoming impatient.

"Come on!" someone shouted. "Let's hear the wall prophecy!"

Orslett told Segalla to mount his horse to get a better view. As he did so, a young man, cloaked in a dark grey gown, climbed the steps and stood on the scaffold, hands outstretched.

"My sister is deep in prayer," he cried. "The angel has not come but soon it will!"

"This has been going on for weeks," Orslett explained. "That precious pair"—he nodded towards the scaffold—"claim that an angel lives in the wall and answers questions about the Queen. Ah, good, it's about to begin!"

The young man handed the woman a white cane, and she tapped the wall.

"I am here!" The voice seemed to spring out of the brickwork.

The crowd fell silent. Even the rooks in the trees seemed to be overawed by this supernatural manifestation.

"Will you listen to me?" the woman asked.

"I shall and the truth shall be given. I am the angel of God. I cannot lie."

Segalla stared in disbelief. In his travels through Europe he had seen the most subtle forms of religious trickery, but nothing to equal this.

"How's it done? Surely there must be someone on the other side of the wall?"

"There isn't anyone or anything," Orslett replied. "Only waste ground!"

"What is the Queen?" the young woman now asked the wall.

"A bloody tyrant!"

The crowd sighed collectively.

"And the Mass?"

"Popish trickery!"

"And the Queen's husband?"

"A foreigner who wishes to take over by stealth the patrimony of England!"

"I did not know angels were biased," Segalla murmured.

Orslett raised his finger to his lips.

"And the Lady Elizabeth?" the woman asked.

"God's chosen one for the throne of England!"

The crowd were now clapping. Orslett suddenly put a

whistle to his lips and blew a long piercing blast. The woman on the scaffold looked up. Heads turned. At the far side of the ruins Segalla noticed a group of men garbed in the royal livery suddenly go down some steps. Orslett raised himself in the stirrups.

"I have a question to ask," he shouted. "What punishment fits those who blaspheme and engage in religious trickery?"

The woman didn't seem so composed now. The young man came beside her, and the crowd's mood, ever fickle, had already changed.

"I have asked a question!" Orslett bawled. "Is it too hard for the angel? Answer it!"

The crowd took up the refrain. "Answer it! Answer it!"

The young woman shook her head. Orslett again blew on the whistle, silencing the crowd.

"Very well," he shouted. "I'll change my question. Is there a God in heaven?"

The woman tapped the wall with the white wand: her voice trembled at Orslett's question, but there was no answer.

"Stay there," Orslett murmured, getting down from his horse. Segalla watched him shoulder his way through the crowd. He glanced across to where the royal retainers had reappeared, a young man, his hands bound, being pushed before them. Orslett had now clambered onto the scaffold. Sheriff's men appeared as if from nowhere. The woman and her companion looked cowed. Orslett had seized the white wand and was tapping the wall, asking a series of ridiculous questions.

"Am I the great Cham of Tartary? Can I fly to the sun?"

This time there was no answer. Now the young man brought from the far end of the ruins was pushed onto the scaffold. The woman crouched down, hands to her face; her accomplice tried to leave but was pushed back. Orslett came to the edge of the platform.

"Good people!" he cried. "You have been tricked and deceived!" He pointed to the ground. "Beneath here are the cellars of the old friary. In the wall behind is an elmwood pipe, cunningly placed there to draw water from a cistern in one of the cellars. These three counterfeits have pretended that the wall housed an angel. What say you to this?"

Orslett immediately jumped off the scaffold as the crowd soon made their feelings felt. Mud, rocks, rotting fruit, the corpses of dead rats, and horse dung were flung at the three miserable counterfeits. Orslett stopped and had a word with the sheriff's men, then swaggered back through the crowd to join Segalla. He swung himself up into the saddle.

"When the crowd have finished, the sheriff's men will take them to Newgate. There will be a few more questions and they'll need all the help the angels can give them." He gathered up his reins. "The Queen will be interested to see who is behind this. Some madcap scheme, or does the Princess Elizabeth and, above all, her cunning Cecil, have a hand in it?"

"What will happen to them then?" Segalla asked.

"Oh, the Queen will show compassion. They'll stand in the pillory for two or three days."

"How did you know?" Segalla asked.

Orslett reined in his horse. "Is there a God in heaven, Nicholas?" he asked. "If there isn't, this trickery is useless anyway. And, if there is, he's far too busy for Greyfriars."

Segalla followed Orslett back up towards St. Paul's and into Bowyers Row. However, they found this street sealed off: chains had been dragged across it, and city beadles stood on guard. Orslett had a quiet word with their leader. Segalla looked down the street at the black and burning ruins and knew they had come too late. The chain was lowered; they dismounted and led their horses along the cobbled alleyway. The air was still thick with woodsmoke, which curled from the baker's shop, now nothing more than a charred ruin.

"We had to let it burn out," the chief beadle explained. "Though we took some water from the Fleet."

"What started it?" Orslett asked.

"Heavens, sir, I am a beadle, not an angel from heaven. I suppose the baker left an oven alight: it happens. The flames jump, these houses are old, the wood is dry. . . ."

"And the woman called Nicolette?" Segalla asked.

The beadle pulled a face and pointed to a dirty sheet in one of the carts.

"What's left of her is there. A pretty wench once, now nothing but burnt flesh and yellow bones. Apparently the fire swept up the stairs, there was no other way out."

Segalla left his horse with Orslett and walked amongst the ruins. The ash and cinders were still hot. Everything was blackened and twisted. Segalla walked over to where the stairs had been and crouched down, sifting amongst the rubble. At the bottom he found pieces of wood, scorched and charred but not totally consumed. He picked these up and sniffed at them. At first he wasn't sure, but, the more he disturbed the ash, the more certain he became: beneath the smell of burning was something which prompted memories of sieges and towns on fire—the terrible stink of oil. Segalla looked back over his shoulder at Orslett chatting with the beadle as if they were acquaintances at some midsummer's fair. It would have been so easy, Segalla thought, to come here, force the locks of the baker's shop, douse the wooden stairs in oil, and turn the whole building into a lighted torch. Segalla threw the wood to the ground, wiped his fingers, and walked back.

"Did you find anything?" he asked.

"Heavens, sir," the beadle replied, "the fire was a furnace." His eyes slid away.

Segalla grasped him by the shoulder; the man tried to squirm away, but Segalla held him fast.

"Come, come, good sir. I am sure you did a very good job, but a woman like Nicolette would have trinkets, coins that might not burn and, as the Gospel says, the labourer is worthy of his hire!"

The beadle smiled, shamefaced, and shuffled his feet.

"We are not interested in what you took," Orslett explained. "But is there anything else?"

The beadle went across to the cart and brought back a coarse cloth sack tied at the neck. He undid this and shook the contents out onto the cobbles: some burnt Ave beads, a book of hours, nothing more than charred parchment and a sheaf of documents probably kept in a chest which had protected it against the flames. Segalla unrolled these. They were singed and holed, merely a list of monies. Segalla rolled the parchment up and put it into his wallet.

"You can't do that!" the beadle declared, his little red face now full of importance.

Segalla got to his feet and slipped a coin into the man's hand.

"Now, sir, you keep what you keep and I'll keep what I've found. Yes?"

The fellow agreed. Segalla and Orslett took their horses and left the street.

"Stephen." Segalla stopped and stroked the muzzle of his horse. "You knew Nicolette?"

"By reputation. I'd been keeping an eye on Dr. Theophilus. When he died, I wondered if his love nest would yield anything fresh."

"Why Theophilus?"

"Because he was so close to the Queen." Orslett pulled a face. "And other little tidbits of information. Anyway, what do you think of this fire?"

"Very little. The documents I found are nothing but a list of monies; for what, or why, is a mystery, as is the fire." Segalla pointed across to a tavern. "Let's go over there, slake the dust from our mouths, and talk about coincidences."

They left the horses in the stables and walked into the taproom, a spacious chamber, clean and well swept, with hams hanging from the rafters to be cured. A fire flamed merrily in the hearth: being midmorning the room was empty, apart from an old woman chewing on her gums in the inglenook and a blind fiddler feeding himself and his dog. The ale Segalla ordered was thick and heavy, well matured and cool.

"When I was abroad," Orslett declared, "I always missed English ale. Well, Nicholas, you mentioned coincidences?"

"Stephen, you studied logic in the seminary, yes? You know there's no such thing as a coincidence. On the night Theophilus was murdered, his mistress, Nicolette, also died in a fire. I am sure that our good and late physician kept documents in her chamber which have also been destroyed, whilst Nicolette could have told us so much about them as well as about her patron. Strange, isn't it? On the night Theophilus died, everything we know about him was destroyed or stolen."

"Stolen? How do you know that?"

Segalla leaned across the table. "Because, Stephen, like you, I visited Theophilus's chamber in Greenwich Palace."

Orslett blinked. Segalla noticed how his hand immediately went beneath the table for his dagger, a typical fighting man's gesture.

"You were there, weren't you, Stephen? When I went into Theophilus's chamber, you came in behind me. You were carrying a small arbalest. You were muffled to hide your voice: it must have been you. Now, it looks as if we have to work together. I do not want to wander the streets of London with an enemy at my back."

"What are you saying?" Orslett declared. "That I came and cleared Theophilus's chamber before going into the city to take care of Mistress Nicolette and whatever else was in her room? If I follow your logic, Nicholas, that makes me a murderer!"

"You could," Segalla replied, "state such a hypothesis, and, Stephen, please put both hands on the table; I am not your enemy. Theophilus was nothing to me." Segalla sipped from the tankard. Orslett did what he asked but watched Segalla intently.

"I am going to be honest," Segalla continued. "I have been sent here by the Holy Father to give good honest counsel to Queen Mary: the Pope suspects she is being poisoned. Dr. Cesar and I are to do all in our power to stop this. If we can, we shall, in a few months, return to Rome, and that will be the end of the matter. If we are unable to help, we shall see what happens and then go back and report that we did the best we could. Queen Mary is the legitimate monarch of this country. She is a Catholic. As a person, I like and respect her. I think her policies are ill advised: her persecution of the Protestants has caused nothing but bloodshed and grief. Nevertheless, as I have said, I am no man's enemy. To whom the Crown of England goes after Mary is not my concern."

Orslett grinned and put his tankard down.

"And now I suppose you want to hear my confession, Father?"

"It's good for the soul, Stephen."

"I believe in neither God nor man," Orslett replied. "I will speak the truth, and, believe me, Nicholas, I very rarely do that. My father died when I was young. I adored him. He was a soldier, a brave man. He went to church and paid his tithes. When he died my mother became the mistress of the

local priest. One of these men who follow the so-called reformed faith. He abused me, as he did my sister, who died of
the tertian fever. My mother I grew to despise, and everything the priest was, I hated. As soon as I was old enough, I
fled abroad and joined the Catholic armies. I saw wickedness,
so deep, Nicholas, it would take your breath away. I lost my
soul and thought I could find it by training to be a priest. I
was a good scholar." Orslett sipped from his tankard. "During Edward's reign, when Northumberland was Protector, I
slipped back into Norfolk, where most of the Catholic families are. I was hunted by the priest catchers. I could trust no
one, moving by night from house to house. Then, one day, I
was celebrating Mass at Thaxted Hall. I met the younger
daughter of the manor lord, Cecily was her name. Nicholas,
I have never seen such beauty before. Every second of the
day I thought of her. For the first time in my life I had met
someone I really believed in. Someone I could not live without. We became lovers, handfasted. When I asked her to
elope with me, she agreed. I came to London. Within a year,
Cecily was pregnant. Twins, Nicholas! Two little jewels! And
that's all I believe in, nothing else. You could say I've lost my
soul."

"Or found it?"

Orslett smiled; this time it was genuine. For a few seconds the hardness disappeared. He looked away to hide the
tears.

"It was good of you to say that, Segalla. So, I'll continue.
I used, well, let's put it this way, I used what I'd collected to

make an introduction to court. When Edward died and Northumberland tried to seize the throne, I was with Mary at Framlingham. How can I put it? I performed certain delicate tasks before she marched on London."

"Such as?"

"Like you saw this morning: unmasking the Queen's enemies. I was one of those who arrested Northumberland and saw him lose his head on Tower Hill. I became the Queen's man in peace and war. Queen Mary trusted me. I was sent as her messenger to her half-sister as well as to keep an eye on Master Cecil's machinations. A dangerous man is Master Cecil. He can read souls. One day he took me into the buttery and talked about the future."

"And now you are Elizabeth's man?"

"I will not betray the Queen." Orslett smiled. "And, there again, I don't believe in Elizabeth. She's not of my faith, she's not of my religion. It doesn't matter to me, Nicholas, who sits on the throne at Westminster. It's all a matter of timing. You must be ready to jump at the right time. To grasp events before they grasp you. Cecil may be upset by my unmasking of those counterfeits at Greyfriars, but he'll see it as all part of the game. When that game changes, so will I." Orslett spread his hands. "I've told you the truth."

"I thought you didn't believe in it?"

"Then I've told you what I think is the truth."

"And these murders?"

"You are right: I was with you in Theophilus's chamber.

But I had no hand in his death or in the whore's. I am an assassin, Nicholas. Believe me, if I thought you were a threat to me, Cecily, or my children, I would kill you, but I have a sense of honour: it wouldn't be a knife in the back or poison in the cup but a sword in some shadowy alleyway."

"So, what do you know?" Segalla asked.

"I am a Judas man," Orslett replied. "That's what Master Cecil calls me. I suspect the Queen thinks the same. A Judas man is ever ready to sell if the price is right." Orslett's voice became hard. "But I'm not. I've told you what my faith is. If I am given a task I will do it. I'll keep my word as long as I can."

Segalla leaned back against the wall. Orslett turned and ordered two more tankards of ale. Segalla was not surprised by Orslett's confession. He had met similar men before. They were no different from mercenaries: men who would take gold and fight. They'd do so bravely and ruthlessly, but they'd be the first to realize when a cause was lost. The guiding light for Master Orslett, however, was not gold but the woman he loved.

"So, tell me what you know," Segalla declared.

"Mary is isolated," Orslett replied slowly. "Her reign has been one mistake after another: the Spanish marriage, the loss of Calais—she has few friends and hardly any allies. Cecil, I am sure, is behind that business we witnessed at Greyfriars, but we cannot prove it. London is full of handbills attacking the Queen. Philip of Spain is tired of her and, I suspect, has eyes on the young Elizabeth. The French, too, are watchful, but the real masters of the game are Elizabeth and Master

Cecil. She is a member of the reformed faith; she has in Cecil a most skilful and subtle secretary. Above all, the populace see her as Great Harry's daughter. But . . ."

"But what?"

"Everybody wants everything to happen quickly. Mary's reign is seen as a limbo to be finished as soon as possible. To put it bluntly, Master Segalla, the Queen is being poisoned, but by whom I do not know: it could be any of the people I mentioned."

"And Mark 15.34?"

"Ah yes. Both Mary and Elizabeth are troubled by that. The Four Evangelists, whoever they are, are threatening to reveal some mystery, some great scandal."

"So, this is not the work of Master Cecil?"

"No. Far from it. Elizabeth is terrified. I am under orders to investigate the source, but I can't fathom it."

"You've been instructed to go to the Tower to search amongst the records there."

"I've been, I've been," Orslett retorted crossly. "But where can I start? Between 1529 and 1535 the Tower saw many parishioners, people coming and going. It's like looking for the proverbial needle in a haystack. I can find no reference to Mark 15.34 or the Four Evangelists. I've returned and told Cecil as much."

"He probably does know more," Segalla replied. "But, of course, Master Orslett, you are a Judas man and must only be told so much. Well, you've been truthful to me. I'll tell you what I know. The Pope, too, received the letter from the Four Evangelists: he did mention one name, Philip Savage."

"Yes, Cecil mentioned him when I visited Hatfield once to report on my lack of success: Savage was controller at the Tower during the years he specified. I told the Queen: she, or Cardinal Pole, must have informed Rome." Orslett pulled a face. "Everyone knows about Savage, but I can't find him. I did discover who might have known him."

"Who?"

"Our good physician, the one who was murdered. He called himself Theophilus, but his real name was John Gresham. He worked in the Tower as an apothecary and physician. He owned a house in Petty Wales and was hired by the lieutenant to tend to prisoners who fell ill. This was some years ago, during the late Henry's reign."

"And Theophilus, or Gresham, and this Philip Savage could be linked?" Segalla asked.

"Perhaps. I asked Theophilus, but he claimed he couldn't remember anyone called Philip Savage."

Orslett, once again, stared round the tavern. He studied a tinker who had come in, put his tray on a table, and was bawling for ale. Orslett smiled and turned back.

"I think it's time we were gone. Look at the tinker, Master Segalla; what's wrong with him?"

Segalla gazed across the taproom. The tinker was shabbily dressed except for good leather boots. Orslett got to his feet.

"They always make that mistake," he whispered. "It's always the boots. Come, Nicholas, we've just been joined by one of Cecil's men!"

Chapter 7

A re you always watched?" Segalla asked as they collected their horses and left the stable yard.

"Who will watch the watchers?" Orslett quipped. "What we do," he said, "is make our way down to East Watergate. We'll pay an ostler to ride our horses back to Greenwich and take a barge downriver to Lambeth."

"I asked you a question," Segalla reminded him.

Orslett gestured round at the packed street. People shoved and pushed. There were merchants in their fine clothes, shabby scholars from St. Paul's, and a couple of city punks in their tawdry finery, fingers drumming on the hilts of their swords. On the corner, a friar begged for alms and tried to ignore the catcalls and jeers of some ruffians. A scold, a brank in her mouth, was being led down to the river to sit in the stocks. The accompanying tipstaffs were drunk, so the woman seized the opportunity to flee, the brank still in her mouth, up an alleyway.

"There are men in London," Orslett declared, "who can move like the air, taking different shapes, assuming divers disguises: the city gallant, the scholar, the beggar, the mountebank, even a woman hooded and cloaked. Like me, Nicholas, they live on their wits. They collect information, juicy tidbits like crows on a midden, and there is always someone to buy. So, yes, I am watched. Some of these spies will die in a ditch; others in a stinking alleyway, a knife in their gullet or belly. Some will do the hangman's dance at Tyburn."

"And you?" Segalla asked.

Orslett stopped and patted his horse's neck.

"I trust you, Segalla, and, believe me, that's a compliment. Every week I take careful note of which ships are in port. I could be across to France or Hainaut in the twinkling of an eye, wife and children alongside me."

"Will you find Philip Savage?" Segalla asked.

"No, but there is someone who might."

They reached the corner of Thames Street and took their horses into the yard of the Three Cranes tavern. Orslett paid a reputable-looking ostler to hire a boy to ride the horses back to Greenwich. A small indenture was drawn up in the small office off the stable yard. Both Orslett and the ostler made their marks; the piece of parchment was then neatly cut, Orslett keeping one half, the ostler the other.

"Oh, and by the way"—Orslett pressed a coin into the ostler's hand—"please don't argue with me, but I want Monkswood here. I know he's back. Tell him Stephen Orslett has business for him."

They crossed the spacious taproom. Orslett hired a

chamber just off the scullery. It was no more than a cell containing a table and a few stools; a window high in the wall provided light. He ordered some meat pies and ale.

"I am sorry," Orslett apologized. "I do most of my business in taverns. The landlord knows me, so we will remain undisturbed."

"How do you know he is not one of Cecil's men?" Segalla teased.

"He probably is; that's why I've hired this room. The walls are of stone and there are no eyelets or spyholes."

"And who is Monkswood?"

Orslett waited until the slattern had served them and left, closing the door behind her.

"Eat your food, Nicholas, and you'll soon find out."

They had barely finished when the door opened and a small, white-haired, cherubic-faced man waddled in. He was dressed like a Carmelite monk in black and white with sandals on his feet. His jerkin came down to his knees, but, as soon as he was in the room, he pulled this up and undid the war belt strapped there: it carried three pouches; each held an Italian throwing knife. The man slung it on a peg on the back of the door. He rubbed his stomach, sat down, and smiled at Segalla and Orslett.

"Pax et bonum, Brothers!"

"Pax et bonum, Monkswood," Orslett replied. "You wish some ale?"

"I've already ordered wine at your expense." The childlike, blue eyes twinkled in merriment. "A large bowl of claret fresh from Bordeaux. I stood over that thieving landlord whilst he broached a fresh cask." He shook his head. "The world is full of thievery and wickedness." His voice took on a high-pitched tone, and Segalla nearly burst out laughing. "And every man is a knave and his woman is a whore!"

"You don't believe that, Monkswood, do you?" Orslett asked.

"The Book of Proverbs says," the villain replied, "that life is a running stream full of rocks and hidden traps. Ah, God bless you."

A slattern came in bearing a large pewter cup brimming with red wine. Monkswood took it with one hand whilst the other gently fondled the young woman's breast.

"Soft and ripe as a summer pear!"

The girl giggled and scurried out.

Monkswood toasted both of them.

"I must come here more often!" He drank but watched Segalla over the rim of his cup. "And who is this stranger, Orslett?"

"A friend, Nicholas Segalla. He's no danger to you, Monkswood."

"I didn't say he was. I know every sheriff's man from Cripplegate to Southwark."

"Let me introduce Monkswood," Orslett continued. "God knows where he comes from and God knows who he really is. He's a self-confessed authority on the Book of Proverbs." Orslett toasted his visitor. "A more villainous rogue couldn't grace any city."

Monkswood smiled so beatifically, Segalla found it almost impossible to believe this cherubic, white-haired man, who looked like a holy friar, was, in truth, a principal denizen of London's colourful underworld.

"We call him Monkswood," Orslett continued, "because of the way he dresses. Some say he was once a friar. He can drink claret until he is fit to burst and still give a sermon. He's as hot and lecherous as a sparrow."

Monkswood's smile widened as if Orslett were complimenting him.

"He has had his fingers in more pies than Master Cecil. He once ran a bordello in Southwark where ageing merchants, for a heavy price, could undress young wenches and smack them to their hearts' content. Monkswood's profits were increased when he made little peepholes into the walls so others could come and watch. He later expanded his business. He began to steal little items from his customers and later wrote to them offering to return these to their wives. Or, there again"—Orslett laughed—"they could buy them back for a considerable price."

"A most lucrative business," Monkswood murmured, shaking his head.

"It was," Orslett continued, "until the sheriff's men became involved. Monkswood moved on to other trades, selling shares for a company to explore the Orinoco, offering to sell the golden crown of an ancient chieftain, not to mention the pile of furs he claimed he had imported from Muscovy!"

"I had the goods," Monkswood intervened.

"Just moleskins sewn together," Orslett countered.

Monkswood spread his hands. "You tell this stranger my business, Stephen."

Orslett opened his hands, and two gold coins appeared on the table. Monkswood groaned with pleasure. He stroked each coin lovingly.

"You could have earned these weeks ago when I first sent for you."

"I had to leave the city for a while," Monkswood murmured, his eyes never leaving the coins.

"Monkswood is a great listener and a keen watcher," Orslett continued. "You can take one of those."

Monkswood went to do so. Orslett gripped his hand, squeezing it tightly.

"Philip Savage?"

Monkswood's face came up. "Never heard of him."

"Then leave the gold alone!"

"I have heard of him."

"What?"

Monkswood's eyes took on a pleading look.

"Don't lie!" Orslett warned. "Don't play tricks with me!"

"He was a royal official," Monkswood gabbled. "He worked in the Tower." He closed his eyes like a scholar remembering his letters. "He became involved in some scandal, I forget now. He took a different name to hide from the sheriff's men. He's been seen at St. Paul's amongst the other wolf's-heads. A mean-spirited man fallen on hard times."

Orslett pushed Monkswood's hand away and picked up the gold coins. The little man groaned, his eyes full of tears.

"Mark 15.34?" Segalla asked.

Monkswood stared back in stupefaction. "That means nothing to me, sir." Monkswood gazed hungrily at Orslett's hand.

"I am hiring you, Monkswood," Orslett declared. "I want to know what Philip Savage calls himself and where he lives. Tell me that. You can leave a letter here with the landlord or deliver it to me personally at Greenwich. You know my word is my bond. Get me that information and the gold is yours."

"Anything else?" Monkswood asked.

"In a while, there may be. I can find you in the Vintry?"

Monkswood smiled. "I have chambers there. A new business venture: an expedition down the Nile where new groves of spices can be found."

"All that glitters is not gold," Orslett declared.

"Ah yes, but it still glitters." Monkswood drained his cup and got to his feet. "That gold will be in my purse within three days." He slipped out of the room as quietly as he came.

"Can he be trusted?" Segalla asked.

"I'd trust him before I would any city official. If Savage is alive and hiding in London, Monkswood will find him."

They left the Three Cranes and went down to East Watergate and hired a barge to take them along the river. The journey was uneventful. Segalla admired the boatman's skill in steering their craft past the heavy-bottomed cogs, war ships, and grain barges which thronged the river. Matters were made worse by a sea mist which suddenly rolled in. Lanterns had to be lit, and, every so often, the bells of the ships rang out giving warning to others using the river. They reached Lambeth. The mist was even more cloying, shrouding the episcopal residence in a veil of grey. Segalla found the palace gloomy, wet, and ill tended.

"Cardinal Pole is a sick man," Orslett pointed out. "His work is finished. There are few who stay to serve him."

They were in the palace itself before anyone stopped to ask their business. When Orslett produced his royal warrant, a rather dowdy chamberlain, who looked as if he had been savouring the ale in the buttery, came lurching towards them. Groaning and muttering under his breath, the fellow led them up some stairs into a hot, stuffy chamber. The windows were shuttered. A few oil lamps burnt. He told them to stay and walked across and rapped on the inner door.

"Come in!"

The chamberlain ushered them forward. If the ante-room was dark the Cardinal's chamber looked as if it dwelt in perpetual night. A fire burnt in the hearth. Above it hung a huge wooden cross, a candle on either side. These flared up, emphasizing the figure of Christ, which writhed in agony, head up, mouth open. At the foot of the cross was a human skull, the white bones glowing eerily in the candlelight.

"Who is it?" The voice was now not so strong.

Narrowing his eyes, Segalla made out a figure seated in a chair before the fire.

"A messenger from the Queen, Your Eminence."

"How is she? How is my sweet cousin?"

"Your Eminence, she is well and sends her love and regards."

"Does she now? Does she now? Simon, is that you?"

"Yes, Your Eminence," the chamberlain replied.

"Light more candles. Put some more wood on the fire. You can drink as much of my ale as you like, but at least keep me warm!"

The chamberlain scurried about, more mutters and curses in the darkness as he stumbled against chairs. Nevertheless, candles were lit. A log was put on the fire and two chairs pushed up opposite the Cardinal.

"Come closer!"

Segalla did so. He genuflected before the Cardinal, kissed the vein-streaked hand, and glanced up: Pole was a very sick man. Segalla had once glimpsed him in Rome, a strong, sturdy figure, glaring eyes, strong mouth and chin. Now all this was gone: the eyes were sunken, the skin an ashen grey, the hair and beard straggling and unkempt. He was dressed in a friar's robe. This, and the blankets heaped about him, were covered in food stains.

"You are Segalla, the Pope's emissary?"

"Yes, Your Eminence."

"And what message does the Pope send?"

"His good wishes and apostolic blessing."

"Don't lie!" Pole snapped. "Carafa hates me as I hate him! And yet"—his voice took on a lighter tone—"once we were great friends: a veritable David and Johnathan. Sit down, sit down! You, too, Stephen."

They did so, and the chamberlain left the room, closing the door behind him.

"The Pope sends me nothing, does he?"

"His Holiness was most concerned about you."

"Aye, I am sure he is, like when am I going to die? How can the Church survive when we fight each other? And the Queen, she is better?"

"She dined well last night, Your Grace," Orslett intervened.

"Do you bring me more medicine?"

"Theophilus died last night," Orslett declared. He glanced quickly at Segalla. "Of . . ."

"He was poisoned!" Pole snapped, pulling himself up in his chair. "Master Orslett, I respect your intentions; I may be a sickly man but I am no fool. I, too, have my spies at Greenwich." His thin fingers clenched on the arm of his chair. "They are killing the Queen," he whispered hoarsely. "And no one can stop them!"

"Who, Your Grace?" Segalla asked.

"That bitch!" Pole's face now contorted with fury. "Boleyn's brat!" His voice became wheedling. "Little, red-haired Elizabeth and her weasel man Cecil. They have got someone close to the Queen. They are killing her and those who try to help her."

"Do you have proof, Your Eminence?"

"Yes, I have, two: history and the truth. When Henry gave up his soul and let his mind be dictated by his codpiece"—the words were spat out—"Boleyn tried to poison both Catherine and Mary. Oh, I lie not." He shook his finger. "Go to the records. Seek out Boleyn's last letter. She publicly confesses the great wrong she did both Catherine and Mary."

Pole's thin body was racked with a spasm of coughing. For a while he just sat catching his breath.

"Elizabeth is young but she has an old head on her shoulders. Cecil's a new breed of man. A master of deceit and rumour. You've been through the city? The broadsheets against the Queen? The whispering campaign? Cecil's behind it!"

"But poison, Your Eminence?"

"Why not? If Mary dies, Elizabeth will seize the throne. If she does, the Catholic faith is finished."

"And Mark 15.34?"

Pole bowed his head. He scratched the lobe of his ear.

" 'Eloi, Eloi,' " he murmured, " 'lamma sabacthani? My God, my God, why have you forsaken me?' " He glanced up. "A fitting prayer for the Queen and myself."

"Do you know what it means?"

"No."

The denial came so fast Segalla doubted if Pole was telling the truth.

"I don't know," Pole confessed. "But, believe me, I'd give everything I own to know why it upsets Elizabeth so much." Pole lifted a hand. "I cannot help you." He sketched a blessing. "Give my love and good wishes to the Queen, as well as my apologies that I can no longer join her council. It's best if you were gone."

Segalla and Orslett left the damp, mildewed palace. They found Dr. Cesar waiting for them in the porter's lodge near the gate. The good doctor was swathed in a thick, woollen cloak; with his red cheeks and pointed beard, he looked like some friendly gnome. Segalla introduced Orslett, and the two men grasped hands.

"I thought I would find you here." Cesar walked between them. "How is His Eminence?"

"Very ill."

"I've left some medicine," Cesar replied. He stamped his feet on the gravelled path and peered through the mist towards the river. "Is this island ever warm?" he murmured.

"In the height of summer." Orslett laughed. "And the thrush sings and the grass is long, lovely, and lush. There's no better place under heaven."

Cesar just grumbled under his breath. They went down to the riverside where they hired a wherry.

"To Greenwich?" Segalla asked.

Orslett shook his head. "No, I think we should go to the Tower."

He settled himself in the stern and they fell silent whilst the boatman pushed his boat away from the quayside.

"Whilst we wait for Monkswood to report, it's best if we do a little searching ourselves." Orslett sat forward. "Cheer up, Dr. Cesar. You missed a beautiful summer but winter has its attractions."

"Why did you come to Lambeth?" Segalla asked.

"I've examined Theophilus's cadaver," Cesar replied. "Slit him from neck to crotch I did. A sturdy man with a good heart and. . . ."

"The poison?" Segalla asked.

"Oh, he was poisoned, something containing mercury. It

rots the inside and blocks the blood, but I can't give it a name." Cesar sighed. "And you, Nicholas, you've been busy?"

Segalla told him what had happened in the city. Cesar pulled a face.

"Poison and arson," he whispered. "A good night's work for our assassin. Do you think we are safe, Nicholas?"

"If you watch what you eat and drink," Orslett intervened, "and take care where you go, you might be."

Segalla pulled his hood up against the clinging cold. It was the middle of September, but such days were common in the English clime: it was as if the seasons became muddled and winter came hurrying in early with a stinging rebuke.

"So we'll spend the day in the Tower?" Cesar asked.

"You need not join us," Orslett replied.

Cesar shrugged. "I visited the Queen this morning and gave her some medicine. The palace is as gloomy as a sepulchre. I'd best be here than anywhere else."

"Why are we going to the Tower?" Segalla asked. "I thought you'd searched the records and found nothing?"

Orslett shrugged. "Cecil was cryptic: it's as if he wants me to stumble on something, the significance of which will mean everything to him and nothing to me." He spread his hands. "After a while I gave up, and, as you saw, the Queen needed me in the city." Orslett turned and spat over the side. "I was looking for any reference to that puzzle: Mark 15.34 or the Four Evangelists. Now, after Theophilus's death, I want to look at the records again, particularly references

linking Theophilus, or Gresham as he was then, and Philip
Savage."

"So, Theophilus lied when he said he did not know who
Savage was?"

"Of course. I informed the Queen, but she ordered me
not to pursue the matter: she did not want her physician
troubled."

"When was this?"

Orslett screwed up his eyes. "Oh, at the end of June or
the first week of July."

By the time they reached the Tower the mist was beginning to lift, the sun breaking through. Nevertheless, the
fortress looked grim with its soaring towers, crenellated walls,
and the decapitated heads of malefactors perched on spikes
above the main gateway. Segalla had been here many times
before and knew this sinister, narrow place like the back of
his hand. However, now he pretended ignorance and allowed
Orslett to lead the way along the narrow gulleys, through
postern gates, and onto the broad expanse of green which
surrounded the soaring Norman Tower. Soldiers stopped
them at every turn, but the royal warrants they carried allowed them through. An officer, Oliver Ingham, one of the
constable's lieutenants, wearily recognized Orslett. He entertained them in the great hall, a smokey, narrow, dark place;
the tables were littered with food. Massive, shaggy hunting
dogs scavenged amongst the dirty rushes. Ingham apparently
wished to be elsewhere but patiently listened to Orslett and
took them across to Beauchamp Tower, where the records
were kept. Ingham handed them over to a red-nosed, watery-

eyed clerk, who led them down to the basement where the manuscripts and parchments were stored.

"The Tower journals from 1529 to 1535." The clerk stood, drumming his fingers against his lips. "You've looked at them before, didn't you?"

"Yes, on the Queen's orders," Orslett snapped.

"Oh, yes, of course you did, I know that!" The clerk seized Orslett's wrist. "There's a chamber above, a fire in the hearth and braziers in each corner. It's where I do my work. There are tables, chairs, and stools, why not work there?"

Orslett glanced at Segalla, raised his eyes heavenwards, but accepted the clerk's kind offer. The man also promised to send refreshments across, and a sullen servant eventually brought these: a jug of ale; three battered, pewter cups; bread; cheese; and rather rancid bacon. Nevertheless, the chamber they were given was warm and clean. A hearth was built into the wall and the log fire burnt merrily whilst in each corner stood a bowl of glowing charcoal. Orslett and Dr. Cesar chatted animatedly about the Tower and its famous prisoners. After a brief wait, the clerk brought in a small chest heaped full of documents which he placed on the table. When he had left, Orslett bolted and locked the doors behind him.

"These are probably all the documents for the administration of the Tower in the years between 1529 and 1535 when King Henry reigned and the Tower was full of his prisoners. Now, I have established that Philip Savage was controller here. We also know that our late lamented physician Theophilus, known as John Gresham, also served as leech to the garrison, as well as the prisoners they guarded."

Orslett tapped the documents. "Somewhere in here lies the solution to the great riddle posed by the Four Evangelists and their cryptic reference to Mark 15.34. Whoever wrote those letters is probably the poisoner. Now, if the sea can give up its secrets, let's see what these can do."

He emptied the contents of the chest onto the table; scraps of parchment, rolls of vellum, books sewn together. In the main they were not exciting: provisions for the Tower; messengers coming and going; where prisoners were held; visitors; the preparations for execution days; wages; salaries; and provisions.

"What are we looking for?" Dr. Cesar asked.

"Anything which catches your eye," Orslett replied. "But, in particular, two men: Philip Savage and John Gresham. I've seen the references. Now I want to read them again as well as ensure I've missed nothing."

The day wore on. Now and again they heard the distant sounds of the Tower: bells ringing, footsteps on the stairs, the shouts of officers. Outside the day changed, the mist lifted, the sun made its presence felt. The room became warm and stuffy, so they opened a window which overlooked the green. At noon they joined the garrison in the great hall for a paltry meal, where at least the meat was of better quality, before returning to their searches. Slowly, they began to rediscover the references Orslett had found as well as new ones. Philip Savage, controller at the Tower, had been a man of great influence. Savage controlled the purse strings and dealt directly not only with the officers and the garrison but also the Tower's notable prisoners. These were many, especially after Anne Boleyn's fall from power.

"What were the allegations against her?" Dr. Cesar asked.

"Basically, King Henry was tired of her," Orslett replied. "He was hot-eyed for Jane Seymour. The accusations against Anne were that she was a witch, that she had been unfaithful with a court musician called Smeaton as well as her brother George, Lord Rochford. They were all rounded up. Smeaton was tortured: Anne, her brother, and a few of their coven went to the block."

"And Savage apparently visited them?"

Segalla pushed across a page from one of the Tower household books.

"Look at this: 'Monies paid to Philip Savage for visiting Anne Boleyn.'"

"Why should he do that?" Cesar asked.

"For many reasons," Segalla retorted. "To her death, Anne always maintained her innocence. King Henry undoubtedly placed great pressure on his Tower officials to elicit a confession from her." He ran his finger further down the page. "Savage also visited her brother George and even Smeaton the musician, who was treated more roughly. The controller was responsible for their comfort. Henry didn't like his prisoners dying of gaol fever; that would be too convenient. He wanted the full rigour of the law carried out. A man of great terror was Henry."

"You speak as if you knew him," Dr. Cesar teased.

"Only by reputation." Segalla turned the pages over. "Ah,

look. Monies were also paid to John Gresham, our good Theophilus. He apparently tended Smeaton after he had been tortured." He turned more pages over. "Well, this is interesting." He pointed to the entry. "It refers to the Christmas following Boleyn's execution: Savage, Gresham, and two others celebrated Yuletide. They held a small party and drew on Tower stores for wine, meats, et cetera."

"Who were the other two?" Orslett asked.

"Peter Dalrymple, clerk of the stores, and Simon Kennet, an official of the Tower chancery."

Segalla put the book down and abruptly left the chamber. A short while later he returned, carrying a wicker basket full of more documents.

"Cecil told you to look at the records between 1529 and 1535?" he asked.

Orslett agreed.

"And you found no reference to Mark 15.34 or the Four Evangelists?"

"I've told you that," Orslett retorted.

"Well"—Segalla emptied the basket onto the table— "let's go a little further in our hunt for Mr. Savage and his friends."

More candles were lit: the Tower records after 1535 were studied, the silence broken only by the crackle of parchment pages being turned over and smoothed down.

"Savage and the others seemed to be great friends," Segalla murmured. "They celebrated Christmas, New Year, Easter, and Midsummer together."

"That's not uncommon," Orslett replied. "The Tower is

like a small village. Household retainers seek out those they like and trust."

Segalla just shook his head. "This seems exceptional." He picked up another household book. "These four seem to have enjoyed a long and fruitful relationship."

They went through more entries over the years. Segalla got the impression that the four men, Savage, Gresham, Dalrymple, and Kennet, admired each other, full of their own importance at the positions they held in the Tower. They were like a small guild or fraternity, meeting to celebrate the great feast days and public holidays. Changes in government, the fall and rise of ministers, did not affect them: Thomas Cromwell, Henry's favourite, created Earl of Essex, controlled the kingdom but ended his days as a traitor in the Tower. The Howards, the greatest nobles in England, also suffered disgrace; the Seymour brothers came and went; but these precious four continued to serve the Crown.

They found no reference to Mark 15.34 or the Four Evangelists until Easter 1552, five years after Henry VIII's death. The young Edward was on the throne, guided and controlled by the sinister Duke of Northumberland. Segalla came across a most interesting entry. On the twenty-fifth of April, the feast of St. Mark, payment was made for "feasting and revelry" by Philip Savage for the "Four Evangelists." Segalla clapped his hands in excitement, and the others clustered round to see what he had found.

"Here we have," Segalla declared, "four men: they formed a coven; they not only worked together but, in their private lives, met to toast their mutual good fortune. Now,

God knows why, but on the feast of St. Mark, who was one of the original Four Evangelists, they undoubtedly held a private party here in the Tower. This entry shows that they called themselves the Four Evangelists."

"But why should they call themselves that?" Orslett asked. "I could understand it if their names were Matthew, Mark, Luke, and John, the same as the writers of the four Gospels."

"I don't know," Segalla retorted. "But I suspect this precious quartet were pompous, arrogant officials living in a time of great change. The great ones, Henry, his wives, his ministers, come and go, but they remain. This inflates their feeling of self-importance. Now, tell me, Stephen, if you were called into court and asked to swear the truth, how do you demonstrate you will tell the truth?"

"By taking an oath, one hand on the Bible." Orslett grinned. "Of course! On the book of the Gospels, written by the Four Evangelists."

"Precisely," Segalla replied. "These four men were bound to each other, not only by mutual admiration but by a great secret which concealed an even greater truth. But, what that was. . . ."

Segalla shrugged and went back to studying the manuscripts. Orslett leafed through another household book and, puzzled, looked up.

"It's strange," he declared. "These four men lived like lords, but abruptly, in 1553, all four disappeared from the Tower. Look." He pointed to entries about their replacements. "Yet, that's not how royal servants are treated. They usually retire with honour, pensions or annuities, benefits to finance their remaining years. And why should all four go immediately together? By July 1553 their names have been removed from the Tower lists."

They went through other documents and found that this was so. Orslett went downstairs to have a word with the clerk and came back a short while later.

"It's as we thought," he declared. "In the summer of 1553, Savage, Gresham, Kennet, and Dalrymple were summarily removed from the payroll of the garrison. They were given no pensions, which means that their dismissal must have been due to disgrace."

"But what?" Dr. Cesar asked. He rose and went to warm his hands by the fire.

"We won't find the reason here," Orslett declared. "That will be kept amongst the Crown's confidential records: letters issued under the Secret Seal." He got to his feet and put on his war belt. "So, the mystery remains. We've found the Four Evangelists, but we don't know what their great secret was!"

Chapter 8

S egalla and his companions stayed in the Tower for a while searching amongst the manuscripts, but they found nothing fresh. The mist had lifted but the sun was setting and the shadows growing longer by the time they left the fortress and made their way down to the Thames. A waiting barge took them along the busy river, now turning a strange orangish hue under the setting sun. Orslett and Cesar discussed the different sights they passed. The physician was particularly interested in the scaffolds and gallows placed along either shoreline: he informed Orslett how, in Europe, the bodies of condemned malefactors were often handed to doctors and hospitals for dissection.

Segalla closed his eyes and pretended to doze, though really he reflected on what they had learnt. He was heartened by the day's work. The Four Evangelists had been named: Gresham, Savage, Dalrymple, and Kennet. They must have discovered a great secret, but did that mean they were now trying to sell it on the open market? Their last letter had named a price but provided no details on how it was to be paid. And how did that link with the murders which had been carried out? First Gresham, or Theophilus as he liked to be called, then his mistress, the woman Nicolette? And were the writers responsible for the secret attacks upon the Queen, or would he have to look elsewhere? Cecil had definitely fed Orslett tidbits of information, hoping his Judas man would stumble on something. Orslett had not, so Cecil had provided a little more, the name of Savage. Did this mean Cecil knew the threat behind Mark 15.34 and the real danger posed by the Four Evangelists? Is that why Theophilus had been murdered? Segalla, try as he might to counter it, had a sense of deep foreboding. On either side of him the city seemed to be busy: ships getting ready to leave on the evening tide; bumboats, wherries, and barges darting about like water beetles. Nevertheless, it was unreal. Pole, Mary's chief councillor, was a sickly recluse at Lambeth whilst his Queen hid away in Greenwich not knowing what to do. All around people were waiting for something to happen.

By the time they reached Greenwich, darkness was falling. Two torches had been lit before the main gateway, and great metal bowls full of charcoal glowed fiercely, sprinkled with incense and herbs to fumigate the air. The guards let them through. In the hallway Sir Henry Grantchester sat at a table drinking with some of his officers. He rose as they entered and came forward to greet them, but it was Cesar's hand he grasped and shook.

"I thank you, sir!"

"Why?" Dr. Cesar raised his eyebrows in surprise.

"The Queen has slept most of the day. She has just

awoken and feels most refreshed. She and Jane Dormer are eating in their chambers. It's the talk of the palace; the Queen seems healthier than she has for many a day. Come, I'll take you to her."

Grantchester ignored Segalla and Orslett, only giving them a cursory nod: he was halfway up the main staircase before he paused.

"Oh, Master Orslett." He made no attempt to hide his disdain. "You had a visitor; dresses like a monk and talks like a priest but he is neither. I had him put in the guardhouse. He claims to have a message for you!"

A soldier took them along a passageway leading off the hallway. Monkswood was sitting on a bench in the guardroom playing Guess a Penny with two of the guards. By the looks on their faces both men were losing heavily. Monkswood got up, scooping the coins into a little cup he carried which disappeared beneath his voluminous robes.

"Ah, Master Stephen, and you, Master Segalla, good evening. I have been waiting some time!"

"You found what we asked?" Orslett demanded.

"Of course, my dear boy, but not here."

Monkswood led them out into the passageway, through a postern gate into one of the small courtyards. A fountain splashed water which twinkled in the light of the cresset torches fixed in the walls. Monkswood looked up at the stars.

"It will soon be winter," he murmured. "I am always pleased when the weather changes."

"Philip Savage!" Orslett demanded.

Monkswood stretched out his soft, white hand. Orslett

pressed a gold piece into the man's palm but gripped his fingers.

"Don't hurt me, Stephen," Monkswood murmured. "If you hurt me, I will not be your friend: there must be honour amongst thieves."

Orslett withdrew his hand.

"Philip Savage," Monkswood continued, "or Francis Tuttle, as he sometimes likes to be called, is a man who fell like Lucifer. Controller in the Tower, he was dismissed from his office."

"Why?" Segalla asked.

Monkswood ran a finger round his lips.

"The information I gathered is not Bible truth. However, Master Savage made the mistake of believing that, because he was a big fish in one pond, he could be a big fish in any. About five years ago he and others entered the city. Rumour had it that they had something to sell."

"And?" Segalla asked impatiently.

"One of my confidants, a lovely boy with a bottom like a peach—" Monkswood licked his lips. "Well, never mind that, he says it was a time of great change. Young Edward was dying. The Duke of Northumberland, his Protector, was wondering who would be the next to sit on the throne at Westminster. Some said Mary, some said Elizabeth, others advanced the claims of Lady Jane Grey. Now, as you know, the good duke put his money on the wrong card and lost everything: that was the time Master Savage decided to dabble. He was trying to sell something. Whatever happened"— he waved a hand—"Northumberland either refused or wasn't able to buy. Instead, Savage became involved with a mysterious stranger, a Master Clarence."

"Clarence?" Segalla asked.

"That's all I know. Anyway, to cut a long story short, I do not know what happened to Master Clarence. Savage was dismissed from his office. Indeed, warrants were issued for his arrest and the sheriff's men were hunting him and others."

"And what happened?"

"One crisis followed another. Northumberland fell from power. Queen Mary, God bless her, swept into London. The sheriff's men had other things to think about, and Master Savage disappeared. He took the name of Francis Tuttle and was last known to have a shabby dwelling place, a garret in a dilapidated house in Dog Leg Lane."

"And have you been there?"

Monkswood laughed softly. "Now, now, Master Orslett, the city is full of men who want to hide. They become very angry if you turn over the stones under which they hide. You have your information and I have my gold."

"There's more," Segalla intervened. He took his own purse off his belt and shook the silver coins out on the palm of his hand. Freshly minted Italian pieces, they glittered in the torchlight.

Monkswood drew his breath in.

"Two more names," Segalla said. "Kennet and Dalrymple."

"Yes, I've heard of them," Monkswood whispered, his eyes never leaving the silver. "In my searches today, their names were bracketed with Savage." He licked his lips. "Master Orslett, what is this all about?"

Segalla touched the tip of Monkswood's nose.

"Curiosity can be a killing infection."

"Aye, it can be," Monkswood replied. "So, I'll give you some advice, Master Segalla."

"Which is?"

"You are not the only ones looking for these men." Monkswood walked towards the door. "The marvellous thing about London, Master Segalla"—he looked round, a smile on his face—"is that, try as hard as you can to hide, you have to come out, take the air, buy the necessities of life, and, isn't it strange, sooner or later, you must cross St. Paul's? Do you know there are friends of mine who spend virtually every day around the great cathedral? They have time on their hands as they sit and watch. They snap up little tidbits, scraps of gossip. So, when I went fishing, I found there's been other nets in the water, but whose, I don't know." He walked back. "And do you know something? Some of the ancient ones recall a man called Segalla, a shadowy figure, a man who stayed out of the light, but, like all others . . . "

"Had to cross St. Paul's," Segalla finished the sentence for him.

"Segalla is not an English name."

"A family of merchants," Segalla replied. "My family have always had close ties with England."

"Of course." Monkswood sighed. He tapped the side of his nose and disappeared into the darkness.

"What was he talking about?" Orslett asked.

"He's like a peacock," Segalla replied. "Monkswood is dangerous because of what he knows and likes to show it.

What concerns me," he continued glibly, wishing to divert the conversation, "is who else is searching?"

"Shall we go to Savage's house?" Orslett asked.

"No," Segalla replied. "It's time to sleep, Stephen, to reflect." He turned to face Orslett. "Monkswood discovered this information quickly. Why wasn't it done before?"

"You heard," Orslett replied. "I sent for Monkswood weeks ago."

"Yes, I remember; he claimed he was out of the city."

Orslett stamped his feet against the cold.

"Perhaps," he muttered. "Or it could be that Monkswood realizes Mary is now lost and wishes to help. Whatever, Cecil will not be pleased."

"Why not?"

"He gave me the task: he will not be happy that, out of desperation and without his consent, I turned to Monkswood for help."

Peter Dalrymple gathered his shabby cloak around him. He grasped the rusty handle of the knife he'd recently bought in the market in St. Paul's graveyard and scurried like a rat down the dark, stinking alleyways towards Cripplegate. Every so often Dalrymple would pause and stare around. He had to make sure he was not being followed. He and the others. Someone had told him how that master of deceit, Monkswood, had been busy around St. Paul's, searching for poor Philip. Dalrymple paused at the corner of an alleyway; a beggar came out of the shadows whining for alms.

Dalrymple held his dagger up and the man slunk away. Dalrymple was worried. They had made a compact never to visit each other. Instead, every so often, they would meet in a ruined house in the fields around St. Mary of Bethlehem, but, on the last few occasions, Savage had never arrived. Dalrymple and Kennet had discussed the matter, but they didn't even know where Savage lived.

Dalrymple turned the corner; at the far end of the alleyway stood an alehouse, the light pouring through the open window of the doorway. He envied the men carousing inside. Dalrymple leaned against the wall, catching his breath, trying to ignore the stench of urine and the putrid smells from the open cesspit which ran the whole course of that narrow, mean runnel. He hoped Savage had been careful: only two weeks ago a bottle of wine had been sent as a gift, brought by a pretty male whore. Kennet had made him drink it first. The whore had died in paroxyms of agony. Ever since, Dalrymple had been most scrupulous in everything he ate and drank, where he went, and to whom he talked. He hurried on, gnawing at his lip. They had had such high hopes, especially when Gresham reappeared under his grand name of Theophilus. He had met them, just once, and promised he would do all he could, but the man was a liar, nothing was done.

Dalrymple left the alleyway and crossed the broad thoroughfare leading down to the city gates. The curfew had not yet sounded, and Dalrymple slipped through a postern door. He went up Grubb Street and onto the open heathland north of the city. He cursed as he stumbled, slipping on the mud, missing his foothold. The wind was coming from the east, and he caught the stench from the deep ditch so bad that, when he crossed it by a small wooden bridge, he held his breath and pinched his nostrils. Once across he stopped; he was in the fields now, full of the scent of approaching autumn. Dalrymple cursed his own misfortune. If only he had not listened! If he'd only ignored Savage's tempting offer! They should have buried their secret and he would now be back in the Tower, acting the lord amongst the prisoners, with a swollen belly and fresh robes.

Dalrymple continued on; somewhere a dog howled, baying at the rising moon. Bats screeched in the twilight and he was startled by the raucous cry of a nesting rook. Dalrymple fought to curb his fear. Near the postern door of St. Paul's Cathedral, Kennet had left the sign that a meeting was planned, and, before him, Dalrymple now saw the decayed mansion where they always met. The roof had long fallen in, the timber and plaster walls were crumbling. He went through the small gap where the lich-gate had stood and around to the door which led into the dilapidated kitchen.

"Simon!" he shouted.

"Here!"

Dalrymple froze. Was that Kennet's voice? And why was he upstairs? They usually met in the disused parlour. Dalrymple climbed the stairs, carefully holding his dagger before him.

"Simon!" he called again.

"I'm in here!"

Dalrymple relaxed; the voice was Kennet's. In a bedchamber, his old friend and acquaintance crouched in a corner, a lantern beside him. He was warming his hands over a small bed of charcoal laid out across a cluster of bricks.

"I found this in the cellar." Kennet spread his fingers. "It can't be seen from outside and I feel so cold."

Dalrymple sat opposite his friend. Kennet looked ill: in the poor light his face was thinner, the eyes large and staring; beads of perspiration ran down his unshaven cheek.

"You have a fever, Simon!"

Kennet coughed, his whole body shaking with a spasm.

"Some contagion," he murmured.

"Will Philip be here?"

Kennet shook his head. "I don't know. But you've heard the rumours?"

"People are looking for us."

"More than that: Gresham's dead. Murdered, so the rumour goes, whilst his whore Nicolette was burnt in a fire. A tinker at St. Paul's lich-gate told me."

"Murdered?" Dalrymple gasped.

"Poisoned!" Kennet snapped back. "And Savage has disappeared."

"What can we do?" Dalrymple asked.

"Leave London," Kennet replied. He patted the bundle beside him. "If we stay, Peter, we are dead men. God damn Gresham!" Kenett continued. "Perhaps he tried to sell the secret: that's why they are now searching for us."

"Where will you go?" Dalrymple asked.

"First, out to a village. Perhaps I can get some work, eat well, cure this ague, and then go west into Cornwall."

Dalrymple got up and walked to the window. He was tempted to follow, but he had a few possessions in the city. Fear curdled his stomach. Was it safe to go back, even now?

"Come with me!" Kennet gasped. "Peter, whatever you have is not worth bringing."

Dalrymple was about to turn away when he glimpsed a shadow in the garden below. He drew back and peered into the darkness. At first he thought he was mistaken, but, no, figures were slipping through the gloom. Dalrymple ran across, grasped Kennet's arm, and pulled him to his feet.

"What's the matter? What's the matter?"

Dalrymple grabbed Kennet's fardel. "Don't ask!" he snarled. "We are not alone!"

Kennet, his body racked with more coughing, allowed Dalrymple to push him out into the dusty gallery. They clattered down the stairs, out through a side door and ran across the overgrown garden. Dalrymple paused. Had he been mistaken? A crossbow bolt whirled above his head. He hurried on: they pushed their way through the hedge, but Kennet collapsed to the ground.

"I can't!" he gasped. "I can't breathe!"

Dalrymple brandished the dagger: his body was soaked in sweat, and at least three of the shapes were hurrying towards them.

"God have mercy on you, Kennet!" Dalrymple whispered. "I can do no more!"

He pushed his way through some undergrowth and ran, fleet as a deer, across the heathland towards the welcoming lights of the city. Behind him, Kennet scrabbled to his feet.

In the poor light, he could make out his pursuers, hooded and masked.

"What do you want?" he stuttered. "I am a poor man."

One of the figures stepped forward and grabbed Kennet.

"You have nothing to fear. We only wish to talk to you. Look, we have brought you a horse."

Kennet turned, and, as he did, the leader of the assassins expertly cut his exposed throat. Kennet slumped to the ground. The assassin wiped his dagger on the dead man's cloak and, helped by his companions, methodically stripped and searched the corpse. The assassin's leader was pleased.

"A good night's work!" he declared. "But we'll have to tell the one who hired us that one of the conys escaped into the hay!"

The next morning, accompanied by Sir Henry Grantchester, Segalla met the Queen in her private chamber; Jane Dormer was in attendance. Segalla was pleased to see the Queen did look more healthy. She had lost that greyish pallor and complained of no pains or aches in her stomach. She smiled as she handed a heavy purse to a beaming Dr. Cesar.

"The potion you gave me, sir, I slept like a babe. I feel stronger, robust enough to do a little hunting in the parks."

"Madame, I would strongly advise against that."

Dr. Cesar helped the Queen gently back into her chair. On the other side Jane Dormer arranged the Queen's dress and pushed a small silver mug into her hands.

"Drink, eat, and rest," Dr. Cesar continued.

The Queen sipped at the ale and nodded.

"And you, Nicholas? A good day's work?"

Segalla briefly described his visit to Pole. The Queen's face puckered in concern. Then he described their searches in the Tower, telling the Queen all they had discovered. For a while Mary just sat, rolling the cup between her hands, eyes half-closed.

"I know nothing of this," she replied. "You say Dr. Gresham was involved? Or Theophilus," she added sourly, "as he liked to be called?"

"You know nothing of this, Your Grace?"

The Queen let her breath out in one long sigh.

"Of course," she replied brusquely, "I knew Dr. Theophilus had served in the Tower and had a good practice in Petty Wales. I also heard rumours that he was not in favour with the Duke of Northumberland, which is one of the reasons I gave him preferment at court. He was a good physician though." She smiled at Dr. Cesar. "Of course, there are better!"

"So, Your Grace, you know nothing about the Four Evangelists?"

Mary shook her head. "Let me remind you, Master Segalla, of those wild, pell-mell days after my brother's death. In July of 1553," she continued, "all of London was in a great tumult. My brother had died, the Duke of Northumberland had proclaimed the Lady Jane Grey as Queen. I was at Framlingham. I unfurled my banner and proclaimed my own rightful claims to my father's throne. The city, the countryside were in uproar." She smiled sourly. "Oh, how things change," she whispered. "In London they tossed their caps into the air and proclaimed 'Long live Queen Mary!' People flocked to my banners. I was not halfway to London when I had three thousand foot and a thousand horse. Now politics is a dirty pool: in the summer of 1553, it was given a good stir with a stout stick. All the filth and muck rose to the top. People swore great oaths only to perjure themselves within the hour. Ah well." She sighed. "That's now history. North-umberland was arrested at Cambridge. He was stripped of all his robes and brought bareheaded into London. His underlings, his minions and henchmen, were swept up like broken shards. All was chaos and confusion." Mary pressed her fingers against her temples.

"What the Queen is saying," Jane Dormer spoke up, "is that many of the documents, warrants, and letters issued by Northumberland's government here in London were either hidden or destroyed. Many men lost their offices. Some household retainers disappeared; fearful of arrest, they have never been seen since. So, we never knew what documents were issued or why certain acts were carried out. It was a hurly-burly time," the lady-in-waiting continued. "North-umberland had proclaimed Lady Jane Queen. However, some in London hoped he'd change his allegiance to the Princess Elizabeth."

"Where are the Duke's papers now kept?" Cesar asked.

"They were taken by my council," Mary replied. "Sifted and put in bundles. They should be kept, like all other records, in the muniment room of the Secret Seal at Westminster. I could have them brought here. Yes, I will. The council clerks have already been through them searching for traitors, Northumberland's accomplices: it would not be a betrayal of any trust."

Segalla bowed his thanks.

"And where do you go to now, Master Segalla?" the Queen asked. She hid the lower part of her face behind her hand. "To Hatfield?"

Segalla caught the satirical tone in her voice.

"Your Grace, let me assure you, neither His Holiness the Pope nor I are involved in any secret business with the Princess Elizabeth: that is not part of my brief. As a courtesy, I must call upon her."

The Queen hitched up her heavy fur robe round her shoulders. She has a healthy pallor, Segalla thought, her face was not so lined, the fatigue and pain had disappeared from her eyes. Jane Dormer caught his glance.

"I have persuaded the Queen," she declared, "to spend some time out at my manor of Sinistrel in Essex. Master Segalla, you are most welcome to join us."

Segalla thanked her, paid his compliments to the Queen, and withdrew. He walked along the gallery and stopped when he heard his name being called. Dr. Cesar hurried up, his bright little eyes sparkling.

"The Queen is comfortable, is she not, Nicholas? Where are you going now?"

"Master Orslett said he would meet me at the pantry. A visit to Master Savage in Dog Leg Lane. Do you wish to come?"

Cesar agreed. They found Orslett booted and cloaked, ready to go. The "Queen's valet or squire," as Orslett liked to describe himself, looked as fresh as a daisy, humming a song, drumming his fingers on the hilt of his sword. They exchanged greetings. Segalla told him about his audience with the Queen, Cesar preening himself at the report of her improvement in health. Orslett clicked his tongue.

"Lackaday!" he murmured. He took Segalla by the elbow and led him down a gallery to a side door. "It does make you wonder, sir, does it not?"

"What do you mean?" Cesar asked sharply, coming up beside him.

"Well, the Queen is sickly whilst Dr. Theophilus attends her. Theophilus dies: a new physician is in residence and the Queen improves quite dramatically."

"You are saying that Theophilus was poisoning the Queen?"

Orslett shrugged. "Possibly."

"I don't think so." Cesar paused. He beckoned both men into an alcove well away from the servants and guards who were going up and down the gallery. "Her Grace is still very ill," Cesar continued. "The medicine I gave her contains both an opiate and something to warm the blood. I think she is also relieved that Dr. Theophilus, not her, was the intended victim. The Queen may well flourish for a while, but I am a physician not a miracle worker. I would be a liar if I told you anything different. Moreover," he added hastily, "you forget two things. First, if the Queen has been poisoned, whoever is repsonsible, the damage may be done. Secondly, for all we know, the poisoner may just be resting from his or her labours for a while. Theophilus was a bit of a fool, perhaps not as vigilant as he could have been." Cesar stroked his burgundy jerkin and adjusted the small ruff round his neck. "The poisoner may," he murmured, "be watching me as well as the Queen. So let's not ride so cock-a-hoop."

They were still discussing the matter as they took a barge from Greenwich across to the city. Orslett was keen to meet Savage and speculated on what they should do.

"I hold the Queen's warrant." He sat forward in the stern of the barge. "We can arrest him and take him upriver to the Tower. The very sight of a dungeon can loosen a man's tongue!"

Segalla heard him out but wasn't too sure: he had a premonition that matters would not go as smoothly as Orslett maintained.

"Surely," he said, "if someone killed Theophilus because he was one of the Four Evangelists, then it stands to reason that the assassin must be watching the other three."

"What is it they did?" Dr. Cesar asked.

"I don't know," Segalla replied. "But if the Queen brings these documents from Westminster they may shed some light."

The spires of the churches came into view. Orslett rapped out an order to turn their craft towards St. Paul's Wharf, a perilous task: it was already midmorning and the river was busy with barges and skiffs going from the city side across to Southwark or downriver to Westminster. They found the streets equally busy. Orslett stopped to take a pot of ale in Knight Rider Street. Segalla made to press on, but Orslett maintained that he was to wait for a sheriff's man. They found the bailiff sitting in a corner of the taproom. For a while Orslett stood over him listening to what the fellow said, nodding every so often and looking back to where Dr. Cesar and Segalla sat drinking just within the doorway. Eventually the bailiff rose and lumbered out. Orslett came and sat down; he toasted his two companions with his tankard and took a deep draught.

"Those mummers arrested in Greyfriars," he declared. "They deny any connection with Master Cecil but believe they were doing God's work against the Queen, whose hands are steeped in blood." He tapped Segalla on the wrist. "And did you find anything in the documents retrieved from Nicolette's chambers?"

Segalla shook his head.

"Ah well." Orslett sighed. "Let's proceed."

They left the tavern. Orslett led them away from the main thoroughfares, slipping up narrow, mean alleyways along runnels, foulsome and dirt-strewn, which wound their way past the houses and shops. At last they reached Dog Leg Lane: Orslett took directions from a beggar boy and led them up to a narrow, decaying mansion which looked as if it had been shoved between the houses on either side. The timber joists were decaying, the black paint had long peeled, the plaster was dirty, the front door swung on its hinges. An old man came along the passageway mouthing on his gums; he gazed bleary-eyed at them.

"Oh yes, oh yes." He scratched his tufts of hair. "Francis

Tuttle lived here, but I haven't seen him for some time. Most of the chambers, well, they are let out on a . . ." He smiled wickedly. "Well you know how it is. Ladies of the town must have their assignations." He waved a hand. "You'll find him at the top."

They climbed the stairs, which seemed to wind forever upwards. Segalla, used to the slums of Rome, was shocked by the foulsome, fetid odours; the rainwater which turned the stairs soggy and slippery; the flyblown windows; and the cracked plaster, some of which had fallen off in great chunks. The old man had been right; most of the chambers were empty. They glanced through one open door which revealed dirty, tattered, dusty cloths on an old bed and a broken stool; an empty chamber pot stood on the stairwell outside. By the time they reached the top, Segalla had covered his nose and mouth. He hammered on the garret door.

"Faugh!" Cesar hissed. "Something's died here!"

Orslett drew his dagger and banged the pommel on the door, splintering the wood. Segalla stepped back.

"The door is new," he remarked. "It's about the only secure thing in this house. Look, the hinges are well oiled, the wood's firm. Master Savage must have paid for such protection."

Segalla peered through the keyhole, but this was blocked by something on the other side. Time and again Orslett kicked at the door with the heel of his boot: eventually there was a crack as the lock broke and the door swung open. The stench forced Segalla to turn away. Orslett went in first. Segalla took one look at the bloated corpse half-lying on the bed and left the chamber, Dr. Cesar hurrying after him. A few minutes later Orslett joined them in the hallway below.

"Dead as a nail!" he declared. "And has been for some time. The body is rotting. I'll get the sheriff's men to come and remove it."

"And the cause?"

Orslett breathed in, even the fetid hallway now seemed sweet.

"Apoplexy, the falling sickness, but, I suspect, Savage was probably poisoned; I can see no wound on his body. More importantly, the chamber has been cleared. No manuscripts, not a scrap of parchment!"

"If I could help?"

Segalla whirled round. Monkswood, looking as cherubic as ever, stood in the doorway, hands up the voluminous sleeves of his gown. He came forward, wrinkling his nose.

"I knew you'd come here. I had the place watched." He blew his cheeks out. "Master Savage is dead, isn't he? Ah well, I've found Master Kennet." He grinned cynically. "But don't raise your hopes: he's in the same state of health as Master Savage!"

Chapter 9

They followed Monkswood through the city streets, north towards Cripplegate. Segalla was quietly amused at how everyone seemed to know Monkswood: many of the rifflers, the naps, the pickpockets and bully boys, all the riff-raff who wandered the streets looking for mischief and victims, drew aside in the most reverential way. Even more surprising, officers of the law, bailiffs and beadles, not to mention respectable clerks and some of the prosperous goldsmiths, all treated Monkswood as if he were some pillar of the Church. This cherubic-faced king of villains acknowledged their salutations as a bishop would the reverential greetings of his flock.

"You are well known, Master Monkswood?" Segalla walked alongside him.

"My son," the cheeky villain replied sonorously, sounding even more like a pompous prelate, "London is a small city and one has a reputation to maintain and preserve."

"For what?" Segalla asked.

"For information, Master Segalla. Information on who is going where and when. Information on stolen property; runaway maids; felons in hiding; bribes offered, bribes received." He touched his ear. "It's all music, and my ears pick it up as sharply as a jackdaw does silver in the grass!"

"And what do they say about Queen Mary?" Segalla asked.

"That she will die, but that's not treason, that's a fact. We all have our invitation to the heavenly court."

"Is she being poisoned? What do the riff-raff say about that?"

"Master Segalla, the riff-raff couldn't give a fig who sits on the throne, but those who matter say Mary is unpopular. And," he continued, "she's alone."

"And when she dies?" Segalla asked.

Monkswood stopped so abruptly that Orslett and Cesar, walking behind, nearly collided with him.

"Why, as night follows day, Master Segalla, the Princess Elizabeth will. She is Great Henry's daughter. She is no foreign prince."

"And Philip of Spain and Mary of France?"

"They can go hang." Monkswood pushed his face forward like a little sparrow. "Tell me, Master Segalla," he continued sardonically. "You are a student of history. When has this kingdom ever sent abroad for a foreign prince to rule it? It will be the Princess Elizabeth and Master Cecil." He pointed at Orslett. "That's the real reason, besides the gold, I intend to help." Monkswood waddled on.

Segalla stood for a while lost in thought. "Always seek the obvious," he murmured.

"Do you always talk to yourself?" Orslett called back.

Segalla shook his head and walked on: Monkswood spoke common sense. Mary was ill, Elizabeth was her natural successor; Philip of Spain could hope, and the French could dream, but what was the reality of the situation? And if Elizabeth was the kingdom's choice, why involve herself in a plot against her sick half-sister? All she had to do was wait. And so, if Elizabeth was not behind the attempts on the Queen's life, who was?

Segalla followed his companions out of Cripplegate: he was pleased to be in the open countryside. The day was proving warm: crickets chirped in the grass, a hunting kestrel hovered over the moorland looking for prey. The narrow lanes and trackways were deserted, as this was not a common route into the city. Segalla loosened his doublet. He must remember to hire horses on their return so they could ride to Hatfield. Orslett looked over his shoulder and grinned.

"Come, Nicholas, an Englishman walks when an Italian would ride!"

They reached a deserted manor: a gaunt, empty shell of a building. Monkswood led them through a hedge and pointed to the corpse, throat slit, lying in a pool of congealing blood in the narrow ditch. Segalla knelt down and turned the dead man over: he was dressed only in a threadbare vest and shabby clouts. He had been stripped of his boots, stockings, and any belt or possessions he carried.

"All the way for this, Monkswood?"

The villain shrugged. "There's something else," he said. "But you asked for Kennet and that's he."

"How do we know it is?" Segalla snapped back, and regretted his words at the look of distaste in Monkswood's eyes. "I am sorry," he murmured, "but the day is warm and I am tired."

"Apology accepted," Monkswood murmured.

Segalla got to his feet.

"I know it's Kennet because one of my lovelies followed him here last night," Monkswood explained. "Apparently Kennet, Dalrymple, and Savage used to meet here: God knows for what reasons. Last night one of my lovelies watched Kennet leave his chamber."

"You found out where he lived?" Orslett intervened.

"Oh yes. Kennet was not as secretive as the others. After he left, my boy broke in, so it's pointless going there. There's nothing left. Kennet took his fardel, a bundle of belongings, left the city, and made his way here: that was just after dark. My boy hid over there." Monkswood pointed to a clump of trees. "A short while later someone else arrived. We think it was Dalrymple. The boy stole into the house. Dalrymple and Kennet met upstairs. Up goes my boy; he could hear them talking but could only catch snatches of words, both men were frightened. Kennet urging Dalrymple to leave the city as it was too dangerous to go back, then something happened. Other night walkers, assassins, entered the house. My boy froze like the little rabbit he is. Kennet was a sickly man:

that's how he was easy to trace. He had a cough like a trumpet and was always seeking philtres and potions. Anyway, Dalrymple fled, but the assassins caught Kennet. They cut his throat like you kill a cony, stripped his body, and disappeared into the night."

"Would you know who they are?" Segalla asked.

"Believe me, sir, I did not send them. Bully boys, assassins, are not amongst my merchandise. They are too untrustworthy. They drink, they brag, and their collars are felt by the sheriff's men."

"So, why have you brought us here?" Orslett demanded.

"I have found something." Monkswood spread his hands. "As the old women say, 'Cross my hand with silver.' There's no trickery."

Segalla handed over two silver pieces. Monkswood beckoned them into the house. They went upstairs and into a room which still smelt of charcoal. In a far corner were scraps of food, a tattered wineskin, and a battered tin cup.

"That's all yours." Monkswood smiled.

Segalla was about to protest when he noticed the scrawl on the wall. He bent down and peered at the letters roughly formed in charcoal. He couldn't understand them until he realized that it was the message he had seen on the manuscript: Mark 15.34, though, this time, Christ's words were rearranged; not "Eloi, Eloi, lamma sabacthani," but "sabacthani lamma, Eloi." Beside the verse, the name "Mark" was scrawled as well as a rough crude drawing of the Tower or part of it. Segalla could make out the huge Norman keep and a tower to its right, round and cylindrical: Kennet—he must have done this while waiting for Dalrymple—had placed a cross in the centre of the Tower. Next to it were other strange symbols and badly formed letters. Segalla took the hem of his cloak and rubbed at the charcoal. He glanced over his shoulder at Orslett, who smiled cynically.

"It's best," Segalla murmured: his eyes slid towards Monkswood.

"You've earned your silver, sir," Orslett declared.

"Then I shall leave you." Monkswood mockingly sketched a blessing in the air. "And I'll go to the sheriff's men and claim the reward for finding a corpse."

"And Dalrymple?"

"If he's in London," Monkswood replied, "he'll be found."

They left the house. Monkswood hastened back into the city. Cesar, too, excused himself and followed. Segalla and Orslett took a different route. They went across the stinking city ditch to the convent of St. Mary of Bethlehem. Orslett explained that the brothers held a warrant from the Crown to stable horses for royal messengers and others from the court. The monastery was dilapidated; many of the buildings were torn down, and only a few brothers had returned after Mary's ascent to the throne. Nevertheless, the brothers were kindly and helpful. They took Segalla and Orslett out to sit in the shade of the cloisters and brought platters of dried meat, fruit, and fresh tangy ale.

"Why here?" Segalla asked. He stretched his legs out and

turned his face to the sun. "I admit it's better than following Master Monkswood through the stinking alleyways of the city."

"It's time we visited Hatfield," Orslett declared. "You've mentioned as much."

Segalla chewed the corner of his lip. He was not too happy with Orslett deciding where and when he should go.

"Won't Master Cecil think it strange?" he asked.

Orslett shook his head. "I never know what Master Cecil thinks," he replied, and took a piece of apple from the trencher. "Never slink around, that's my motto. Be bold, act the part: it creates the least suspicion."

In his chamber, Peter Dalrymple crouched on his straw-filled mattress and bit the quick of his thumb. He had come back late last night, soaked in sweat: he'd spent the last of his coins on some wine and drunk himself into a stupor. He had woken late that morning, his mouth and throat sore, his head aching. Dalrymple was a man at the end of his tether. What could he do now? If he stayed here he'd starve. Or, worse still, the assassins would come and snuff his life out as they did to poor Kennet. But where could he go? Dalrymple leaned back against the damp wall. He picked up the scrap of parchment he had been working on, a detailed confession, but that was useless. What could he do with that? He tore the parchment into shreds and threw them into the cracked pisspot. Dalrymple closed his eyes. He went back to the beginning: he and the others in the Tower. They had found that damnable secret and, in the tumultuous days following King Edward's death, had tried to sell it to Northumberland's council here in the city. But something had gone wrong. Master Clarence had appeared. He had promised them good silver. Where had they met him? Ah yes, in the Bishop's Mitre on the edge of Smithfield. A shadowy figure, Master Clarence had invited them to a chamber late at night, his face masked and cowled. He'd kept in the shadows, a tall man, his voice cultured like a scholar's. They had handed no documents over. However, when he had produced a bag of silver, throwing it contemptuously into the pool of candlelight on the table, Savage had talked, chattering like a squirrel. Master Clarence had sat, quietly listening. Every so often he would betray surprise, a sharp intake of breath or an exclamation of disbelief, but, in the end, they had convinced him. The candle had been doused, Master Clarence had left, and they were counting the silver when the law officers had broken in. Dalrymple wiped his mouth on the back of his hand. If only they had been more prudent, but, in their greed, they had walked into the trap. Master Clarence must have invited the sheriff there, and, when he left, the sheriff's men waiting below had swept up to arrest them. Their lives could have ended there, but Savage had been adroit. In return for the silver, they had been spared their lives, allowed to flee, each to go his separate way. Two days later fresh warrants had been issued for their arrest. Sheriff's men and paid informers hunted them around St. Paul's or along the narrow, mean alleyways of Whitefriars. Gresham, more prudent than the rest, had silver from his practice as a physician; he had fled abroad, but the other three had been left to their own devices. They had only been saved by Queen Mary's entry to the city and the fall of Northumberland. The city forgot about the three wanted men. The sheriff's posse had bigger quarry to hunt.

Dalrymple started at a tap on his door. He swallowed hard and brought out the dagger hidden beneath the blankets. Again the tap.

"Master Dalrymple?"

"Come in."

The rickety door swung back on its hinges. The man who stepped into the room was dressed like a monk, snowy white hair, a cherubic face. Dalrymple held the dagger out.

"I know you!" he gasped. "Or, at least, I've heard of you!"

"My name is Monkswood." The man leaned against the closed door, hands still up his sleeves. "Master Dalrymple, I suggest you put that dagger down. I have two friends outside. What can you do? Where can you go? Kennet is dead. Naked as a worm, his corpse still lies in that derelict house where you met him last night."

Dalrymple put the dagger down. Monkswood glanced around the chamber.

"How the mighty have fallen!" he murmured. "I come to give you life or death, Master Dalrymple. There are those in the city who would love to talk to you. They will pay me good silver and perhaps reward you for what you know."

Monkswood, uninvited, sat down on a rickety stool; he

still kept his hands up the sleeves of his gown. Dalrymple was sure the man was armed.

"What do you want?" Dalrymple croaked.

"Well, you can stay here and be slain: those who killed Kennet will come looking for you."

"Or?"

"Or," Monkswood breathed, "you can come with me to Greenwich Palace, surrender to the Queen's justice, throw yourself upon her mercy and speak to those who wish to speak to you."

Dalrymple blinked and wetted his lips.

"You are alone: you are starving; you are penniless," Monkswood insisted. He drew his hands from his sleeves. "Come with me and you are safe."

Dalrymple looked up at the flies squashed against the dirty plaster. Suddenly he felt tired, weary of all this.

"I have your word?" he muttered.

"You have my word." Monkswood got to his feet. "You'll be safe!"

"Why are you here, Master Segalla?"

Princess Elizabeth sat back in her chair and stared at the two men seated opposite. At her side Master Cecil leaned against her chair, one hand just above her shoulder. Segalla studied both of them carefully. Outside, darkness was falling; he had been surprised that the Princess had granted him an audience so quickly. He and Orslett had spent most of the day riding to Hatfield. The journey had been pleasant enough, the trackways dry; they had stopped to rest their horses in the early afternoon and arrived at Hatfield just before dusk.

"I am sorry." Princess Elizabeth's pale face broke into a smile; her green catlike eyes scrutinized Segalla and Orslett. "You wish some refreshments?" She gazed at her secretary. "Master Cecil, if you would be so kind?"

Cecil filled the cups; the wine, white and cool, slaked the dust from Segalla's throat.

"I have come because your sister the Queen graciously agreed for Master Orslett to bring me here. I bear the good wishes and blessings of His Holiness Pope Paul IV. . . ."

Elizabeth started to laugh, a deep throaty chuckle. She smoothed the folds of her red and gold damask dress, her long, slender fingers playing with the cuffs. For a while she just rocked backward and forward, the tears glinting in her eyes. Even the black-garbed, grim-faced Cecil allowed himself a sly smile. So infectious was the Princess's laugh that Segalla shuffled his feet in embarrassment.

"Carafa." Elizabeth patted her chest and, with the back of her hand, wiped the tears from her eyes. "Carafa sends blessings and greetings to Boleyn's brat! That's what he calls me, isn't it?"

"His Holiness is concerned . . ."

"His Holiness," Elizabeth snapped, her face becoming hard, "couldn't give a fig about me and would dance a jig if I died. So, why are you here, Segalla? No, no." She shook the small, leather glove she carried in one hand. "Indeed, I know why you are here. My sister is not well."

"Your sister, madame," Segalla decided brusqueness was best, "is dying. Some say from poison."

Elizabeth's face grew paler still. She lowered her head, then looked up, her green eyes enlarged, hard as glass, no merriment now. She shook off Cecil's warning hand.

"Master Segalla, I know you are a member of the Jesuit order, a priest. What I am, and what I believe in, is a matter of my concern. What other people believe in is theirs. I don't make windows into men's souls. If my sister is ill, God save her. If she is being poisoned, then God damn those responsible. I am no assassin, Master Segalla."

"I did not say you . . ." Segalla tried to gain control of the conversation.

"I did not say you were saying!" Elizabeth spat back. "But I want to make two things very clear. First, I do not plot against my sister's life. Secondly, God forbid Her Majesty should die, but, if she does, the Crown of England comes to me, not to some foreign potentate or a slip of a girl mooning over her new husband at the French court. Cousin Mary Stuart should keep her nose out of matters which do not concern her!" Elizabeth paused and grasped her jewelled stomacher, breathing in through her nostrils. "I will not, do you understand, Master Segalla, I will not give up my birthright for any foreign prince!"

"And Philip of Spain?"

Elizabeth forced a smile. "Philip of Spain acts the alley cat. He has ruined my sister, Mary, and now he would like to come tiptoeing into my bed. You have my answer."

"And Mark 15.34?"

Elizabeth covered her mouth with her hands. She glanced sideways at Cecil.

"We have heard of this madcap nonsense," the secretary smoothly intervened. "Letters which claim that Mary is dead and buried and ask what price the Crown of England."

"What does it mean?" Segalla asked.

Cecil drew his brows together. Segalla could see the secretary was nervous. The fellow turned his head, scratching at his brow, glancing surreptiously at Orslett; then Cecil abruptly got up and walked to the window.

"Have you noticed, Master Segalla, how fast winter comes? In a few days it will be Michaelmas, the end of September. You have been to London, you have noticed the restlessness."

Segalla realized Cecil was now behind him, able to communicate with Elizabeth without being watched.

"And?" he asked.

"All things change, Master Segalla. This kingdom is restless. It needs peace and security."

"And does Mark 15.34 threaten that? No one knows," Segalla continued, "what it means: yet it causes consternation both here and at court."

Segalla studied Elizabeth: she was watching her secretary intently.

"We do not know what it means," Cecil replied flatly. "Yes, there is a threat, but we do not know what it is."

Segalla could tell from the Princess's face that Cecil was lying.

"The Four Evangelists." Segalla's eyes never left Elizabeth. "The Four Evangelists," he repeated, "are now depleted in number. Savage is dead, poisoned in his garret. Dr. John Gresham, better known as Theophilus, has also been murdered. Kennet's body was found in Moorfields, his throat slashed from ear to ear. Dalrymple is hiding in London, and, tomorrow, madame, the Queen has graciously allowed me to search the records of the Secret Seal. Soon Dalrymple will be found, and perhaps even more?"

The change in Elizabeth, though she tried to hide it, was noticeable. A brave, resolute young woman, Segalla thought, with a will of steel and a sharp brain to match. Nevertheless, she was agitated. First she glanced at Orslett, then at Cecil standing behind them.

"I do not know what you mean." The Princess tried to keep her voice steady. "Master Cecil, I think I have spoken enough. Darkness has fallen; you may, if you wish, Master Segalla, stay here for the night. I beg you to be gone by morning."

Segalla got to his feet and bowed. He was almost at the door when Elizabeth called his name.

"Madame?"

Elizabeth had also stood up, her face full of fury. She pointed a finger at him.

"Master Segalla!" Her voice was harsh. "As I have said, God forbid my sister dies, but, if she does and God is gracious enough to grant the Crown to me, do not let me find you in my kingdom!"

Orslett, who had also risen, was about to follow Segalla out of the chamber.

"You will stay!" Elizabeth commanded. "I have messages for my good sister!"

Segalla left the chamber. Cecil followed him out: the secretary plucked at Segalla's sleeve.

"You may stay the night," he declared; his shrewd eyes held Segalla's gaze. "You meddle in matters that do not concern you." He pointed to the gallery beyond the antechamber. "Wait there for Orslett. He'll be out shortly."

Cecil returned to the chamber. The Princess was still standing, Orslett on his knees before her. The Princess waited until Cecil closed the door.

"My lady, he's out of hearing."

Elizabeth walked around Orslett. "Well, well, Master Stephen." Her voice was low, purring, her fingers tightly clenched. "Here's a pretty mess. I am threatened and I ask you to investigate; you come back empty-handed, but the Pope's minion can wander into England and ferret out secrets!"

"Who told you to hire Monkswood?" Cecil snapped. "If I'd wanted to, I could have done that!"

"I had no choice," Orslett retorted. "Nothing came of nothing. Monkswood was hired." Orslett snapped his fingers. "And all manner of things are known."

"Be careful!" Elizabeth kicked the sole of Orslett's boot. "Monkswood and his ilk work for money and for favours."

"My lady," Orslett replied, "I do what I can. If I have gone too far, I beg pardon."

"Ah, yes, there's the rub." Elizabeth crouched down. "Sly Master Orslett with a foot in either camp. I think you are my man and my sweet sister thinks you are hers. But what are you really, Master Orslett, eh?" Elizabeth rose to her feet and walked around and again, drawing back, she kicked Orslett viciously in the shin. "The Four Evangelists, these men of subtle trickery: So three are dead, eh? And the fourth is soon to be caught? So, what will you do for me?"

"My lady." Orslett winced at the pain in his shin. "I have no choice but to work with Segalla. I do not think. . . ."

"You do not think what?"

"I do not think Savage or any of his colleagues have anything to do with the letters you have received. They are weak, helpless men hiding from their own shadows."

"So?" Elizabeth sat back in her chair.

"They discovered a secret, my lady. Now, I suspect, they are terrified of it. They are not the authors of the letters you have received. Someone else has that secret: this is the person we must find."

"No, Master Orslett," Elizabeth snapped back. "That is the person *you* must find, and do so quickly!"

Orslett moved his leg to ease the pain in his shin. Elizabeth's mood suddenly changed. She went over, stretching out her hand.

"Come, Master Orslett, stand, stand!" She declared wearily. She helped him to his feet and gestured to a chair. "I am sorry for the blow." She smiled impishly. "My temper got the better of me."

Orslett sat down, eyes watchful.

"I know." Elizabeth waved a hand. "You must serve my

sister as well as me and you can only do, well, what you call your best. Master Cecil, make sure Orslett leaves Hatfield well rewarded."

She bowed her head, and Orslett, thinking the interview was over, got to his feet.

"Oh and Stephen!"

He turned; the Princess was smiling dazzlingly at him.

"When you find Master Dalrymple and whoever was responsible for those letters. . . ."

"Yes, my lady?"

Elizabeth's smile faded. "Kill them!" she whispered. "Do you understand me? Quickly, without mercy!"

Orslett left the chamber, and, try as he might, he had to hobble through the anteroom and out along the gallery where Segalla was waiting. A chamberlain hovered nearby. Orslett winked slyly at Segalla and they kept their peace until they were shown to their quarters at the far end of the rambling palace. Orslett sat on the edge of the bed, kicked off his boot, pulled down the woollen stocking he wore, and rubbed at the purpling bruise.

"The Princess wasn't pleased?" Segalla asked.

"Elizabeth is a fiery girl." Orslett put his foot down. "She has her father's temper. She can punch and kick like a man and the next minute rub up against you like a loving cat."

Segalla walked round the chamber tapping at the wooden-panelled wall.

"Let me see," he mused. "It must be hard for you, Stephen, serving two masters?"

"It's like standing with one foot on either side of a campfire," Orslett replied. "You tend to get your breeches singed."

"And that's why the Princess was angry," Segalla continued. "Because you are also Queen Mary's man, you have to work with me. You discovered three of the Evangelists and they are now dead. We have a good chance of trapping the fourth, which leaves two problems. First, what is the secret they hold?" Segalla clicked his tongue.

"And secondly?" Orslett replied impatiently.

"Oh, I am sure you have reached the same conclusion as I, Stephen. John Gresham may have lived like a hog but his three companions were frightened, impoverished men. They may know the secret but they are certainly not writing the letters. Someone else is. Which brings me to a third, more frightening conclusion." Segalla glanced through the window. "I believe," he continued, "that the Princess Elizabeth has no hand in these attacks upon Mary. However, Elizabeth is terrified of some secret which might debar her from the throne or interfere with her right of succession. There was a drawing on the wall of that derelict mansion . . ."

"Yes, I glimpsed that," Orslett interrupted. "A sketch of the Tower."

"And the place Kennet had marked with an X?"

"The Bloody Tower," Orslett replied. "The chamber is on the second floor."

Segalla kicked his own boots off and sat on the bed.

"Then tomorrow, Stephen." He glanced across. "It will be the Tower again!"

Chapter 10

Two days later they reached the Tower just before noon. Segalla paid an ostler to take the horses back to St. Mary of Bethlehem. A surly officer met them on Tower Green and waved them to what Orslett had described as the Bloody Tower.

"For the moment," the officer declared sourly, as if he bitterly regretted it, "there are no prisoners. The doors to all the chambers are open."

Orslett thrust his warrant into the man's face.

"We are not peasants from the country," he snapped, "coming up to admire the sights. I bear the Queen's warrant!"

The fellow stepped back. "What do you want?" He tried to sound more polite.

"First, your good manners, and secondly, your cooperation."

The officer took them across into the Tower. The walls were cold and clammy with mildew on the steps. The ground

floor served as a guardroom, now disused. On the first floor
a small gallery led into two connecting chambers, where the
arrow-slit windows provided little light. Under Orslett's
instructions the officer lit sconce torches as well as a tallow
candle. Both chambers had been swept clean. There was
nothing on the floor or walls, and only a few sticks of furniture remained.

"What was so special about this?" Segalla asked.

He then glimpsed the inscriptions on the wall, the marks
made by prisoners over the years. He began to study these,
Orslett joined him, and they went round the walls. Segalla
found it a gloomy task. One of his own nightmares was being
caught and imprisoned in a place such as this. The walls bore
evident testimony to the wretched condition of the prisoners over the years: "Jesus have mercy on Adam Belcher."
"May the Lord deliver us from our snare." "Pray for my wife
and family." Sometimes it was merely names followed by a
date: "Michael Foliot 1487." Other messages were obscene or
curses against enemies now long dead. A few were macabre:
gallows; the execution block; a dancing skeleton. Some parts
of the walls were covered in these messages. They moved into
the chamber beyond and, just beneath a window, Segalla
found what he was looking for.

"Eloi Eloi lamma sabacthani: Mark 15.34." "Jesu have
mercy on us," then, "Smeaton, Rochford, and Norris."

"Anne Boleyn's purported lovers," Orslett explained.
"They must have been imprisoned here before their sen-
tences were carried out. Rochford and Norris had their

heads struck off. Smeaton, being a commoner, a mere musician, was racked until his limbs fell apart before he was hanged at Tyburn."

"What year were they executed?"

Orslett narrowed his eyes. "In 1536; eleven years before Henry's death."

"Did they confess?"

"Henry was tired of Anne," Orslett explained. "He had already decided that Jane Seymour would be his new wife. Anne was a flirt; she liked to tease the King with her admirers: their confessions, however, taken under torture, are meaningless."

They left the Tower, thanked the officer, and went down to the riverside where they hired a barge near Custom House; this took them downriver to Greenwich. The afternoon was a fine one, the sun quite strong, and, as they pulled into the palace quayside, they saw the Queen's banners being hoisted, a sign that Mary was still in residence. They found Monkswood waiting just outside the gates of the palace: he was grinning from ear to ear, skipping from foot to foot.

"Master Orslett, Master Segalla, thank God you spoke to Monkswood!"

"Now, why is that?"

"I've found Dalrymple." He chortled at their surprise. "He's inside, guarded in a special chamber by the Queen's men."

"Is Dr. Cesar here?" Segalla asked.

"He claimed to have pressing business in the city: potions and powders to buy. Anyway, the Queen has set a strong guard on Dalrymple. No one is to approach him until Master Orslett gets his confession. I persuaded him to surrender." Monkswood skipped alongside them. "Promised him a fine reward. Did I do right, Master Stephen?"

Orslett clapped the cunning man on the shoulder.

"You did well, good and faithful servant," he declared. "Your reward will be great."

They climbed the long staircase into the gallery leading to the royal quarters. Sir Henry Grantchester ushered them into the Queen's chamber. Mary was sitting before the fire at a small writing table, surrounded by clerks busily sealing letters. Jane Dormer, leafing through a book of hours, sat on a chair opposite. Orslett and Segalla sank to one knee. The Queen smiled at them, beckoning at them to rise and sit before her. Lady Jane came across and served them goblets of wine.

"Does not the Queen look well?" she whispered. "She is finishing these letters and has agreed to come with me to Sinistrel. The country air will do her good."

Segalla glanced across: the Queen's movements were vigorous; she looked healthy, no trembling or clutching at her stomach. She took the pile of letters a clerk handed across; she imprinted the soft wax with a seal and briskly gave them back.

"And Dalrymple?" Segalla asked.

"He was brought here by a strange man," Lady Jane replied. "A monk?"

"Monkswood," Segalla explained.

"That's right. Dalrymple surrendered to Sir Henry

Grantchester. He is now under close guard at the far end of the palace."

"What did the Queen say to him?"

Jane raised her lovely eyebrows. "I don't know," she replied. "The Queen asked for the chamber to be cleared, and, for the first time ever, that included me. She must have been alone with Dalrymple for about a quarter of an hour." She smiled. "I admit I eavesdropped, but the Queen was speaking softly. I think she was asking Dalrymple questions. Sir Henry Grantchester was also concerned, pacing the ante-chamber like an angry dog. I thought he'd break the door down, but anyone can see that Dalrymple is a sickly man, a threat to no one."

"Right." The Queen clasped her hands, joining them as if in prayer. "If I seal another document, my fingers will fall off! I have done enough!"

The clerks bowed and made their way out. Whilst the room was cleared the Queen made conversation: How had their journey been? How was her good sister? She graciously thanked Orslett for "resolving that mummery at St. Paul's." The Queen did seem well; her eyes were bright, her face had lost its sickly pallor, and Segalla wondered once again whether Theophilus had been secretly poisoning her.

Once the room was cleared, the Queen stopped her chatter.

"The documents you asked for from the Chancery are here in the palace," she declared flatly. "For what good they may do you. Is there anything else you require?"

Segalla described his visits to Hatfield and the Tower and what they had discovered.

"Yes, quite." The Queen pursed her lips primly.

"And Master Dalrymple?" Segalla asked.

"Ah." The Queen smiled. "I met him once before, you know, years ago when I was in the Tower." She blinked, tightening her lips, running a finger backward and forward round her mouth.

"Your Grace, I must ask you again," Segalla insisted. "Theophilus, who recommended him to you?"

"Oh, he came well accredited about two years ago. Why, yes, with letters from Paris and Rome. It was after"—she paused—"after the time I thought I was pregnant." She tilted her head back. "The court were sniggering at me. Dr. Theophilus came, he was a member of the Guild of Physicians and, when I was in the Tower, he treated both myself and my mother. He did good work."

"Your Grace, do you realize that the so-called Evangelists, Savage, Dalrymple, Gresham, and Kennet, are not responsible for these letters you and others have received?"

"I appreciate that," the Queen replied.

"Madam, then who else could be responsible?"

The Queen stared at a point behind Segalla's head.

"Madam, this person may have designs on your life."

"I don't think so," the Queen replied tersely. She sighed, flailing her hands in her lap. "But, what does it all matter?"

"Your Grace." Segalla leaned forward, rubbing his hands together. "Madam, you are the Queen. Whom you see, and the reason for it, is a matter for you. But why did you question Dalrymple by himself?"

The Queen glared across at Jane Dormer.

"I don't know. I can't tell you why." She drew her breath in sharply. "I wanted to know about Theophilus." The Queen was trying to be truthful, but Segalla could see that she did not like his questions. "Enough is enough!" She sighed. "This evening"—she glanced at Lady Jane—"I intend to leave for Sinistrel in Essex. Tomorrow is October; winter draws on. Soon the air will turn cold and it would be pleasant . . ."

She was interrupted by a loud hammering on the door and Grantchester burst in.

"Your Grace." He paused, gasping for breath. "My apologies. Master Segalla, Master Orslett, you'd best come quickly! The prisoner Dalrymple, a fire has broken out in his room!"

Segalla and Orslett left the Queen, following Grantchester as he hurried along galleries and down the stairs. As soon as they reached the ground floor Segalla smelt burning. Smoke was wafting its way through the palace, and he heard the cries of servants and scullions. They bypassed the kitchens and entered a stone-flagged corridor full of smoke. One of the royal bodyguard had established a chain of water carriers, buckets were being quickly passed up along the line. Segalla and his two companions, covering their mouths and noses, pushed their way through. The fire had been doused, the windows opened, but the chamber where Dalrymple had been placed was now a blackened, charred shell. Segalla glimpsed a pair of legs sticking out from beneath a dirty horse blanket.

"That's Dalrymple," an officer declared. "Or what's left of him!"

"What happened?" Orslett demanded.

He and Segalla stepped into the room. The plaster, the ceiling and floor were totally scorched: the bed and furniture simply charred scraps. There was a barred window over-looking the bed; its shutters, badly burnt, were now pulled back to let out the smoke and provide fresh air.

"Dalrymple was put here?" Segalla asked.

"At my orders," Grantchester declared, coming into the room. "There were two guards in the gallery outside and two in the courtyard beyond. The window was closed."

"And?" Segalla asked.

"The guard outside noticed the smoke first. By the time he had come in, the guards in the corridor were also alerted. The door was locked from the outside. The soldiers kicked it down. Apparently Dalrymple had been on the bed: he, the bed, and the sheets were just one great tongue of flame. Dalrymple was screaming. My lads did what they could; there's a well in the courtyard, and water was also fetched from the kitchens. The floor is made of stone, that's how the fire was so easily contained, but there was nothing they could do for Dalrymple."

Segalla crouched down. Most of the rushes had been consumed, but scraps remained. He felt these; they were hard and dry.

"What was this room used for?" he asked.

"By one of the clerks of the stores. Her Grace told us to keep Dalrymple comfortable but well guarded. Apart from our dungeons, this seemed the best place."

Orslett walked to the door. "Clear the gallery!" he ordered an officer.

Segalla got to his feet, brushing his hands.

"And who visited him?"

Grantchester shook his head and wiped grey ash from his doublet.

"According to the guards, no one."

Segalla walked out into the passageway. The smoke still swirled so he went into the courtyard; Orslett and Grantchester followed him.

"Look, Sir Henry," Segalla began, "here is a man who could have given us vital information. He is put in a stone chamber with guards in the passageway as well as outside. No one visits him, yes?"

Grantchester nodded.

"You are sure of that?"

"As I am of the sun in the sky."

"Dr. Cesar?"

"He was here when Dalrymple surrendered to the Queen's justice but the only person that came into that room was myself. I brought some food and drink, and the only light he had was a candle and a tinder. I gave the guards strict instructions." Grantchester fought hard to keep his temper under control. "I gave strict instructions," he repeated, "not to let anyone in or out. The Queen had impressed upon me how important Dalrymple was."

"You are sure of that?" Orslett demanded.

"Interrogate the guards yourself!" Grantchester snapped. "The only person who went into that room, between yesterday afternoon and the time of the fire breaking out, was myself."

"How many times?" Segalla asked.

"Yesterday evening, early this morning, and just before noon. On each occasion I brought food."

"And how was Dalrymple?" Segalla asked.

"At first very frightened, a sickly man. By this morning he was more reassured, more confident. He claimed he wished he had surrendered himself years ago."

Segalla glanced over the captain of the guard's shoulder and glimpsed Monkswood standing in the doorway.

"And how long has he been here?"

Grantchester followed his gaze.

"He arrived with Dalrymple yesterday."

"Tell him to wait," Segalla ordered. "Sir Henry, can you bring me the soldiers who were on duty when the fire broke out?"

Sir Henry stalked off, pushing Monkswood back into the passageway. Segalla and Orslett went and sat on a bench against the far wall. The four soldiers were burly young men used to carrying out orders. They listened to Segalla and Orslett's questions and shrugged.

"We just walked up and down," the one who introduced

himself as Corporal Tipping declared. "Suddenly we hears a scream. I was in the passageway: I ran for the door and couldn't believe my eyes. The rushes, bed, and the poor bastard who had been sleeping on it were a sheet of flame, as if hell had broken through the floor."

"And no one approached?" Segalla asked.

"I tell you, sir," another interrupted. "I was with Corporal Tipping here. Browngate and Hallam here were outside. No one approached that room. The fire just seemed to happen so quickly. They noticed the smoke curling outside just as we realized something was wrong."

"By the time we broke the door down," Tipping intervened, "well, the chamber was just a wall of fire. I alerted the captain of the guard and ran for people to bring water from the well. Much good that did!"

Segalla gave the corporal a piece of silver and dismissed him and his companions. Grantchester then brought Monkswood across. It was the first time Segalla had seen that sanctimonious villian look upset.

"I've lost the reward," the fellow moaned. "I've lost all my silver!"

"No, you haven't!" Orslett snapped. "I'll see you well provided for, Monkswood. You went nowhere near Dalrymple's cell?"

"What do you think?" the rogue scoffed. "I was barely tolerated. Mind you, I was given a warm bed and some food."

"And you never went near that chamber?" Orslett insisted.

"Sir, sir." Monkswood rubbed his face. "I've told you

what I know." He looked wistfully over his shoulder. "Now, I'd best be going. I have more business in the city."

"Not so soon," Segalla retorted.

Monkswood sighed and looked heavenwards.

"You found Dalrymple in his chamber, yes?"

Monkswood nodded.

"And you persuaded him to surrender to the Queen's justice?"

Again the nod.

"Surely, Dalrymple spoke to you on the journey down here?"

"Tight as a miser's purse," Monkswood retorted. "He said he'd keep his mouth shut until he spoke to the Queen's men. From what I can gather, Her Majesty, God bless her, was waiting for you to return. Now, Master Stephen, if you don't mind?" Monkswood held his hand out. "Cross my palm and I'll disappear until you want me again!"

Orslett threw him a piece of silver. Monkswood caught it and waddled across the cobbles. Orslett shouted at the soldiers to let him through. Grantchester returned.

"Her Grace leaves for Sinistrel later this evening," he declared. "Certain chests have arrived for you, sirs."

Grantchester's voice was clipped, his face impassive.

"And will you stay with us?" Segalla lifted his head, squinting against the weak sun.

"Where Her Grace goes, the captain of her guard follows." Grantchester replied wearily. He bowed. "Dalrymple is dead, the fire is out. You may wish to examine his room more closely."

Orslett made his excuses and left with Grantchester.

Segalla sat for a while staring up at the sky, trying to sift through what he had learnt. He wished he hadn't gone to Hatfield. If he had only been here when Dalrymple had arrived. Now, all of the Four Evangelists were dead; the Queen had a new physician and seemed much better; the game was over. In which case he should leave. Segalla stiffened. He watched a sparrow peck at a seed on the cobbles. Is that what his silent enemy wanted? To pretend that all was well? Segalla was no longer needed and so he'd be down to Tilbury and on the next ship to France or some Italian port? Segalla wiped some ash off the back of his hand. If only life were so easy. He heard a sound and looked up. A casement window was opening slowly. Segalla recognized the danger signs. He could see no hand, no face: he threw himself sideways just before the crossbow bolt smacked into the wall. Segalla, on all fours on the cobbles, looked up. The casement window, high in the wall, was now closed. Segalla picked up the bolt, its sharp edge flattened by the impact, and walked quickly back into the corridor, which still stank from the fire. He stood within the doorway. Servants cleaning up the mess stared at him curiously. Segalla undid his jerkin and ran a finger round his neck, wiping away the sweat. He would love to go racing up the stairs, but what good would that do? It was better to stop, wait, and watch. Who was in the palace? Cesar was in London. Where was Grantchester? And why did Orslett excuse himself so abruptly? Segalla recalled that the Queen's man had said that he had other business to attend to.

Or was it someone else? Someone yet to show his hand? How did he know that Monkswood had left? Or pretty Jane Dormer? A woman could loose a small arbalest as quickly and as accurately as a man, and hadn't Jane said how much she liked to hunt? Or, again, there was Elizabeth at Hatfield with the silent, subtle Cecil. They must have agents at Greenwich. . . . Or was it the men who had slain Kennet? The work of a professional assassin, someone hired specially . . . ?

"Excuse me, sir."

Segalla moved out of the way so a scullion could sweep the dirt into the courtyard. He walked into the chamber where Dalrymple had died. The water had turned the floor into a black, wet sludge. All the consumable items in the room had been reduced to ash. Segalla picked up a twisted candlestick. It would be foolish to dismiss the fire as an accident. A single, solitary candle couldn't have turned the room into a raging inferno.

"Is there anything else, sir?"

Segalla looked round. Corporal Tipping was standing in the doorway, staring at him curiously. Segalla noticed that a small arbalest hung from the hook on his leather sword belt.

"Are you skilled in that?" Segalla asked.

Tipping stared at him open-mouthed then threw his head back and laughed.

"Good! I am one of the best archers in the royal household. If you want to wager, sir, another piece of silver?"

Segalla shook his head. The man's reply was so honest it put him beyond suspicion.

"I'll take your word for it, but . . ." Segalla took a silver coin out of his pocket; he walked towards the soldier, who licked his lips, eyes on the coin. "Come on, Corporal Tipping," Segalla murmured. "Someone must have come down to see the prisoner?"

Tipping, his eyes still on the coin, shook his head.

"Sir, I'd love to say there was, I really would. But, even when Sir Henry took his food in, it was only for a matter of seconds. Don't forget, sir, we might have wanted to talk to Dalrymple, but he didn't want to talk to us. Whenever Sir Henry brought the food, the man always lay on his bed, his back to the door."

"And where were you when the fire started?"

"As I have said, outside in the passageway, sitting in the alcove, wondering whether to take a barge to the stews this evening. It's a lonely life without a doxy. Now that I've earned more money here than I would in a month, I'll put that right."

"So, it will be a tankard of ale and a pretty girl on your lap?"

"Yes, sir, before I'm much older."

"You smelt the smoke and heard the man scream?" Segalla asked.

"Yes, I did." The soldier narrowed his eyes. "But there was something else, sir: just before the fire started, I heard, well, it sounded like a rush of air, but that may have been my imagination."

Segalla flicked him the coin; Tipping caught it deftly.

"I'll look round for a while," he declared.

"Much good it will do, sir; there's nothing left."

Segalla inspected the shutters and then the door. He could find nothing amiss. Both were badly scorched but there was no sign of the fire being started through any of these. He looked up at the ceiling; it was hard brick, not a crack, not a gap.

"Of course," Segalla reasoned, "a storeroom would have to be kept dry."

He stood in a corner, trying to visualize what had happened. If Dalrymple had knocked his candle over, it would take minutes for a good fire to ignite and the man would have simply been able to douse it or escape. So, what was the sound Tipping had heard? Like that of rushing air? Segalla recalled a siege outside St. Quentin: engineers and masters of ordnance firing a fuse, the sudden spurt of fire as a flame caught the powder and raced along the line. But how could that have happened here? People can smell gunpowder, saltpetre was so pungent; moreover, the door and windows were closely guarded.

Segalla went to the window. He leaned out, breathed in the fresh air, then turned and looked at the floor. He noticed the filthy water swirl slightly. At first he thought this had been caused by himself, but the water seemed to be seeping towards the far wall as if there was a drain or hole. Segalla took his dagger out and, crouching down, jabbed, but he could find no outlet in the floor. However, when he reached the wall, he found there was an aperture; placing his hand under the water, he realized the gap was shaped like a half-moon. Why this? Segalla looked up at the beams and noticed the blackened hooks. Of course! This would have once been used to hang freshly cut meat; and there had to be a drain for the blood. Segalla walked briskly out of the cell and along the passageway to the adjoining chamber. The door was un-locked; he pushed this open and went in. The air smelt sweet, of sugar and other spices. Shelves ranged around the room bore small casks and bottles; the window high in the wall was shuttered, allowing in only faint cracks of light. Segalla searched around and found a candle. He took his tinder, lit it, and, crouching down, saw there was a slight gulley across the floor running from the far wall. He edged across and, placing the candle down, glimpsed the gap; some of the dirty water from the adjoining room had already begun to seep through. Segalla pushed his hand though the gap, withdrew it, and wiped it on his jerkin. He searched around either side of the gap, brushing the floor with his fingers and sniffing at the grains of wet dirt he lifted.

"Gunpowder and oil!" he murmured.

Segalla got to his feet, blew out the candle, and went to the door. He went outside into the courtyard and stared at his fingers. Yes, what he had discovered was not dirty water from the fire-blackened room; the texture was thicker; he could even see the small grains of powder. So, what did it mean? The hole he had discovered was barely big enough for a man to put his hand through, and the wall separating the rooms was at least a foot thick.

"How could the assassin put oil and gunpowder in a chamber through a hole like that?" he murmured.

A small cloth ball soaked in oil and powder, pushed on a stick? Yet that wasn't possible: it might start a fire, but nothing like the conflagration Tipping had described. Segalla went back in and looked down the gallery, the corporal and his companions still lounged on a bench. Segalla called them over.

"I want the cell cleared," he ordered.

"What's the hurry?" Tipping went to argue.

"Just clear it!" Segalla snapped. "And I want the chamber adjoining it opened. You"—he stopped a scullion who tried to brush past him—"bring me a pot of ale and some bread from the kitchen. Corporal Tipping," Segalla ordered, "I'm going to show you something, and you may end the day much richer than you think!"

Segalla went outside and sat down well away from any window. The scullion brought out a trencher: the bread was soft and white, there was a strip of cooked bacon, rather pungent cheese, and a frothy tankard of ale. Segalla ate and drank slowly. He resolved he would do that as long as he stayed at Greenwich. Be wary of any who prepared him a meal or cup of wine or platter of food left in his chamber. Inside he heard Tipping's shouts: the servants had reassembled. Brooms and shovels were brought and a good hour passed before Tipping shook Segalla awake from where he was dozing in the corner of the wall.

"It is as clean as it ever will be, sir. You could eat your meal off it!"

Segalla followed him back into the storeroom. The floor

was now clear of all debris and dirt. It was hard and cobbled, like the yard outside, but the small drain running into the aperture against the far wall was now very distinct. Segalla led Tipping and the other three curious soldiers into the storeroom next door. Candles were lit; Tipping exclaimed when he saw the muck seeping there.

"Whoever killed Dalrymple," Segalla explained, "used that drain hole."

"But that's ridiculous!" One of the soldiers spoke up. "You can just about get your hand through, let alone anything else!"

Tipping crouched down.

"Now, when the fire started," the corporal declared, lifting a finger, "the room beyond was full of dry rushes. The gully to that drain hole would be hidden. So, whoever was looking to kill Dalrymple came into this storeroom and found this."

"Now, what you heard," Segalla added, "was the same sound as when a fuse trail is lit."

"Aye, that's right." Tipping got to his feet. "Are you saying that someone laid a trail of gunpowder from here into that room?"

"Not only gunpowder, Corporal, but oil as well. Tell me, what did Dalrymple do in his cell?"

"He slept," the soldier replied. "Slept as if he hadn't done so for weeks!"

"Well, now here's a problem for you, Corporal," Segalla declared. "How would you get oil and gunpowder into a room through a hole or drain as small as that? And there's two silver pieces in it for the answer." Segalla clapped the man on the shoulder. "So, there's a puzzle for you, my lad. And, if you find the solution, bring it only to me!"

Chapter 11

Segalla returned to his chamber: he fell asleep and was woken up by Dr. Cesar anxiously bending over him.

"You heard what happened?" Segalla declared, swinging his legs off the bed.

Cesar stroked his moustache and nodded.

"I was across at the apothecary in Hind Street." He shook the leather bag he carried. "And then"—he smiled—"I dallied along the way with some young wench who wished to talk to me at the Golden Mitre."

"Why the apothecary?" Segalla asked.

"Potions, powders." Cesar clutched his cloak around him. "The weather is changing. Soon it will be winter. Nicholas, how long are we going to stay in this cold, forbidding isle?"

"I don't know," Segalla replied. "You heard Dalrymple was burnt to death?"

"Yes, I met Orslett on the stairwell. He's helping the Queen and Jane Dormer. They intend to leave before dusk.

Probably stay at some royal manor and arrive at Sinistrel tomorrow."

"Did you meet Dalrymple?" Segalla asked.

"From afar. I heard the rumours. The Queen was quite adamant. No one was to approach him until you and Orslett returned."

"It was murder," Segalla declared flatly.

Cesar raised his eyebrows in surprise.

"I've talked to the guards. The fire started too quickly and spread so rapidly."

"But how?" Cesar breathed. "If he was kept under strict custody?"

"I don't know," Segalla replied. "But it looks as if the Four Evangelists are dead. Theophilus, Savage, Kennet, and Dalrymple."

"But you don't think they were sending the letters?"

"No, I don't."

"And neither do I." Orslett pushed the door open. He carried a scroll of parchment, the red ribbon hanging loose. Orslett handed this to Segalla, who took it to the window to read.

Again in the same copperplate hand, the letters perfectly formed:

Ave Maria sepulta? What price the Crown of England? Priceless beyond measure. Pearls should not be cast before swine. Remember Mark 15.34.

The Four Evangelists

"When was it delivered?" Segalla asked.

"Sometime last night or early this morning. We don't know," Orslett replied, sitting on a bench just inside the doorway. "It was left just within the gateway: it must have lain there some time."

Segalla felt the texture of the parchment; it was costly, the work of a scholar, the words expertly set out. He got to his feet to ease the ache in his back.

"What," he declared, "have we learnt? First, the Queen was undoubtedly being poisoned—possibly by Theophilus—but Dr. Cesar has put matters right."

"No, no, as I have said," Cesar interrupted, "the Queen is a very sickly woman. I have given her good medicines and potions, but she suffers from the dropsy and high fevers and is generally depleted. I am a doctor, not a miracle worker, nor must we dismiss Mary's state of mind. Now she feels relieved, slightly happy, but God knows what the future will bring!"

Segalla pulled a face. "Be that as it may, I still suspect Theophilus was the poisoner, though who hired him and why is a mystery. All his papers have been taken and those kept by his doxy consumed in a fire. The other three Evangelists have also met untimely deaths. We now know they were not the authors of this." He tossed the scroll back at Orslett. "They were too frightened. Poor, miserable men: they never had the means, nor the will, to plot, but their deaths are as mysterious as the secrets they held. So, we come to a conclusion. Someone else knows the secret and is penning the letters. He, she, or they, regard Mary as dead. They keep jibing about the Crown of England." Segalla paused. "I wonder what they mean by 'pearls before swine'? The mystery is contained in that verse, Mark 15.34: it also has something to do with the entourage of Anne Boleyn and their sojourn in the Tower before execution. We also know the Four Evangelists, in their prime, learnt a terrible secret which they sold to a mysterious Mr. Clarence. What else do we know?"

"That the Queen does not like these letters," Orslett replied. "Nor does the Princess Elizabeth. So, if neither of these can be the author, who is it?"

"The French," Cesar offered. "They are watching Mary's health with great interest. They spin their own webs."

"True," Segalla murmured. A suspicion started, something intangible. What if Cesar was right? Would the French try to kill Mary? Clear the way for their own candidate, the Dauphiness? Catherine de' Medici was the Queen of Poisoners and a born intriguer.

"Philip of Spain is not as innocent as he appears," Orslett added. "He is tired of Mary and has now turned his hand against her."

"But the letters?" Segalla asked. "Could the French really know some great secret?"

"Philip of Spain could," Orslett offered. "He is the Queen's consort. He would have access to records, manuscripts. God knows what he's learnt."

"Then, if that is the case"—Segalla sat down upon the bed—"tomorrow morning, after the Queen has left. . . ." He looked towards the window and noticed how grey the sky had become. A wind had risen and splattered spent leaves against the mullioned glass pane. "Tomorrow, we search the records!"

Orslett and Cesar left. Segalla stayed for a while, going over and over what he had learnt. He heard a bell ring followed by trumpet calls. Putting on cloak and boots, he went down to the hall where the Queen and Jane Dormer, together with other members of the royal household, were preparing to leave. Mary was dressed in Lincoln green, her face freshly painted. She moved with vigour, thanking those officers who would stay at Greenwich: she took Dr. Cesar aside and gave him a small purse, patting him affectionately on the shoulder. She also took leave of Segalla; he knelt to kiss her fingers, and the Queen leaned down.

"Nicholas, I feel better. I thank you for Dr. Cesar. Perhaps you could convey my gratitude to the Holy Father."

Segalla glanced up quickly. He caught the hint: the Queen now believed the danger had passed and there was no further reason for him to stay in England.

"It's up to you," she murmured, and passed on to talk to Orslett.

"She is not as strong as she appears."

Lady Jane was smiling at him. She pulled back the light gauze veil which covered her face. She looked pale, her eyes brimming with tears.

"What do you mean?" Segalla asked.

"I don't know," she murmured. "But have you seen a flame just before it goes out? It seems to spring up and burn more strongly, merrily."

"And that is the Queen?"

"Yes, Nicholas, that is the Queen."

Lady Jane Dormer swept on. Segalla walked back to the stairs and stood, his hand on a newel.

"Sir?"

Segalla whirled round. He nearly burst out laughing as Corporal Tipping came out of the shadows, his face smeared with black, a triumphant smile on his lips.

"I'm really glad I met you, sir."

"How's that now, Corporal?"

The soldier beckoned him closer. "Come with me, sir! Come with me!"

He led him down to the back of the palace and into the storeroom where Dalrymple had been imprisoned. Segalla was surprised. The room was still scorched, but dry rushes now lay on the floor, a new pallet had been brought, and a carpenter had rehung the door, which Tipping now closed.

"Stay outside! Watch the candlelight!"

Segalla stared through the grille. A lit tallow candle had been placed on the table. Tipping went into the adjoining chamber. Segalla heard him moving about, cursing under his breath: he went to the door but it was locked.

"Go back, sir!" Tipping called. "Just watch the candle-wick!"

Segalla did so. He heard a slight sound but nothing un-toward, then started in surprise. At first smoke and then tongues of flame shot up from the rushes. Within seconds a small but vigorous fire burnt. Tipping came running out of the adjoining chamber. He carried a huge pair of bellows made of black leather and wood, steel-tipped with a short funnel at the end. He dropped this at Segalla's feet and, taking a rough piece of sacking, opened the door and began to beat down the hungry flames. At first Segalla was alarmed, thinking the fire would spread, until he noticed how the rushes had been pulled away from the bed. At last the flames were out. The smoke still curled out along the passageway. Tipping, chest heaving, came out looking even more like an imp from hell.

"That's the mistake we made," he declared, throwing the piece of sacking down on the floor. "You'd never put an oil fire out with water but smother the flames."

Segalla, intrigued, followed him to the adjoining room.

"It's quite easily done," Tipping explained. "What the assassin did, sir, was put gunpowder into the bellows. I've seen it done as a madcap trick in kitchens."

"Of course!" Segalla breathed.

"The bellows were put into the small hole." Tipping showed him how: he shook some gunpowder from a horn into the black canvas bag inside the bellows. The handles of the bellows were squeezed together and the gunpowder spurted out, sprinkling the floor.

"And the same was done with the oil?" Segalla asked.

"Even easier," Tipping replied. "That being liquid it goes further."

Segalla crouched down by the small sluice hole in the wall.

"And that can be done?"

"I did it," Tipping observed. "It's very quiet and very quick. Remember Dalrymple was asleep a lot. If he heard any rustling he'd think it was a rat or a mouse. The palace is full of such vermin. Also the rushes were very dry, and they were then soaked in materials which would cause conflagration: oil and a little gunpowder."

"And how was it lit?"

Tipping smiled and walked into the corner of the room. He brought back a long rod with a half-burnt taper at the end, the type used by sextons to light tall candles on the high altar of a church.

"Of course." Segalla took the pole out of the man's hand. "You simply light this, slip it through the hole, and light those rushes near the bed."

"I think so," Tipping agreed. "The flames would spread as fast as the wind. The bedding is caught, poor Dalrymple wakes up. He's wrapped in a cloak, he's in stockinged feet, these and some of his other clothing could have been stained with the gunpowder and oil. The fire spreads to him." The soldier shrugged. "The rest you know."

Segalla walked to the door.

"And you discovered this all by yourself?" he called out over his shoulder.

Tipping followed rather shamefacedly.

"I'd like to say I did, sir. I agree with you, the assassin visited the adjoining storeroom. I looked around; there was oil, then I pulled away some of the caskets. I found a small basket containing grains of gunpowder next to the taper on the wooden pole. I guessed what had happened."

Segalla walked outside, it was cold and growing dark. The wind whipped the leaves across the small, deserted courtyard. What Tipping told him made sense. It could be quite easily done, dried rushes soaked in oil and gunpowder, lit with a taper. He'd seen the defenders of many a castle or wall use such materials against the enemy's siege machinery; it was very cheap, easy to prepare, and deadly in its effect. The assassin, disguised as a servant, had secreted those materials in the storeroom. No one would ever suspect: that room hadn't been guarded; servants could come and go. Yet, something was wrong.

"The prisoner's food?" Segalla asked. "And drink? Where were these prepared?"

"Oh, in the palace kitchens, and left out on a tray. I brought it down for Sir Henry Grantchester, who took it in to the prisoner."

"So, anyone could have prepared an opiate? A sleeping draught?" Segalla explained.

"Was that necessary, sir?" Tipping shook his head. "Dalrymple was exhausted: we always took him wine and he had been starving."

Segalla nodded. "But you were the guard. You'd see someone slipping into the adjoining chamber?"

"Would I, sir? These are palace storerooms. Servants came in and out whenever they wished. My task was to guard the prisoner and nothing else."

Segalla breathed in and looked up at the sky.

"What time did the fire start?"

"About one o'clock."

"And what time did the palace servants take a break from their duties and eat?"

"About one o'clock."

"And what time was the prisoner fed?"

"About noon."

Segalla took two silver coins out of his purse and pressed them into Tipping's hand.

"You did good work, Corporal, but tell no one else what we have discovered. The bellows and the oil. Get rid of them, then clean the cell."

With the soldier's thanks ringing in his ears, Segalla reentered the palace and made his way back up to his chamber. He now knew how Dalrymple had died. The assassin, disguised as a servant, had been able to move in and out of that storeroom unimpeded. The oil, bellows, and taper would already be there. The gunpowder could be brought and the conflagration started when the rest of the palace retainers were in the communal refectory. Corporal Tipping's remarks reflected the soldiers' attitude. They were to guard the prisoner and would never dream of challenging a servant who entered the adjoining room. And the assassin? A professional, consummate in disguise: he would know the prisoner was closely guarded and so look for a safe way to kill Dalrymple. He would realize there were storerooms, the same in every great mansion, and look for the weakness; that adjoining chamber provided it. Dalrymple would be an easy victim: tired, frightened, having just eaten and drunk wine, he would be fast asleep upon the bed. The assassin struck. Dalrymple, woken abruptly from his slumber, floundered about. In such an enclosed space, the dry rushes, soaked in oil and gunpowder, would be a death trap.

But who? Segalla sat at his desk. Sir Henry Grantchester? Orslett was with him when the conflagration started. Dr. Cesar was in the city, so there must be someone else. Segalla ruefully concluded that he had gone as far as he could. The Four Evangelists, that secret little group from the Tower so many years ago, were all dead, but still the letters were coming. Segalla went down to the kitchens: a sullen-faced cook brought him a cold pie, some bread, and ale. Segalla ate and then retired to bed.

The next morning he, Orslett, and Cesar gathered in the small muniment room where coffers, chests, and panniers full of documents had been brought from Westminster. They began to sift through the different memoranda, household accounts, letters, and warrants. These dated from January 1553 through to February 1554, the period of confusion following Edward VI's death. Segalla and his companions soon caught the excitement, the shifting political scene as Northumberland tried to exclude Mary, who bravely fought back. There were reports from spies trying to determine who would win: the sheriff, merchants, and leading citizens of the city sending letters to either camp. The raising of troops, the sealing of ports, and the desperate attempts by either faction to control London permeated the documents.

"It's an impossible task," Orslett declared after their first week closeted in the chamber; he gestured at the pile of discarded documents on the floor.

"A waste of time!" Dr. Cesar snapped.

The physician had lost his cheery, devil-may-care attitude. He was beginning to hint that he and Segalla had finished their task so they should return to Rome. Segalla had ignored him, but, by the end of the week, Cesar was more insistent.

"Nicholas," he declared as they walked along the passageway after Segalla had celebrated Mass in one of the small chantry chapels, "we are finished here. The Queen is in good health, or the best she'll ever be. We can do no more. London has a surfeit of skilled physicians. The Four Evangelists are dead whilst the anonymous writer seems to pose no danger to our Queen."

Segalla shook his head. He went across to a window embrasure and they sat on the cushioned seat.

"How do we know," he replied, "that, as soon as we disappear, the assassin does not strike against the Queen? Moreover, we have no evidence that the anonymous writer means the Queen well. He does hail Mary as dead and buried!"

Segalla scratched at a piece of candle wax on his sleeve.

"If you wish, Dr. Cesar, you may go. I am sure the Queen will give you licence. I am going to remain until this matter is finished."

Dr. Cesar sighed despondently but did not broach the matter again.

The days passed into weeks: Segalla and his companions became part of the routine of the nearly deserted palace. The cooks fed them, the servants cleaned their chambers, the atmosphere remained desultory. Now and again, they'd take a break from their labours and visit the city or stroll along the riverside. Letters came from Jane Dormer and the Queen: all seemed to be well. Segalla secretly wondered whether they were wasting their time, when, just before All Hallows Eve, Orslett seized a piece of paper, waving it excitedly around. He passed it over. Segalla pulled the candlestick closer and studied the cramped writing. It was from one of the aldermen, a member of the city council, "To the Sheriff's men, bailiffs, and beadles of the Ward" asking them to search out for three traitorous former officials from the Tower: Dalrymple, Kennet, and Savage. It accused them of "doing great mischief" and specified the offences: extortion and blackmail. A brief description was given; at the end of the proclamation was a curious reference to a Master Clarence.

Segalla recalled the mysterious stranger who bought the great secret before turning these three conspirators over to the sheriff's men. They continued their searches: more references were found to Master Clarence, as well as reports from spies about Kennet, Savage, and Dalrymple.

"Good Dr. Theophilus," Segalla observed, "appears to have kept in the shadows."

A short while later they found the reason why: a copy of a licence for Dr. John Gresham, "formerly the King's physician in the Tower, to go abroad to foreign parts."

"Ah!" Orslett remarked. "That explains a great deal. Theophilus was one of the Four Evangelists, but he may not have been implicated as deeply as his companions."

October passed into November: they still made no real progress. On the eve of the feast of All Souls, Segalla and

Orslett decided to take a break and left the palace for an evening walk along the embankment to a riverside tavern. They discussed what they had found, as well as the cessation of letters from Sinistrel about the Queen's condition.

"What will you do?" Segalla asked as they took their seats in the warm tavern close to the roaring fire.

"What will I do when?" Orslett replied, ordering two large cups of posset.

Segalla waited until these had been served.

"If the Queen dies," he continued. "I and Dr. Cesar will probably leave the country, as quietly and as speedily as possible. But you?"

Orslett rubbed his unshaven cheek. "Tonight," he said, "I am going back to visit my wife and family to make sure all is well. You've read the documents, Nicholas. What happened in 1553, when our late good King Edward VI died, will happen again. There may well be a time of flux, of sudden change." He removed the linen cloth, picked up the warm posset cup, and sipped at it. "As I've said," he murmured, "it's all a matter of knowing when to jump!" He put the posset cup down. "And I tell you this, Nicholas." He peered round the tavern full of fishermen, people who plied their trade along the river. "Do not make the mistake of thinking that you will be allowed to go unchecked. If Mary dies, God forbid, Elizabeth will succeed. Cecil is the most craftiest spider, a most subtle snake. He'll have his henchmen in every city and port. I already know he commands the fleet. So, forget Spain, France, and the power of Rome: this kingdom will declare for Henry's daughter. Make no mistake of that." He lowered his voice. "So, Master Segalla, member of the Jesuit order, I wouldn't tarry long if I were you."

Segalla took the warning and, in his suspicious mind, wondered how much and how far he could trust Orslett. They left the tavern. A river mist was boiling up the Thames, its ghostly wisps blurring lights and deadening sound along the riverside.

The silence was oppressive. Segalla went to ask Orslett some questions about his family when his companion seized his wrist and stopped. Orslett lifted a finger to his lips. Segalla stood listening into the darkness, then he heard it: a dull footfall behind them, followed by the clink of metal. Segalla's hand went under his cloak to the hilt of his sword. Orslett had already stepped back, throwing his cloak over his shoulder, quietly drawing sword and dagger. He motioned with his head that they walk on; they did so, slightly apart, Orslett looking to the left over the river, Segalla to the right. There was the sound of running footsteps. A man, cloaked and muffled, appeared out of the swirling mists. Two more stepped out of the darkness, sword and dagger whirling. Segalla and Orslett stood back to back. The silence was broken by the sound of grunts and muttered oaths as the assassins struck and then withdrew, surprised at finding their quarry so well prepared. Segalla was used to such murderous forays. Time and again along the stinking alleyways or on the lonely heaths of Europe, he had fought off cut-throats and paid assassins. This was no different. Instead of a wall or a tree, he only had Orslett's back to defend him; he quietly prayed that Orslett was not an accomplice. Segalla knew he could not die or be killed, but he had, in his long career, sustained grievous cuts; his body was criss-crossed with scars. Orslett, however, was an accomplished swordsman. He took care of one assassin and turned to help Segalla, sword and knife blade flickering out. Segalla managed to pierce one of his opponents high in the shoulder, and their assailants fled, as quickly and as silently as they had come.

For a while both men stood panting, their sweat rapidly cooling. They sheathed their weapons and wrapped their cloaks about them. Segalla went back and turned over the dead assassin. He pulled the vizard from his face. In the murky gloom Segalla made out sharp, sinister features. Orslett deftly went through the man's pockets but could find nothing.

"A professional killer," he declared, kicking the corpse with the toe of his boot. "Nothing on him to say who he was or where he came from or, more importantly, who paid. Ah well, leave him there: the river people will soon strip him."

"Was he one of Cecil's men?" Segalla asked as they walked back to the palace.

"I don't think so," Orslett replied. "Cecil moves in more subtle ways." He turned at the porter's lodge and patted Segalla on the shoulder. "Cecil still needs me, and he'll watch to see where and when I jump. Remember that!"

He slipped out into the darkness. Segalla returned to his chamber. He went along the gallery and pushed open the door to Dr. Cesar's room: the good physician was lying on the bed, a wineskin in his hand, his snores echoing round the chamber. Segalla returned to the muniment room. He was still agitated, fearful of what had happened. He lit more candles and sifted through the documents. At last he calmed his mind: he was about to give up and retire when he came across a rough draft of a letter drawn up, at the behest of one of Northumberland's henchmen, to his spies in the city. He ordered them to investigate rumours that Mary Tudor's principal lieutenant, "the attainted traitor Reginald Pole," may have slipped into the city. Segalla, curious, read it again. Pole had been hated by King Henry VIII: Reginald had fled abroad and attacked the English King's divorce from Catherine of Aragon and the consequent break with Rome. Pole had been Henry's inveterate enemy and that of his successor Edward VI. Segalla tapped his fingers against the parchment.

"There was more to it then, wasn't there?" he murmured to himself. "Reginald Pole was the son of Margaret, Countess of Salisbury, a niece of Edward IV who was the daughter of the Duke of. . . ." Segalla smacked the heel of his hand against his forehead and sprang to his feet. "Of course! Of course!" he whispered. "George, Duke of Clarence!"

Segalla walked to the window and peered out: mist swirled in the courtyard below. Segalla no longer felt sleepy. Let us imagine, he thought, these four men, the so-called Four Evangelists have discovered a secret. In the turbulent days of 1553, when the kingdom was divided between Mary Tudor and the Duke of Northumberland they, or at least three of them, tried to sell the secret to both camps. Northumberland reacted by hunting them down, but Mary responded more skilfully, sending her most trusted friend and minister, Reginald Pole, into London under the guise of Mr. Clarence. Pole had bought the secret but betrayed the Evangelists to the sheriff's men.

"Which means," Segalla declared, "that Mary recognized that the secret was vastly important, so. . . ."

Segalla wondered if he should ride out to Lambeth or even to Sinistrel in Essex, but, as the Queen and Pole had refused to tell him earlier, why should they do so now? Segalla folded the piece of parchment and slipped it into his pocket. And what if Mary and Pole were responsible for the murders of Savage, Dalrymple, and the rest? Perhaps he could discover it himself?

Segalla sat down, took a pen, and wrote "Mark 15.34," followed by "Eloi, Eloi, lamma sabacthani? My God, my God, why have you forsaken me?" He placed the candle on the edge of the parchment and watched the large letters he had formed dance in the flickering shadows. So far, Segalla reasoned, he had tried to discover the mystery behind this reference but what had he achieved? It was something which worried both Mary and Elizabeth as well as those who'd been executed for their involvement with Anne Boleyn.

"In what year?" Segalla asked himself. He wrote the answer out. "In 1536."

"And in 1534? What had happened in 1534?"

Segalla racked his brains: it was the year Loyola founded the order of the Jesuits: there was an uprising in Munster and Suleiman the Magnificent captured Baghdad. And in England? Henry VIII had broken from Rome. What else? Segalla paused, pen over his parchment. Ah yes, Anne Boleyn had given birth to a daughter Elizabeth in 1533 and, in 1534, by the Act of Succession, Elizabeth replaced Mary as Henry's legitimate heir. Segalla recalled the drawing on the wall of the Bloody Tower: Mark Smeaton, the musician accused of adultery with the Queen, the only member of Anne Boleyn's coven who had been racked and tortured.

Segalla looked at the words: "Eloi, Eloi, lamma sabachtani." He wrote them out as Kennet had done, jumbled up with Smeaton's first name, Mark, beneath. He began to strike out the letters of the Hebrew phrase. Segalla closed his eyes: the quotation from St. Mark's gospel was the anagram of a name! Now he knew why Elizabeth and Cecil were so frightened: he had also guessed the name of the anonymous letter-writer, surprising though it was. But the assassin? The person responsible for so many deaths? Segalla rolled the piece of parchment up. Now he could see a way forward. The assassin had nothing to do with the anonymous letters, but who he or she was remained a mystery.

Chapter 12

S egalla did not reveal what he had discovered to the others. He and Orslett mentioned the attack, and Dr. Cesar
murmured that perhaps they all should be careful and not
leave the palace. They worked for two more days but discovered nothing else. Segalla's mind was really elsewhere,
turning over and over again his new discovery. He was certain that if Pole knew the secret then so did Mary.

Just after the Feast of Saints Elizabeth and Zachary,
Segalla was making preparations to go along the river to
Lambeth when a messenger, booted, spurred, and covered in
mud, arrived at Greenwich. The news he brought caused
gloom and consternation. Orslett met Segalla and Dr. Cesar
in the small chancery, his face grim and slightly pale, the first
time Segalla had seen this most secretive of men agitated.

"The Queen is being brought back to Greenwich," he
declared. "She had a relapse: her condition is very frail. God
knows how, but the news is all over the city. Already the
French and Spanish ambassadors have sent messengers en-
quiring."

Cesar sat down in the chair and rubbed his cheeks. "There is nothing I can do," he murmured. "I suspected as much."

"You suspected what?" Segalla snapped, wishing the physician could be more precise.

"Well, we know the Queen had dropsy," Cesar continued slowly. "But I suspect that she has a growth, a tumour, inside that is sapping away her strength." He glanced pleadingly at Segalla. "I told you I was a physician, not a miracle worker. If I had been here years ago, perhaps. I can almost guess the symptoms. The Queen will be dizzy, her belly will swell up, her legs become thick and fat with water. She'll be weak and in continuous pain."

"They say she'll be here by tomorrow morning," Orslett interrupted. He waved his hand around. "I say we bring all this to an end." He went over and closed the door. "Nicholas, I beg you; Cecil will soon make his hand felt. It is time you and Dr. Cesar returned to Rome."

Cesar loudly agreed. Segalla just shook his head. He went back to the manuscripts. Cesar declared that it was futile and left with Orslett. Segalla sat in the muniment room, but he found it was difficult to work. He went down to the kitchen; already some of the servants and retainers were deserting the royal household, going into the city to wait and see what would happen.

Late next morning Mary returned, carried into the palace on a litter. Segalla and the other officers met her in the hallway, and Segalla's heart sank as the curtains were pulled back. The Queen was lying against cushions, her pallor was grey, her half-open eyes ringed by black shadows, her skin tight and leathery. She moved her head, went to speak, but then wearily lifted her hand. Jane Dormer looked as if she hadn't slept for days: when the Queen was taken up to her chamber, she stayed behind. She plucked Segalla's sleeve and took him over into the shadows. For a while they stood watching the liveried retainers lift the Queen up the stairs to her chambers.

"It is finished," Jane whispered.

"What happened?" Segalla asked.

Dormer shook her head. "At first the Queen was merry, more vigorous than I have seen her for months, but, five days ago, she woke complaining of severe pains in her abdomen. We had Dr. Cesar's medicines and a local leech was summoned: the fellow just shook his head and fled. She's bleeding internally," Jane continued. "I wish she'd stayed, but she was insistent on returning here."

"Where's Sir Henry Grantchester?"

Lady Jane smiled bleakly. "He brought us into the city but said he had business there. It's starting already, Nicholas. The Queen is dying and every day the number of people around her will diminish. Oh, Grantchester will return, I am sure, after he's finished his business with Master Cecil's agents. If the Queen dies," Lady Jane continued, "I shall not remain in England."

Segalla made to go, but she caught his wrist.

"Stay," she murmured. "At least let the Queen see you about."

Segalla agreed. In the next few days Greenwich became

a mausoleum. Grantchester returned, but it was apparent his mind was elsewhere, and, although he did his best, he could do little to stop desertions both amongst the household and his own guard.

"There's nothing I can do," he informed Segalla.

"I suppose the road to Hatfield's packed!" Segalla snapped.

Grantchester lifted his head. "Don't judge us so hard, Master Segalla. You are a stranger, but we have to look to the future, just like Master Orslett has."

Orslett had now become a shadow, spending more time outside the palace than within. Already a distance was growing up between them. Orslett never came to their chamber and showed no interest in the Queen: he seemed to have more business in the city, going out early and coming back late.

Segalla, as promised, visited the Queen regularly. He even celebrated Mass in her bedchamber. Dr. Cesar was also assiduous in his attentions and, by the twelfth of November, had managed to give the Queen some comfort. She became more alert and dispatched writs ordering her Privy Council to meet her at Greenwich. Once again the palace became busy as different lords and their retainers assembled. Grim-faced men, they soon made their wishes known. The Queen was so ill, they declared, she should seal her will and proclaim that Elizabeth was her successor. Mary was reluctant to do this. She was supported by some of the Catholic bishops, who realized that when Elizabeth became Queen they would be summarily removed from office.

Segalla used the confusion to leave the palace and go along the fog-bound river to Lambeth. The archbishop's palace was almost deserted. It was ill-kept, unswept, and dirty, and only a few retainers remained. Segalla found the Cardinal lying on his great four-poster bed, head back against the bolsters, Ave beads wrapped around his fingers.

"Why have you come, Segalla?" he asked, face grey with exhaustion. "Haven't you heard I am dying? My Queen is dying? My servants can draw you a map to Hatfield."

"Mark 15.34," Segalla replied. " 'Eloi, Eloi, lamma sabacthani?' "

Pole gave a laugh which ended in a fit of coughing.

"What nonsense is this?" he stuttered.

"No nonsense, Your Grace. A secret you've known for the last five years when you slipped into London under the name of Master Clarence and did business with the Four Evangelists."

Pole gave a dismissive wave of his hand.

"Your Grace, don't lie. You are at death's door and I am a priest."

"Aye and both are true of Carafa!" Pole's lips curled in a snarl.

"You wrote the letters, didn't you?" Segalla continued. "In 1536 Mark Smeaton, court musician, was arrested and imprisoned in the Tower on a charge of adultery with Anne Boleyn. After he was racked and tortured, Smeaton was attended by the Tower physician, John Gresham, whom we know as Dr. Theophilus. Now Theophilus was a friend of three of the officials in the Tower: Kennet, Dalrymple, and

Savage. They learnt a terrible secret. Anne Boleyn was not only unfaithful to Henry but the child she'd conceived was fathered by Mark Smeaton. The poor musician's mind, disturbed by torture, had locked the secret in the verse Mark 15.34. Mark was his first name; 1534 was the year Princess Elizabeth was made Henry VIII's legitimate heir by the Act of Succession. Finally, the phrase: 'Eloi, Eloi, lamma sabacthani' contains the letters which formed Smeaton's surname."

Pole wiped the phlegm from the corner of his mouth.

"Subtle Jesuit," he murmured.

"Now, the Evangelists kept it a secret," Segalla continued. "After all, whilst the great tyrant was alive, who dared whisper or murmur what they knew? The same is true during the reign of Edward VI. Who would be bothered with such scandal? Edward was a young boy, he could live for another fifty years with Elizabeth being married off to some foreign princeling. However, in 1553, everything changed. Young Edward died rather suddenly. Three contenders for the English throne emerged: Mary, the rightful heir; Elizabeth, her half-sister; and Lady Jane Grey. The Duke of Northumberland, who had exercised complete power during Edward's reign, chose to ignore Mary and Elizabeth and advanced the claims of Lady Jane Grey."

Segalla paused whilst Pole had another fit of coughing.

"The Duke chose wrongly," Segalla continued. "Like a gambler at hazard, he picked up the wrong cards; Lady Jane was not the offspring of Henry Tudor. Our Evangelists, or at least three of them, made their move: they offered their secret both to the Duke of Northumberland and the Princess Mary."

"Why should they do that?" Pole asked.

"Oh, for a number of reasons. Northumberland knew he had chosen wrongly. He might decide to support the Princess Mary. Such information, if published abroad, would dash Elizabeth's hopes for good. No one would recognize her claims to the throne. If Northumberland brought such information to Mary, who knows, he might have received a pardon. Or curried favour as Mary's troops advanced on London. Northumberland, however, was confused and losing his grip. He sent out warrants for the arrest of these men: they, now committed to their course of action, opened up negotiations with Mary herself."

Segalla studied the Cardinal's face and he knew he'd hit his mark. The Cardinal's eyes had a faraway look, as if he were back in those turbulent days five years ago.

"Mary was more adroit and decisive," Segalla continued. "She shared everything with her great friend Reginald Pole, a man skilled in intrigue. Who knows: Pole may have had suspicions of his own. He is already returning to England to join Mary's party. Now he slips into London. He calls himself Master Clarence after his Yorkist grandfather George, Duke of Clarence."

Pole's dry lips cracked in a smile.

"You opened negotiations with these hucksters. You took their secret and God knows what else they gave you. You also informed the sheriff's men. I suppose you thought the Evangelists would die, either on the scaffold or rotting in some prison. In all their misfortune they had one glimmer of hope: London was in chaos. They offered the gold you had given them in return for their lives. Am I correct, my Lord Cardinal?"

Pole sighed.

"You are the author of those letters, aren't you?" Segalla insisted. He sat and watched the candle flame on the far side of the bed rise and fall from a draught through one of the casement windows.

"I am dying," Pole began. "My Queen is dying. Everything breaks down, Segalla. Henry VIII, God curse him, sowed a poisonous seed, and now it's reached full fruition. The Catholic Church in England is destroyed. The rightful heir, her mind and soul racked by years of torture, will soon be with God. Henry did that. He drove Catherine of Aragon to her grave. He tortured his own child Mary Tudor. Oh, not in the Tower with the rack and the thumbscrew but through indifference, insults, and studied contempt. Henry's lusts destroyed the Church: good men like More and Fisher went to the scaffold. He turned on my family because we had Yorkist blood in our veins. Yes, I am the grandson of George, Duke of Clarence. Some might say I have a better claim to the throne of England than Henry Tudor." Pole paused to cough and clear his throat. "Henry hated my family. My own mother, Margaret Pole, Countess of Salisbury, was sent to the block like some attainted traitor. And, as for that strumpet Boleyn!" Pole turned his head, eyes gleaming with hatred. "A strumpet!" he spat out. "She knew more about the arts of love than any whore in the city! Shall I tell you something, Segalla? Henry was frightened of Boleyn. He could not make love to her, as impotent as a eunuch. Oh, he fumbled and he bumbled. Do you think I jest?" Pole swallowed hard. "Search amongst the records. You'll find the letter from Boleyn, dispatched from the Tower only a few hours before her execution. She turns the insult back at him. She hints quite openly at the King's impotence, the final snub, the studied insult." Pole smiled. "No wonder the King went hunting the day she died. He wanted to shut her up. He wanted to be rid of her. He never believed that Boleyn would proclaim him a cuckold to Europe, but he had to make sure. Boleyn must have laughed. Henry now had the Princess Elizabeth to look after and what could he do? Reject her? Say that a common musician could achieve in bed more than the great Henry of England? I watched all this from afar. Henry chose his third wife more carefully. Little, docile Jane Seymour, the quietest filly in his stables: she gave the King his powers back." Pole paused. "Some water?" he gasped.

Segalla rose, filled a goblet, and held it to the Cardinal's lips. He sipped carefully.

"Oh there were rumours," the Cardinal continued, wiping his mouth on the back of his hand. "Right from the start there were rumours about Princess Elizabeth's paternity. However, Boleyn and all her entourage are dead, whilst the birth of Prince Edward silenced the clacking tongues for good. I was abroad, you know why?"

Segalla nodded.

"If Henry had found me, I would have gone the same way as my mother and my brothers. Oh, I listened, my ear close to the keyhole of the English court. I recognized Catherine of Aragon as my true Queen and the Princess Mary as the rightful heir to the crown of Edward the Confessor. I hoped that one day Mary might perhaps marry some foreign prince, but then little Edward died and the game changed." Pole chuckled deep in his throat. "Oh yes, how it changed! During Edward's final illness, Mary, God bless her, began to move. I made preparations to return to England. I landed at a small fishing port near Ipswich, met with Mary, then travelled disguised into London. The Queen had informed me how these Evangelists had a great secret they wished to sell. In ordinary circumstances we would have ignored them, but they had been officials in the Tower and made some reference to Anne Boleyn." Pole looked up at the red-gold tester covering the bed and closed his eyes.

Segalla thought he had fallen asleep, but the Cardinal, fingering the rosary beads, continued.

"London was in turmoil. Northumberland had lost his grip: the Evangelists gave me the name of a tavern; well, the rest you know."

"But what proof did they provide?" Segalla asked.

Pole chuckled again. "A document you'll no longer find. Smeaton's own confession giving times and dates as well as his assertion that Henry and Anne Boleyn . . . well." He waved a hand. "The King could not fulfil his lusts. God's curse on him!"

"So, Queen Mary knows all this?"

"Yes, she does."

"But there's no love lost between the Queen and her half-sister. Why not publicize it abroad?"

Again Pole laughed, drily, shaking his head.

"You'll never understand, will you? Queen Mary may be Catherine of Aragon's daughter, the Catholic wife of King Philip of Spain, but she is, first and foremost, a Tudor." Pole pointed a finger. "Don't ever forget that. Mary Tudor adored her father. Don't you realize that? Whatever he did to her mother, whatever he did to her, deep in her heart, Mary loved her father with a passion beyond all understanding. You've got to love with all your heart, soul, and mind, Segalla, before you can hate." Pole fell silent, his lips moving as if he were talking to someone else. "There were other reasons," he continued. "Anne Boleyn begged for forgiveness of Mary before she died. Very few people have done that with the Queen. Mary never forgot. Moreover, despite sibling rivalry, I think Mary is genuinely fond of her sister, and Elizabeth returns this in kind. In truth, whatever I have said, Elizabeth would have no dealings with an assassin plotting to kill her half-sister."

"Do you think the Queen is being poisoned?"

"Yes, I do, but I don't know how, why, or by whom. Mary should never have married Philip of Spain, a spider in silk that one. Moreover, I wouldn't let any lackey of that French queen within walking distance of Mary. God knows, it could be anyone!"

"There's another reason, isn't there," Segalla asked, "why Mary didn't publicize the news?"

"Of course." Pole sighed. "Once you start a rumour like that, once you let the poison out of the jug, who knows where it would stop? If Elizabeth might not be Henry's daughter, was Edward his son . . . ?"

"Or Mary his child?" Segalla finished.

"Precisely." Pole pushed himself up on the bed.

"But you think differently, don't you?" Segalla continued. "To quote your own phrase, Your Grace, the game is over. You hated Henry VIII, you hated Anne Boleyn. Your Queen is dying and so Master Clarence became the Evangelists." Segalla pointed to a writing desk in the corner of the shadowy room. "You wrote those letters, baiting Elizabeth with copies here and abroad. You reminded her that Mary would die, but her succession might not be as easy as she thought. You asked for money but you did not intend to collect. It was a game you enjoyed, the hurt you caused. I suppose the Queen protested, but you still carried on."

"And I will do so," Pole retorted. "Look at me, Segalla!" he hissed. "Look at Mary! Look at our Church! All is ruined. Go back to Rome. Tell Carafa to fall to his prayers because, like me, he cannot have much time left. I do wonder." Pole narrowed his eyes.

"What, Your Grace?"

"Why Carafa didn't tell you." The Cardinal chuckled at the surprise in Segalla's face. "I found that surprising. Our Holy Pontiff, God's Vicar on earth, Pope Paul IV, knows all about Mark 15.34, the Evangelists, and Master Clarence, for the very simple reason I told him!"

"When?" Segalla felt his body turn clammy with sweat.

"Years ago, when Mary succeeded to the throne, all looked golden and rosy. My letters are in Rome giving chapter and verse. I thought it would please Carafa. I thought it would make him support Mary all the more, if he knew that Elizabeth was not only a Protestant heretic but base born."

"And what else do you know?"

"That the physician John Gresham, who called himself Theophilus, when he returned to England carried letters of accreditation from Carafa. I am sure John Gresham visited Rome: the price of papal support was that he confirmed everything I told Carafa."

"But the Queen must have known Gresham was one of the Evangelists?"

"He cleared himself, with some truth: he was not as guilty as the others." Pole smirked. "He was a good physician and Mary could keep an eye on him."

"Surely the Queen objected to you sending those letters?"

"The Queen can refuse me nothing!" Pole snarled. "It is a dying man's revenge!"

Segalla stared at this cunning prelate. Pole was dying. He had nothing to lose so why should he tell lies? Segalla realized how adroitly he had been tricked. He felt a sense of despair at the implication of what Pole had confessed. He got to his feet and bowed to the Cardinal.

"Your Grace, I must go!"

Pole raised his hand in blessing. "Master Segalla, so must I. We shall not meet again."

Segalla left the palace. Outside, on the fog-bound quayside, he paused, breathing in deeply, trying to control his teeming thoughts. He hired a barge to take him along the river to Greenwich. When he arrived at the palace, he had something to eat in the buttery and went straight to the muniment room, where he continued his searches. Of Dr. Cesar and Orslett there was no sign. Now and again Segalla broke off his work to pay a visit to the Queen. One look at her ashen pallor, the sunken eyes, the dry, cracked lips, her chest rising and falling as she panted for breath, and he realized the Queen would not last long. Lady Jane Dormer told him news of the court.

"Four days earlier," she whispered, "the master of the rolls and the comptroller of the household were sent to Hatfield to inform Elizabeth that she would succeed to the Crown. Mary asked her half-sister to make two promises. The first to maintain the old religion, the other to pay the Queen's debts. Elizabeth did not even bother to reply. The Spanish and French ambassadors had also been in attendance at Hatfield."

By November 16 the Queen was losing consciousness. On that evening Segalla was present when Mary drifted out of her deep sleep. She comforted Lady Jane, who was sobbing beside the bed, and told her not to grieve for her but that she had good dreams: she had seen many little children, like angels, playing around her, singing pleasing notes. The Queen fell asleep again. Segalla celebrated Mass in the Queen's chamber. There were now only Lady Jane, a few maids, and, to his credit, Sir Henry Grantchester present.

Afterwards Segalla returned to his searches and found

what he was looking for. He then began to construct his own hypothesis, listing all the murders: Theophilus, Nicolette, Savage, Kennet, and Dalrymple. He dozed for a while and was woken by a servant banging on his door.

"Lady Jane wishes to see you now." The man's face was tear-stained. "The Queen." He swallowed hard. "The Queen is dying."

Segalla grabbed his cloak and hurried down. The Queen's bedchamber was insufferably hot. A fire burnt in the hearth, dishes full of charcoal were placed around the room, and the windows were shuttered. Every available candle had been lit. On one side of the Queen's bed a priest knelt, face in his hands, murmuring the Office of the Dead. On the other, Lady Jane, kneeling on cushions, mouthed the responses. Segalla went over and joined her. The Queen's head lolled to one side of the pillow: her veil had been removed, her sweat-strewn hair fanned out across the bolsters, her eyes were half-open, and a dribble of saliva snaked out of the corner of her mouth. Only a faint pulse in her throat showed that she was still alive. Segalla joined in the responses. He must have knelt there for half an hour and, just as the bells of the palace were chiming the hour of six, Lady Jane got to her feet.

"She has left us," she murmured. "The Queen is dead!"

Segalla leaned over and felt the dry, cold skin: the pulse had gone, the eyes remained half-open.

"God rest her," he confirmed. "But the Queen is dead!"

Dr. Cesar was summoned and, together with other physicians, asked the others to withdraw whilst he examined the corpse. It did not take long. Cesar drew the sheet over the Queen's face. Lady Jane ordered the bed drapes to be pulled close. They left the death room and gathered in the antechamber, where a thoughtful Grantchester had laid out some watered wine, bread, cheese, and dried meats. Lady Jane sipped at her cup. She was not crying but seemed peaceful and determined.

"I have done all I can," she declared, putting the cup down. "My Queen is no more, my friend is dead. I do not even wish to attend the funeral. I will not see people weep hypocritical tears. I shall go to Sinistrel and, as soon as possible, leave for Spain." She breathed in. "Father Segalla, I give you good advice. You should do the same. Any commission given to you by the Holy Father and validated by the Crown is now dead. Cecil's men will already be busy in the city. You should look to yourself."

Segalla made no reply. He glanced at Dr. Cesar who, according to the Queen's will, was now richer by a hundred pounds in gold.

"Lady Jane speaks the truth," he said, hitching his furred robe round his shoulders. "We have no business here now."

"Will Philip of Spain move?" Segalla asked. "Or Catherine of France?"

Lady Jane went to a window. She pulled back the shutters and opened a small casement door.

"There," she said, pointing out to the boiling mist. "Over there in the city. They will decide who is crowned at Westminster. They have prepared for this day. The great merchants in their gabled house, the apprentices of Cheapside, the mob around Whitefriars. Go out into the countryside, Master Segalla; the great lords with their retinues, they will make their decision. I have told as much to Philip of Spain."

"We should go," Cesar declared.

"In a while," Segalla replied. "I promise you. We shall not wait long. Lady Jane, before I leave, I would like to call on you at Sinistrel. Is that possible?"

Lady Jane nodded. Segalla went back to his own chamber. The records in the muniment room he ignored. Any notes he had drawn up, he cut with his dagger and burnt on the fire. Cesar came up to enquire about the exact date for departure but Segalla put him off, saying he had other business to finish though he would not tarry long. Later that day, when the palace retainers, those who had stayed by their posts, prepared for the Queen's funeral, Segalla disguised himself and went out across the river into the city. He made enquiries, obtained certain purchases, and frequented the taverns along Cheapside. He found everything Lady Jane had said was true. There were deep regrets for Mary's death but also subdued rejoicing that Elizabeth would succeed. Cecil's men had been very busy. Proclamations had been posted at St. Paul's and at the cross in Cheapside. The royal ships in the Thames had declared for Elizabeth, and what had been a steady flow of would-be supporters to Hatfield had now turned into a triumphant procession. Indeed, Elizabeth was already issuing proclamations. The soldiers in the Tower had also declared for her, whilst, rumour had it, an army of at least twenty thousand men would camp outside London to ensure that Henry's daughter Elizabeth succeeded to the throne.

By the time Segalla returned to the riverside, bonfires had been lit at many crossroads. Apprentice boys were hailing Elizabeth and cursing the power for Spain. At Greenwich he even found members of Elizabeth's household had joined the guards at the gate, but he was allowed through without any trouble. Segalla returned to his own chamber and quickly packed his few belongings. He paid a heavy bribe to Corporal Tipping, for horses and sumpter ponies to be set aside for himself and Dr. Cesar. When he returned, Orslett had lit a candle and was lounging in a chair.

"You've come to arrest me, Stephen?"

"Not yet," Orslett smiled thinly. "But the order will go out if you tarry too long."

"So, you have jumped?"

"Of course! Queen Mary is dead! Long live Queen Elizabeth!" Orslett got up and closed the door, then leaned against it. "You've discovered the secret, haven't you?"

"Whom am I speaking to? Elizabeth's man or Stephen Orslett?"

"Stephen Orslett, Nicholas. I may be treacherous, but not to my friends. The Queen wants to know."

At first Segalla thought he was talking about Mary, then he laughed.

"I am going to give you good advice, Stephen," he replied. "And, believe me, I tell the truth. When the Queen or Cecil asks, did I know the secret, you are to reply 'No.' You must not give any hint that I have been successful: if you do, I cannot vouch for myself and I would certainly worry for you and your family." Segalla grasped the cross on the chain round his neck. "I swear, Stephen, by all that is sacred: you must not know the secret!"

"You are to be out of London within the day," Orslett replied. He put his hand on the latch. "And, within a week, out of England. How you go, or where you go, is no business of mine." He put a hand out. "Pray for me, Nicholas. Pray that in the future, not for my sake but for my wife and children"—he smiled—"I never jump too late!"

Chapter 13

The following morning Segalla received news that Cardinal Pole had died at the same hour, on the evening of the same day as his Queen. He would have liked to have paid his respects to the Cardinal's corpse: Pole was a prince of the Church and protocol had to be observed. However, he heeded Orslett's warning and spent the day making his final preparations. The Queen's funeral was fixed for the twelfth of December. Lady Jane Dormer changed her mind and said that she would return to the capital to observe the last rites. Nevertheless, she was unable to cope with Elizabeth's retainers now thronging Greenwich Palace, taking over the principal posts, so she left immediately for Sinistrel. Segalla, harassed by Cesar to accompany her, still had certain affairs to complete in the city. Despite the physician's remonstrations, they stayed in a tavern near St. Giles and, on November 21, travelled across the wild Essex countryside to Sinistrel.

The journey was uneventful, the weather cold and hard. The mist hardly lifted, yet the ground underfoot was firm and made their journey speedier. Cesar chattered about how much he would enjoy returning to the warmth of Italy, loudly bemoaning Mary's death but proclaiming her lavish generosity to him. Segalla let him talk. Three days later they passed through a small village and took the trackway up towards Sinistrel. Despite its sombre name, the manor was pleasant enough; the ground floor was of red brick, the upper stories were of timber and white plaster, the mullioned lead-pane glass was bright and shiny. The roof was tiled with lead slates and large, intricately carved chimney pots soared up to the grey Essex sky.

Segalla would have led his horse round to the stables at the rear, but the main door was opened: Lady Jane, preceded by servants, came out to greet them. Even though they had parted only a few days earlier, Lady Jane's pleasure in their arrival was obvious. She looked beautiful, her ivory pale face emphasized by a long, black velvet dress adorned with only a silver-encrusted cross on a silver chain around her neck, her lustrous hair caught up behind a gauze veil.

"I am glad I came," she declared. "I could not stand Greenwich much longer. Let the physicians embalm the Queen's body and then I'll return. Come in, you look cold."

She took them into the warm, oak-panelled hallway along the gallery and into the parlour. The remains of the Queen's previous visit were still there: cushions bearing the royal insignia, chests and coffers. Lady Jane caught Segalla's glance and smiled sadly.

"These will all have to go back." She looked round the warm, decorated room. "And I'll have to leave all this."

"You will travel to Spain?" Segalla asked.

"Oh yes, I will not live in England under Elizabeth. Tell me"—she ushered them to seats before the fire—"did you ever discover the identity of the anonymous letter-writer or what it meant?"

Segalla shook his head. "No, my lady. What does it matter now? Cecil's men will be all over Greenwich. We have no authority to look at the documents the Queen brought from Westminster." He smiled across at Cesar. "And our good physician wishes to return to the warmth of Rome."

For a while they sat and sipped at the mulled wine, chatting about the coming funeral and what Elizabeth's accession would mean. A servant showed them to their chambers on the second gallery: clean, well-polished rooms with fresh sheets and linen. Segalla could see that Lady Jane wanted to make them as comfortable as possible. She was also aware of the possible dangers and sent some of her servants to watch the trackways into the village lest Cecil sent a party of men after them. On the morning after they arrived, Segalla celebrated Mass in the small manor chapel and took Lady Jane aside.

"We must be gone soon," he declared. "But, tonight, Lady Jane, I need to have private words with you. Is it possible to have the meal served and the servants dismissed?"

Lady Jane looked alarmed.

"It is important," Segalla insisted.

Lady Jane reluctantly agreed: she jokingly added that her future bridegroom, the Count de Feria, a stickler for protocol, might raise concerns at her dining alone with two gentlemen. Nevertheless, she kept her word. Later that evening, when darkness had fallen and the candles had been lit, she entertained Segalla and Cesar in the small parlour. The cooks served roast chicken in lemon sauce with vegetables and bread, followed by mince tart. The food was laid out on a small side table: Lady Jane insisted on serving them herself whilst Segalla said he would pour the wine.

For a while they ate in silence. Segalla answered Lady Jane's and Cesar's questions as quickly and sharply as possible. He listened to the sounds from different parts of the house as the servants made to leave and go back into the village. At last there was silence. Segalla caught Lady Jane looking at him strangely; he raised his glass.

"To you, my lady, to your husband to be. May you have a long and fruitful life in Spain. May the Lord bless you with health and children."

Cesar joined in the toast; Lady Jane smiled.

"And to the memory of the Queen," Segalla added. "May God take her to a place of light and peace and exact true vengeance on her murderer."

Lady Jane's goblet slipped in her hand, the wine splashing out like blood on the white tablecloth. Cesar looked sharply at Segalla. He put his own goblet down, rubbing his stomach; Lady Jane dabbed at the wine stain.

"Nicholas, what do you mean?"

Segalla pushed back his chair and got up. He walked to the door, turned the key, pulled it out of the lock, and put it into his wallet. Then he went to the window and stared out into the night.

"Tenebrae factae," he said, quoting the Gospels. "And

darkness fell. A dramatic line, is it not, my lady? We have Christ's own words." Segalla paused to listen to an owl hooting from the mist-strewn orchard at the far end of the house. "We have Christ's own words," he repeated, "that those things done in the dark will be judged in the light. Mary Tudor, God rest her, was poisoned: her assassin now sits in this chamber." He ignored the sharp intake of breath behind him. "Mary Tudor was poisoned," he repeated, not even bothering to turn round, "slowly, subtly: her assassin had nothing to do with those anonymous letters." He walked back to the top of the table. Cesar and Lady Jane sat staring at him. Segalla gazed into the fire flickering under the manteled hearth; the dancing flames seemed to bring to life the serpents carved on either side.

"What nonsense is this?" Lady Jane stammered.

"Oh, it's no nonsense, my lady. Is it, Dr. Cesar?"

The physician pushed back his chair.

"Dr. Cesar," Segalla continued, "physician and personal assassin to His Holiness Pope Paul IV in Rome."

"This is nonsense!" Cesar snapped.

Segalla noticed how his cheery face was now ashen.

"Nicholas, I don't feel well. I should not listen to this nonsense."

Lady Jane, fingers tightly clutching her goblet, gazed in horror at Cesar.

"Time is short," Segalla continued. "Justice must be done and I must be gone before daybreak. Cecil's men may well pay Sinistrel a visit. I do not wish them to catch me here, so I shall be short and to the point. Pope Paul IV, for God knows what reason, did not welcome Mary Tudor as Queen. His Holiness, I believe, hated the entire Tudor clan: the idea of Mary married to a Spaniard, of bringing England under Philip's sway, was equally distasteful. Dr. Theophilus, whom we know as John Gresham, was bribed, inveigled to return to England. Slowly, but carefully, he began to poison Mary. Gresham had a great deal to hide, and he did so not only by a change in name but through papal protection. He wasn't very effective: a timid, anxious man, Gresham began to have scruples, so he was replaced by our good Dr. Cesar."

The physician made to get up, but Segalla shook his head.

"The door is locked, Cesar," he murmured. "I know you are not armed; I am, and Lady Jane is now all attention. You arrived in England with me. Your first task was to remove Dr. Theophilus from the scene, and you did that most professionally. On the day he died you gave him a poison, sometime earlier in the afternoon, a slow-working potion: you then made it look as if Theophilus had been poisoned at the banquet."

"But the cup?" Lady Jane exclaimed.

"Yes, that mystified me: both the wine in one of the jugs and that in Theophilus's cup were tainted. However, I drank from that wine and felt no ill effects because the poison was not put in until Dr. Cesar joined us in the hall. You remember him sniffing at the cup and taking the jug out into the kitchen with Grantchester?" Segalla pointed to the heavy rings on Cesar's fingers. "I wonder how many of them have cavities to conceal poison?"

"But the rats died immediately," Lady Jane intervened.

"Oh, a different poison was used. A powder which worked more quickly. Dr. Cesar could act the innocent. He deliberately absented himself from the last banquet; it would be easy for him to simulate illness. He could calculate how long the poison would take and make sure he was nowhere about, an easy enough task. Theophilus loved his comforts, and I suppose it would not be difficult to slip into his chamber late that afternoon and put the potion in his wine jug."

"What wine jug?" Cesar snarled.

"Oh, that's the other reason you never came to the banquet," Segalla added. "You used the time to visit Theophilus's chamber, not only to remove the offending wine but also any documents and memoranda. When I later visited Theophilus's chamber all such documents had gone. At the time I knew something else was missing, but couldn't place it, not till much later. Theophilus loved his belly: there was no wine. Now . . ."

Segalla noticed the sweat breaking out on Cesar's brow. The physician dabbed at this with a napkin, blinking and wetting his lips.

"Theophilus had a chamber elsewhere, and you, Cesar, had been well advised. So, after Theophilus's death, you slipped out into the city. A simple enough task: with a flask of oil you wet the wooden stairs leading up to the chamber where Theophilus kept his mistress and started the fire. You never cared about the woman. All that concerned you was that Theophilus's possessions, including any incriminating documents or letters, were consumed in the raging inferno."

Cesar pushed back the chair. "I suppose," he jibed, "you are going to accuse me of poisoning Philip Savage?"

"Oh no, you didn't kill Savage. Theophilus did that. On the orders of His Holiness."

"I don't understand," Lady Jane broke in; her face was now ashen white.

Segalla noticed she'd brought out a dagger from underneath the table.

"There's nothing to fear, madam," Segalla declared. "I assure you, you are in no danger, certainly not from me or Dr. Cesar. Theophilus murdered Savage, and you, Dr. Cesar, because of what you'd learnt in Rome and from Gresham's papers, were able to hire those assassins to attack Kennet and Dalrymple. You also hired the same ruffians to attack Orslett and myself on the riverbank as we walked back to Greenwich. It must have been someone in the palace who could pass the word where and when we would be so vulnerable."

"I wasn't here the day Dalrymple—"

"Oh yes, you were," Segalla interrupted. "You're a master of disguise, Dr. Cesar: put on an old cloak and a hood, adopt a shuffling gait, stain those moustaches with a sprinkling of dust, carry a bundle on your back, and you're a servant. You didn't leave the palace, you just became disguised. You went into the storeroom and, with the bellows, oil, gunpowder, and taper, committed murder. It would have taken no more than a few minutes. The guards were dozing, only concerned about Dalrymple: the rest of the palace servants had stopped work for the midday meal. When the confusion broke out, you simply left the storeroom, one of the many servants milling about." Segalla tapped the table top with his knife. "You were also concerned about me. I was not proving to be the amenable travel companion you thought. Did you intend to kill me with the crossbow bolt or was it just a warning?"

"You have no proof!" Cesar riposted.

"You are a physician skilled in poisons. If I searched your saddlebags I'd find the evidence. I don't have to do that. On the day you said you were absent from Greenwich Palace, you claimed you had gone to an apothecary. When I visited that apothecary he said that you'd visited him the day before, and he showed me the entry in his ledger listing the poisons you bought."

"Poisons!" Lady Jane broke in.

"Oh yes, Dr. Cesar took over from that villain Theophilus: he continued to poison the Queen. Lady Jane!"

Segalla sprang to his feet as the beautiful young woman, her face twisted in a snarl of rage, rose with the knife blade pointed towards Dr. Cesar. The physician seemed unable to move. Segalla went along the table and wrestled the dagger from her hand and made her sit back in the chair.

"Dr. Cesar continued what Theophilus was doing slowly, poisoning the Queen." Segalla walked back to the door. "At first he made her feel comfortable, gave her a respite, then he simply finished what another had begun!"

"Why?" Lady Jane Dormer hissed. "In God's name why?"

"The answer to that lies in Rome."

Cesar lurched forward, his hands clutching the table; his face was grey and sweat-soaked.

"I have pains!" he gasped.

"Of course you have," Segalla replied quietly. "The wine I gave you contains enough belladonna to kill us all!"

Cesar pushed the chair back; his breathing was more rapid, his face had turned a dreadful pallor.

"You murdering bastard!" he gasped. "You of all people, Segalla . . . !"

"A case of the kettle calling the pot black," Segalla replied. "Is that the real reason why we visited Catherine de' Medici in France? That Queen of Poisoners! That lady of the night with her elixirs and potions, powders and philtres. Did she give you something special? When I was going through those documents at Greenwich, I noticed that Theophilus had not only been recommended by Pope Paul IV but by Catherine de' Medici." Segalla got to his feet. "You'll die quicker than the Queen," he declared. "You are skilled enough to know there is no antidote. The windows are closed and narrow: the doors are bolted. Come, Lady Jane."

The woman, wan as a ghost, allowed herself to be escorted from the chamber even as Cesar slouched down, lost in his ever-increasing circle of pain. As he closed the door and locked it behind them, Segalla turned a deaf ear to the dying physician's heart-rending groans. Lady Jane sat at the foot of the stairs and put her face in her hands.

"It would be a mercy to put a ball in the back of his head," she declared.

"He's being hanged by his own halter! Think of the cruelty he and Theophilus caused. Because of them Mary knew no peace whilst Dalrymple, Kennet, and Savage died horrible deaths. Moreover, these were not their only victims."

"Who else?" she asked.

"Reginald Pole, Cardinal of the Church. Go back through your diaries and journals, Lady Jane. The Cardinal fell ill at the same time as the Queen. No one can really accept that their deaths on the same day are mere coincidence."

Lady Jane got to her feet. "But why? The Pope! A priest! A man of God! Christ's Vice-Regent on earth!"

"Carafa is a prince, steeped in the complex, violent politics of the Italian States. In his own mind he sees himself as doing God's work with Cesar and Theophilus as mere tools."

"Why don't you tell me the truth?" Lady Jane pleaded. "Why was it so important to kill the likes of Dalrymple? You've discovered a terrible secret, haven't you?"

Segalla crouched down beside her.

"Yes, but I cannot, I will not, tell you. If I did, if Cecil suspected for a moment that you knew the full truth behind Mark 15.34, you would never leave England!"

Segalla heard a movement from the room they had just left and got up.

"Tomorrow I'll be gone and the secret with me."

He went back to the door and turned the key. Cesar, slumped from the chair, was kneeling in a half-crouched position, head against the table, eyes sightless, saliva dribbling out of the corner of his mouth. Segalla tapped the corpse with the toe of his boot, sending it crashing to the floor.

"That's murder!" Lady Jane stood in the doorway. "Aren't we both guilty of murder?"

"Cesar was a criminal and a poisoner," Segalla replied. "I hold the commission from the Holy Father. I am his plenipotentiary, to do what is necessary. I also hold a similar commission from the Queen."

"She is dead."

"Elizabeth is not yet crowned Queen and, according to English law, Mary's writ still runs." Segalla went and opened the casement window: he looked up at the star-strewn sky. "I have not committed murder but carried out God's and Man's justice."

"And Carafa?"

Segalla looked over his shoulder. "As you rightly said, Carafa is God's Vice-Regent on earth. He will answer to God, perhaps sooner than he expected."

"And Cesar's corpse?"

Segalla chewed on his lip. "I could bury it out in the woods."

"No, no, there's another place," Lady Jane interrupted.

Under her directions "Segalla brought up an old arrow box from the cellar. Cesar's corpse was put in it and, with hammer and nails, Segalla fastened down the lid. He then fetched a small handcart from the stables. Lady Jane led him out along the gallery and into the kitchen. For a while she searched under the mantel of the huge hearth. Segalla exclaimed in surprise as part of the wall to the right of the fireplace swung open.

"A contrivance of my great-grandfather," Lady Jane explained.

Segalla pulled the handcart up over the steps and onto

the earth-beaten floor beyond. Muttering and gasping for breath, he followed Lady Jane, who hurried before him carrying a cresset torch which spluttered against the Stygian darkness. The passageway broadened, then stopped before a red-brick wall. Again, Lady Jane, murmuring to herself, searched about. Segalla heard a click and realized that part of the wall was really painted wood which now swung away: he pushed the casket through. Lady Jane told him to wait. Segalla did, sitting alone in the cold blackness on the coffin of a man he had just executed. An eerie experience. The house was dead silent. Lady Jane had not left any light, and, for a while, Segalla panicked: this was his nightmare, to be incarcerated, to be walled up alive in some forgotten oubliette or dungeon. He stretched out his hands and touched the wall, forcing himself to think rather than panic. Apparently this secret gully and chamber had been built against the huge kitchen hearth. He heard a sound. Lady Jane returned, dragging a pick and mattock with her.

"The floor is of earth," she explained. "It would be best if he were buried."

She also offered some rags from the kitchen. Segalla wrapped these round his hands and began to hack at the earth. Lady Jane brought more candles. Segalla worked for hours, taking sips of ale and bites of the dry meat Lady Jane brought. At last a shallow grave was dug: the coffin was lowered, and the earth piled and beaten around it. The candles were extinguished, and they returned to the kitchen.

"It will soon be dawn," Lady Jane observed. "The servants will return."

Segalla, his hands chapped, his muscles aching, slept for a while and, just after daybreak, collected his horse and bade Lady Jane farewell in the stable courtyard.

"We shall not meet again." Segalla took her hand and kissed it: her fingers were ice cold. "What I did," he continued, "was just and fair!"

Lady Jane stood on tiptoe and kissed him on the cheek.

"The Queen's justice was done," she whispered. "But it's best if you were gone: Cecil's men will soon be here. I will take care of Cesar's horse. As you say, we shall not meet again!"

Peter Carafa, by divine election, Supreme Pontiff, knelt in the small chapel of San Angelo overlooking the Tiber and stared at the pure beeswax candles burning so vigorously before the statue of the Virgin Mary. Carafa felt his old bones ache, and, closing his eyes, he prayed that the winter would be short and spring would soon return to Rome. He was here not just because it was the Eve of the Purification of Our Lady, Candlemas, but also to meet his emissary, lately returned from England. The Swiss mercenaries guarding the door, and every door beyond, had strict orders to let no one in but Segalla. Carafa slipped the Ave beads between his fingers. Things had not gone according to plan. Mary Tudor was dead, buried under the cold slabs of Westminster Abbey, but Elizabeth had proved herself to be a redoubtable opponent. Sly and devious, Elizabeth had swept to the throne on a wave of popular acclamation: the Protestant faith had been reaffirmed, the prisons opened, the Catholic bishops removed; and yet Elizabeth had been adroit. Oh, she had promised this and she had promised that: friendship with France, Scotland, Spain, and, through secret channels, the papacy. Little, red-haired Elizabeth, Boleyn's brat! She was dangling them all on a string. Carafa heard the door open and footsteps behind him. For the space of three Aves, Carafa waited. He then opened his eyes, crossed himself, but didn't turn round.

"Nicholas, Nicholas!" he murmured. "Welcome back to Rome!"

"Thank you, Your Holiness."

"A safe journey?"

"Safe but arduous."

"But God guides his elect."

"Undoubtedly, Your Holiness, though we could all debate who is his elect?"

Carafa chuckled merrily and eased himself off the priedieu: wheezing and puffing, he went and sat in the great episcopal chair set against the wall; he waved Segalla to the bench before it.

"And the good Dr. Cesar?"

"He is dead, Your Holiness; I killed him."

Carafa pulled a face. "Thou shalt not kill, Nicholas!"

"Is Your Holiness talking about yourself or my actions in carrying out lawful execution of an assassin?"

Carafa held up a podgy finger. "Touché, Segalla." He studied the Jesuit's secretive face. "And you want the truth?"

"I know how it was done," Segalla retorted. "But why?"

Carafa breathed in deeply. "What year is it?"

"It is 1559."

"For one and a half thousand years," Carafa replied, "the Catholic Church has been here in Rome. Empires come and go." He waved his hand. "Princes rise and fall." He snapped his fingers. "Nothing but puffs of dust under the sun. The Catholic Church was in England, the Mass was being celebrated, long before the legions left Britain." He scratched his face, then clutched his stomach as it curdled. He was sorry Cesar was dead, but, there again, Carafa never fully trusted any man, and how long would Cesar have kept his mouth shut?

"Your Holiness, Mary Tudor was a legitimate Catholic ruler!"

"The Catholic Church," Carafa continued, "had its roots in England when the Tudors were still grubbing in their caves. It was the Tudors who tore the edifice down: all because Henry wanted to get rid of his wife."

"Yet Mary Stuart," Segalla countered. "She's a descendant of the Tudor line."

Carafa laughed, a sharp bark, and leaned forward, elbows resting on his knees, his small eyes full of merriment.

"Do you think I care about Mary Stuart? I hate the Tudors and I hate Spain." He breathed in deeply. "Years ago, when we were friends, Reginald Pole told me about the great secret of the Four Evangelists." Carafa rubbed his hands. "First, however, let me present you with our world picture. Spain, under Philip, is no friend of the papacy or the Catholic Church. The Spanish bishops take their orders from Madrid, not from Rome. Spain is a powerful country; it also controls the wealthy Low Countries to the north of France, which gives it a springboard for England. Spanish fleets range over the great western oceans, their hulls full of gold and silver from the new lands. Europe has always been kept safe by a balancing act between France and Spain, with England moving from camp to camp. But can you imagine, Segalla, a world where Spain controls England and eventually, perhaps, even Scotland? Philip would then have France surrounded. His fleet would control the narrow seas. He could overawe France, and what would happen then, Segalla, eh? His eyes would turn to Italy. It's only thirty-four years since his father's Spanish troops sacked Rome. Philip's marriage to Mary was part of this: if Mary gave birth to a child, the Tudors would be replaced by a Spanish dynasty."

"But Mary was a devout Catholic!"

"Oh, for the love of God, Segalla, don't be so naive!" Carafa sighed. "I realized that Mary had to die. I managed to get my hands on Dr. Theophilus, or Gresham as he was called in a previous life, one of the Four Evangelists, a weak, venal man, much given to wine, food, and soft, perfumed flesh. I gave him letters of accreditation as well as secret instructions and packed him off to Paris, where Catherine de' Medici did the same. Theophilus was under strict instructions: no children for Mary and the shortest of reigns."

"And when Mary died you'd support France?"

"I'd support no one. I encouraged France to further the claims of Mary Stuart. Catherine de' Medici is no fool: she, too, feared Philip. If Mary Tudor died, Philip would undoubtedly make an offer for Elizabeth's hand and the same old dance would begin." Carafa clicked his tongue and looked up at the ceiling.

"Chaos!" Segalla remarked. "That's what you wanted to cause. Chaos!"

Carafa lifted his hand to his face and smiled.

"Now you have it, Nicholas. Mary dies: Philip is still her consort, he might further his own claims, offer betrothal, protection, to Elizabeth, whose claim to the throne, never mind the Four Evangelists, is fairly weak."

"And, of course," Segalla added, "France would intervene?"

"Exactly, Nicholas, a three-cornered fight. Elizabeth, Philip, and the French. All circling each other. Each advancing their claims. Scotland is already under French influence, Catherine de' Medici will not let the game slip so easily. . . ."

"But why were the Four Evangelists murdered?"

"Ah." Carafa leaned back in the chair, hands resting on its ornately carved arms. "Something I never anticipated. At first I thought Theophilus was the blackmailer, but he had all the courage of a mouse. Those letters were very dangerous, Nicholas. If it became public knowledge that Elizabeth was not the true heir of Henry VIII, that would strengthen not only Philip's hand but also that of Mary Stuart." He smiled at the surprise in Segalla's face. "I don't want," he added waspishly, "Mary Stuart on the throne at Westminster, bringing France, England, and Scotland under one ruler; that would upset the balance."

"What you wanted," Segalla retorted, "was everyone at

everyone else's throats. If it was rumoured abroad that Elizabeth was a bastard, it would have only strengthened Philip's hand." Segalla leaned forward. "So that's why the Evangelists were killed?"

Carafa breathed out noisily and flapped his hands.

"You deserve to know, Nicholas. I would have told you eventually."

Segalla ignored the lie.

"I knew about the secret of the Four Evangelists and, as I have said, I dispatched Theophilus to England. His instructions were quite clear: he was to offer medication to both Mary Tudor and Pole, her interfering Cardinal and First Minister." Carafa spread his hands. "I assured Mary that Theophilus could be trusted. After all, he, or his associates, had tried to discredit Elizabeth: he would be the last person to be suborned by Cecil."

"Of course," Segalla agreed. "Cecil must have also found out about Mark 15.34: anyone else knowing would, in his book, be marked down for destruction."

"You have it." Carafa smiled. "Theophilus was an excellent choice, but either he had a tender conscience or became frightened. Now, when that first anonymous letter was circulated, I told Theophilus to take care of his former colleagues. He murdered Savage, but his heart was not in it. I suspected that Theophilus would either confess all or flee."

"And that was the reason for my mission to England: I was really to take Dr. Cesar. He would pose as the benevolent physician, the Queen's saviour, and, at the same time, take care of Theophilus and the remaining Evangelists."

Carafa nodded. "You were a pretext: your mission to save Mary merely a cover. She was already a dead woman." He wagged a finger. "You're sharper than I thought. Ah well." He sighed. "Cesar visited Catherine to collect a certain potion as well as ensure that, if Theophilus fled to France, he would not live long."

Segalla smiled thinly. "What you didn't know was that the letters were being sent not by Theophilus or his former colleagues but by Pole."

"Pole?" Carafa's hand went to his mouth. "Ah!" He smiled. "I see. My old friend was dying. He hated Boleyn and her brat more than I did."

"He was baiting her," Segalla retorted. "Pole was simply lashing out at the inevitable."

"The inevitable?" Carafa queried.

"For all your plots," Segalla replied. "There will be no three-cornered fight between France, England, and Spain. Elizabeth is cunning and astute, more so than Mary. Cecil is a veritable snake. They'll both lie, cheat, but keep their own counsel. They are supported by the Commons, the London merchants, and the fleet. I suspect Elizabeth will accept the reformed faith in a much more moderate version if the papacy leaves her alone." Segalla fought to control his temper. "You say the Church has flourished for hundreds of years. Then, Your Holiness, you should have learnt the English are not partial to having their princes thrust upon them by foreign troops."

"I still have Mark 15.34."

"Who would believe you now?" Segalla scoffed. "It

would be dismissed as a piece of popish trickery." He got to his feet. "It's all been trickery!"

Carafa just shrugged. "But you'll stay with me, Nicholas?"

"No. I'll go to one of our houses in Paris. I am sure Your Holiness has other things to do." Segalla walked to the door and then turned round. "How do you sleep, Your Holiness?"

"Very well, Segalla." Carafa did not even move his head. "What I have done, I have done for the sake of the Church."

Segalla walked back. "But you had a hand in the murder of a Catholic monarch as well as that of her First Minister. You were responsible for Cesar's death and those whom that assassin murdered. And for what? To plan for something which will never happen?"

Carafa smiled, licking his lips. "But, in the end, Segalla, in the end . . . Philip has lost England, and, in time, the Church will return."

Segalla bowed and walked to the door. He looked around. Carafa was at his prie-dieu, face in his hands, praying before the stark crucifix displayed above the chapel altar.

Epilogue

Segalla and Ann Dukthas stepped out of the taxi which had taken them along the Essex lanes and up the leafy trackway to Sinistrel Manor. Ann felt unreal: so strange to be visiting a place which she had read about only the night before, the silent witness of dramatic events four hundred years ago. Sinistrel was an elegant Tudor manor with long red-brick chimneys, ornate gables, and bay windows full of mullioned glass.

"It's changed somewhat," Segalla declared, clasping her by the elbow and ushering her towards the main door.

"What happened to Jane Dormer? Please!" Ann grasped his hand. "Before we go in?"

Segalla looked at his fob watch. "We are a little early, and the officials from the English Heritage may not be ready for us." He pointed across to a wooden bench on the far side of the gravel-strewn trackway. "Let's enjoy the sunshine and the fresh air."

They sat down; Segalla pulled out a hip flask and offered

it to Ann, who shook her head. He took a sip and squinted at the house, a dreamy look in his eyes.

"What happened to Jane Dormer?" Ann repeated.

Segalla put the stopper back on the flask. "She married the love of her life, the Count de Feria, and went to live in Spain, where she wrote her memoirs. You should read them, Ann, the excellent London Library in St. James's Square has a copy. Jane remained a Catholic, as well as Mary's most fervent supporter for forty years after the events described in my papers. Jane never accepted that Mary died of natural causes. She spent a great deal of her life, time, energy, and money plotting against Elizabeth."

"But is it true?" Ann asked.

"Look at the facts." Segalla stretched out his legs. "Mary Tudor was born in 1516. Of robust health, she becomes Queen only to fall prey to the most dreadful catalogue of diseases. At the same time, her very close friend and councillor Cardinal Reginald Pole becomes ill. Coincidence?" Segalla shook his head. "Coincidence that they both died on the same day? You'll find such facts mentioned in any common history book of the period."

"And Carafa?" Ann asked.

"He died shortly after I left his service. A ruthless and wily politician, Carafa hated the Tudor dynasty. He loathed Elizabeth and he had no great love for Cardinal Pole. Carafa was obsessed with the Spanish controlling Europe, Italy, and, above all, Rome. He spent most of his time and energy countering Philip's ambitions."

"But would he stoop to murder?"

"Yes, he certainly would," Segalla replied drily. "Being a priest, even one who holds high office, has never stopped hate seething in the human heart. And Carafa knew how to hate."

"But the story of the Four Evangelists?"

Segalla rubbed the side of his nose. "A lot of the evidence has disappeared. However, the Public Record Office in Chancery Lane contains a letter, written by Mary to her husband, Philip, in which she confesses that she holds a great secret about her half-sister Elizabeth. In the same archives you'll find the Venetian State papers. Now the Venetians ran the best spy service in sixteenth-century Europe. The Venetians also allude to Mary possessing such a secret about her half-sister. Finally, as Reginald Pole was the Queen's confessor and adviser, he undoubtedly would have known it, too."

"But Mary hated Anne Boleyn," Ann countered. "Doesn't Anne Boleyn, in one of the last letters before she was executed, imply that she had tried to harm the young Mary?"

Segalla shook his head. "True, Mary had no love for Boleyn, but she had a genuine affection for Elizabeth. Mary could have had her young half-sister executed, but she did not. Mary, despite being the daughter of Catherine of Aragon, was a Tudor through and through. She adored her father and would not allow any slur against Henry's name to be broadcast abroad."

"But you imply that Henry was impotent?"

"He was and he wasn't," Segalla replied. "Undoubtedly, when Henry first married Catherine of Aragon he was virile, a veritable lady's man: Mary was his issue. He also had young Fitzroy by his mistress Bessie Blunt. However, by the time the King had married Anne Boleyn, he was nearly twenty-five years older, suffering from syphilis as well as a myriad of other infections. These undoubtedly affected his sexual prowess."

"But was he frightened of her?"

"Yes. Boleyn was a vibrant, young, charismatic woman. According to all reports, she exuded sexuality like other women do a perfume. Henry was not, perhaps, the lover he had led her to believe. Go to the archives. Read the last letter Anne Boleyn dispatched to Henry on the eve of her execution. It contains a very clear hint that Henry's impotence had been a problem between them."

"But would she commit adultery with a commoner like Mark Smeaton?"

"Anne, of course, always denied it, but it's possible. One of Henry's other queens, little Catherine Howard, despite the fact that she was Henry's fourth wife and knew, only too well, the fate of her distant cousin Anne Boleyn, still had an association with Thomas Culpepper. Catherine died with his name on her lips. Anne Boleyn may have made a similar mistake. No wonder Henry struck out against her entire family. He must have felt a cuckold, but how could he proclaim to Europe that his own wife had betrayed him? He had no choice but to accept young Elizabeth as his daughter. I doubt if it would have troubled his wily mind. After all, Seymour gave birth to a male heir, and there was always Mary. I suppose Henry, in his worst nightmare, never imagined that young Elizabeth would ever accede to the throne. Anne Boleyn may have protested her innocence, but her relationship with Smeaton does make you wonder." Segalla got up and stamped his feet. He looked at his fob watch. "Of all Henry's children, Elizabeth, unlike the other two, very rarely mentioned her parents." He peered up at one of the windows and waved at a person standing there. "We'll have to go in soon," Segalla declared.

"And the murder plot against Mary?" Ann asked.

"Oh, there was Dr. Theophilus," Segalla replied. "And a certain Dr. Cesar. Mary's will bequeaths this Cesar a hundred pounds. Mary was definitely poisoned. The historian J. M. Stone, in his book on Mary published in 1953, actually quotes a Venetian letter which states Mary had been poisoned by 'an Italian physician.'" Segalla put on his gloves. "Yet, if you go to the Public Record Office, you'll find no trace of this Cesar in the records after Mary's death." He nodded towards the house. "This is his last resting place."

The door to the manor suddenly opened. An elderly man in a grey suit, wearing the insignia of the English Heritage, came out onto the porch and waved them over.

"Dr. Segalla, we are ready."

"In a minute!" he called back. "I'll be with you soon."

"Have they discovered Cesar's remains?"

"They discovered the arrow chest," Segalla replied. "They are going to bring it out now."

"How did you arrange this?" Ann asked.

Segalla laughed. "I am a most fervent supporter of English Heritage. But come, I'll tell you later why I had to be here."

They walked across. Segalla introduced Ann to James Broadway, an official from English Heritage who was to supervise the bringing out and opening of the casket. Ann shook his hand, and they were led inside. Ann recalled Segalla's description of the manor and hid her thrill of excitement.

"You haven't been here before, have you?" Broadway asked.

"Not really," Segalla enigmatically replied.

"And you, Miss Dukthas?"

"Oh, I have dreamed of coming to such a place." She winked quickly at Segalla.

Broadway led them into a small anteroom where others were waiting, sipping at coffee. Broadway poured cups for Ann and Segalla then moved around introducing them to the other officials, representatives from the Home Office and a pathologist from the London Hospital. A short while later they were taken into what must have once been the kitchen with bare walls and a stone-flagged floor. It was devoid of any furniture except for a table covered in plastic, on which a long casket lay, also protected by layers of transparent film. The air was musty; Broadway explained that all light and fresh air had to be kept out. In the far wall was a great gap where the stones and brickwork had been pulled away. Broadway, wielding a powerful torch, took Ann and Segalla down the cold and musty passageway. Ann felt uneasy, slightly light-headed: she was taking a journey back through time. They entered the cavernous chamber. Segalla kept a firm grip on Ann's hand.

"Nothing much here," Broadway declared. He pointed to the shallow grave. "We filled most of that in, as it's rather dangerous: the coffin was buried two or three feet deep in packed earth."

"You know how he died?" Ann asked.

"That," Broadway declared, "is what we are going to discover. Dr. Segalla, I would like to thank you for your very generous contribution both for the renovation of Sinistrel and this excavation."

They returned to the kitchen; the coffin was uncovered and the yellowing skeleton carefully laid out on the table beside it. All clothing and flesh had rotted away. Only shards of cloth and pieces of the leather belt and boots remained. Ann studied the skeleton: the remains of Dr. Cesar, the jovial yet sinister sixteenth-century physician, who had done so much to influence the course of English history. Segalla appeared noncommittal, cold, and impassive. He paid more attention to the possible contents of the coffin than to the skeleton itself. The pathologist made a quick study.

"Nothing," he declared. "But I have yet to make a bone analysis. There is no obvious mark of violence caused by dagger, pistol, or garrotte, but the corpse was buried secretly. So, perhaps it was poison."

He stood back so the others, Segalla and Ann amongst them, could take a closer look. Half an hour later they left. Segalla kept silent until the waiting taxi had returned them to the White Hart. They went up to Ann's room. She and Segalla washed their hands and prepared for lunch. Segalla came out of the bathroom, carefully wiping his fingers on a towel.

"You didn't seem very interested in the remains of your old comrade."

Segalla pulled a face. "One skeleton tends to be like another."

"Didn't Catherine de' Medici ever enquire after her good friend? At the beginning of your paper, her designs, as well as her murderous liaison with Cesar, receive great emphasis."

"Catherine de' Medici emphasized anything," Segalla retorted, "which concerned her or her power. She really did believe that Mary Stuart could succeed to the throne of England: her husband, Henry, even had the royal arms quartered on his daughter-in-law's escutcheon. If Henry II had lived," Segalla continued, "the French would have made some attempt against Elizabeth, but, a year later, Henry was killed jousting with a young nobleman, Montmorency."

"Ah yes, the young lion killing the older lion, and there was a reference to a cage?"

"Henry II's insignia was a lion rampant," Segalla replied. "Montmorency's was a silver one. In the fatal joust, Montmorency pierced Henry's helmet, the golden cage, and struck him in the eye. The King died in agony a few weeks later."

"So, Nostradamus's prophecy was proved correct?"

"All prophecies are self-fulfilling. I often wonder if Catherine de' Medici gave her amorous husband a helping hand up to the court of heaven. Whatever, Henry's death did not bring Catherine's ambitions to full realization. Her sons proved to be incompetent; the dispute with the Huguenots slipped into civil war, and Catherine had enough problems without fishing in England's troubled waters."

"But you and Catherine met again?"

"Of course!" Segalla returned to the bathroom. He came out and picked up his jacket from the back of a chair. "That visit to Sinistrel was essential," he declared. "You see, Carafa was a vindictive, vicious, old man. I suspect he knew my secret. A few days after I left his service he wrote to me; he hoped I had carefully searched Cesar's corpse before I disposed of it as Cesar had collected information about me." He sat down in the chair.

"And you were worried that such secrets were buried at Sinistrel?"

"It's possible. I never searched Cesar's body. I was in too much of a hurry. I did wonder whether Cesar died with secret information about me. But what could I do? I returned to England on many an occasion, but"—he grinned—"until this morning I couldn't walk up to the front door of Sinistrel Manor and ask to examine a corpse buried in a secret grave." Segalla got to his feet. "Ah well, they've all gone. Let's have lunch, Ann." He walked to the door. "And do the only thing we can: as the poet says, 'Sip the blood-red claret and salute the dead'!"